Voted Most Likely to Murder

Voted Most Likely to Murder

A MYSTERY

Lacey Moone

NEW YORK

Books should be disposed of and recycled according to local requirements. All paper materials used are FSC compliant.

This is a work of fiction. All of the names, characters, organizations, places and events portrayed in this novel are either products of the author's imagination or are used fictitiously. Any resemblance to real or actual events, locales, or persons, living or dead, is entirely coincidental.

Published in the United States by Crooked Lane Books, an imprint of The Quick Brown Fox & Company LLC.

Crooked Lane Books and its logo are trademarks of The Quick Brown Fox & Company LLC.

Library of Congress Catalog-in-Publication data available upon request.

ISBN (hardcover): 979-8-89242- 567-4
ISBN (paperback): 979-8-89242-568-1
ISBN (ebook): 979-8-89242-569-8

Cover design by Dàlia Adillon

Printed in the United States.

www.crookedlanebooks.com

Crooked Lane Books
34 West 27th St., 10th Floor
New York, NY 10001

First Edition: May 2026

The authorized representative in the EU for product safety and compliance is eucomply OÜPärnu mnt 139b-14, 11317 Tallinn, Estonia, hello@eucompliancepartner.com, +33757690241

10 9 8 7 6 5 4 3 2 1

To my grandmother, Kathleen, who I miss greatly. I still have the pen.

Chapter One

High school reunions should be outlawed. Especially when the last time you saw your classmates, you were driving off in a blaze of glory after vowing to never again step foot in that dinky Nova Scotian town.

I stared up at the entrance to my old high school, dread bubbling in my stomach. The building looked exactly as it had the last time I graced its front steps. It reminded me of a photograph left too long in the sun, brittle and yellowing around the edges. A drab, industrial brick structure looming over the surrounding square Loyalist-era houses. The only thing remotely cheerful about the property was the small wooden replica of the town's lighthouse, painted in the school colors, white, gold, and blue, on the grass next to the entrance. A large banner hung above the main doors, welcoming back my graduating class.

If I didn't know better, I'd think the reunion committee conspired to ensure this event was held at the lowest point in my life. Whoever heard of a fourteen-year reunion? It was ridiculous. What was their door prize going to be, a fistful of Canadian Tire money?

I shifted my weight between my already aching feet. I didn't want to go inside, but I promised my mother I would drag myself out from under the storm cloud that had been hovering over my head since my less-than-dignified return to Little Blue Harbour three months ago, and at least attempt to socialize with humans again. She'd also threatened to drive me here in her housecoat and fuzzy shark slippers, and drag me inside by my ear if I refused. While the chances of her following through on such a threat were low, they were never zero, so here I was.

Besides, I'd actually made an effort with my appearance for the first time in months, and it seemed like a shame to waste it. My normally bare cheeks were rosy, thanks to my new Summer Kiss blush, and I'd managed to wrangle my curly brown hair back into a bun.

Unfortunately, my wardrobe was limited at the moment; black cotton capris paired with a white top and a gray blazer was the best I could manage. At the last moment, I'd also slipped on a pair of sparkly white heels in an effort to avoid looking like the lead female cop in a crime drama.

I stood on the sidewalk, wondering if I should just call it a night and see if the Little Blue Beanery café still made those honey crullers I used to love, when I heard someone approach behind me.

A tall woman with freckled cheeks and an indigo blue bob rushed up to me, her smile stretched wide with excitement. Before I could react, she threw her arms around me, encasing me in her green leather jacket. By some miracle, I managed not to topple us both. She rocked me back and forth, causing my round, tortoiseshell spectacles to slide down my nose.

I met Stephanie "Stevie" Hart when I was fifteen years old in third period art class. This unbelievably cool new girl from Alberta, already a hot commodity with her purple lipstick and Harley-Davidson motorcycle boots, strolled right past the popular students and asked me to be project partners. It wasn't until we turned in our clay sculpture a week later that I learned Stevie wasn't even enrolled in art class; she'd been skipping geometry the entire time.

Obviously, we had no choice but to become friends.

Stevie held me in front of her, grinning at me. "Belinda Bishop back in Little Blue Harbour, Nova Scotia." She dropped her arms and took a step back. "Wait, is the apocalypse coming? Is this the first sign?"

I broke into my first genuine smile in months. "Sorry, no apocalypse," I said. "My mother just guilted me into making an appearance."

Stevie bumped me playfully with her hip. "Well, whatever the motivation was, it's awesome to see you again."

Little pinpricks of guilt nipped at my skin. While Stevie and I touched base occasionally on social media, our friendship had dwindled since leaving high school. "I'm sorry I haven't come by the tearoom."

She held up a hand, cutting off my apology. "You don't owe me an explanation. I know your move back home wasn't under the best circumstances. I don't blame you for wanting to keep a low profile."

My face lit up with bright sarcasm. "Oh, you mean because I'm a thirty-two-year-old failure who lost her job, her boyfriend, and her apartment, and now has to work for her parents?"

Stevie nodded approvingly. "Impressive summary."

I shrugged. "I've been practicing. It's not like it won't come up at some point tonight."

I imagined the Pageant Minions, a group of beauty queen wannabes who used to pride themselves on making my life as unpleasant as possible, would take particular delight in reminding me of my recent downfall.

As a teenager, I promised myself I wouldn't end up trapped in Little Blue Harbour like how I envisioned most of my classmates. I was going to be an investigative journalist like my idol, *Dateline*'s Keith Morrison. Exposing corrupt corporations. Staring down ruthless killers as I pressed them for answers. Uncovering the truth.

Unfortunately, the universe had other plans. After graduating with a degree in journalism in Ottawa, my only successful job offer was from the *Bytown Freebie*, a publication every bit as glamorous as its name. Occasionally, I supplemented that income with freelance writing gigs, but my poor networking skills, coupled with a tendency to be somewhat overzealous in pursuit of a story, left my side hustle with something to be desired.

I met Craig when I covered an independent film festival where they were showing his film, *Saturday Brunch with Arthur*, in which the main character is forced to share a meal with the three parts of his psyche: the Ego, the Id, and the Superego.

The film was not great.

Neither was the relationship. But, with my writing career flatlining, I needed a win. So I ignored enough red flags to throw myself a parade. Craig never showed any genuine interest in my career or hobbies. He wouldn't defend me when his friends mocked my job. Birthday and holiday gifts usually consisted of a twenty-five-dollar gift card for his favorite store. It all finally came crashing down when I returned home to our shared apartment and found him with another woman. On the same day I'd been let go from my job.

After weeks of no apartment prospects and a rapidly shrinking savings account, I had no choice but to break down and call my parents in Nova Scotia. Luckily for me, one of their front desk clerks had recently moved to Amherst, so they offered me the job as well as my old bedroom. Officially, it was only until I got back on my feet, but every day I woke up to my old *Pan's Labyrinth* poster, the odds of that ever happening felt diminished. Still, I couldn't bring myself to give up all hope of salvaging my writing career just yet. All I needed was one amazing story.

However, Little Blue Harbour wasn't known for its breaking news.

Stevie hooked her arm through mine as we started up the school steps. "You're going to be helping out your parents with their cottage rentals and RV park. I think it'll be a great way to spend the summer; you'll have a gorgeous view of the harbour, surrounded by those adorable cottages your parents built, and you'll get to meet people from all over."

"Ah, yes, people. My favorite," I deadpanned.

She laughed. "I work in customer service too. And work for my mother. We're the same. Don't be such a sook."

I bristled at the accusation. "I am not being whiny. It's not the same at all, you and Diane are business partners. You work with your mother, not for her." Stevie and her mother operated a popular Loyalist-themed tearoom on the town's historic boardwalk, the Osprey.

"You think that matters to the Pageant Minions?" she asked.

A chilling thought occurred to me. "Does that mean Jolene Dexter is coming to this too?"

Stevie made an apologetic face. "She's the head of the reunion committee."

I rolled my eyes. "Little Blue Harbour's answer to Tracy Flick." *Jolene Dexter, my childhood best friend and high school nemesis.*

Stevie bounded forward and pulled on the double doors, holding one open for me. "Don't worry, I'm only staying long enough to confirm that everyone has aged as badly as I hope they have."

"Most of them still live here," I said, following her up the steps. "You already know how they've aged."

We headed for the gymnasium, but a male voice in the lobby called us back. "Sorry, ladies," he said, "you have to check in here before you can go inside."

The man waved us over to a folding table arranged in front of the trophy case. His navy blue checkered suit was snug across his stomach, and his smile reminded me of a used car salesman. Instantly, I recognized the black hair, slicked back with just as much hair gel as it was fourteen years ago.

"Is that Big Andy?" I asked Stevie, surprised.

She nodded, rolling her eyes. "Brace yourself, he still flirts with anything that moves," she murmured as we approached the table. "Hey, Andy. Did Jolene rope you into volunteering?" she asked at normal volume.

"You know me, can't say no to a pretty face," he said. "You're looking good as always, Stevie." His flirty smile slipped a little when he turned to me. "Oh, hey. Um?"

He cocked his head to the side like a confused dog. Not that I actually expected Andrew Perch to remember me. Handsome, popular, and athletic, he and I didn't exactly run in the same social circles. It would have been like a dolphin hanging out with a sea cucumber.

"Belinda Bishop," I said, a little deflated.

His eyes lit up in recognition, and he gave me a double snap with finger guns. "Oh, yeah, Belinda. Sorry about that. How are your folks doing? Ellie and Kenneth, right?"

"They're fine." I scanned the rows of name tags laid out on the table, thankful for an excuse to avoid eye contact. "You're still living here in town?"

Andy nodded proudly, looking around the lobby. "Still at the school too. I'm the history teacher and the coach for the football team."

"Makes sense. You played running back. Right?" I didn't go to many games, and when I did, it was usually to hang out under the bleachers rather than watch.

"Yup," he said. Like most Maritimers, he said it with a short inhale, my least favorite aspect of the East Coast accent, and one I made a point of losing when I moved to Ontario. "Played in university too, until I blew out my left knee," he continued. "Now my biggest victory is if I can get the kids to remember who Laura Secord is."

His carefree tone dipped a little. Something told me I was not the only one there tonight worried about living up to expectations.

He slid two drink tickets across the table. "The awards ceremony begins at nine."

"Is there an open bar?" I asked, only half joking.

Andy laughed. "Sorry, one free drink each. After that, it's cash only."

I cast a wary glance at the gym doors. "I guess I should get this over with." I sighed, affixing the name tag to my lapel.

"Be strong, Bishop," he said, clenching his fist in solidarity. "Say hi to your dad for me. My buddies and I are looking for a new member for our weekly poker game, if you think he'd be interested."

Another couple arrived behind us, and we let Andy get back to his greeting duties. "He knows my father is retired RCMP, right?" I whispered to Stevie as we walked away.

She laughed. "Your father would destroy those guys. Nothing gets past Kenny. Remember when we tried to sneak out to Nina Gould's clambake party?"

I grimaced at the memory. I love my father, but having a cop in the family, especially one who could smell BS from the next town over, didn't exactly rocket me to the top of the social food chain as a teenager.

"What awards ceremony was Andy talking about?" I asked her.

"It's this dumb poll they had on the reunion's website. They came up with a bunch of different categories, like Teacher's Pet or Class Clown, and then everyone voted on a winner. It's basically just a way for the popular crowd to relive their glory days," she said. "I just voted for myself in every category."

I laughed. "They should give out real high school reunion awards, like Most Regrettable Tattoo."

"Most Divorces Before Thirty," snickered Stevie.

"Biggest Waste of a College Degree. I'd probably win that one."

"Oh, stop it," said Stevie. "Everyone knows the truly talented are underappreciated in their youth. Look at Van Gogh."

I raised my eyebrows. "That's the example you chose?"

"He is one of the most renowned artists in the world."

I snorted. "Yeah, after he died."

People crowded the dance floor in the center of the gym as the DJ on the assembly stage blasted an old Britney Spears song. The walls were covered in sparkly blue tinsel with white streamers and gold balloons. Small round tables surrounded the dance floor where a few people were seated, chatting. Each table had a blue tablecloth, a decorative gold centerpiece, and white flameless candles. A crowd of people mingled in front of a folding table with rows of award trophies next to the bar, while a hired photographer made his way through the guests, taking both candid and posed photos.

A massive balloon depicting the school mascot, Manny the Muskrat, stood in the back corner of the gym, its face illuminated by the spinning lights of the disco ball hanging from the scoreboard.

Stevie stared up at it. "Oh, that is creepy."

"It's like the eyes follow you," I said, swaying back and forth.

"You can thank the school spirit committee," said Stevie. "Those kids had to sell a lot of very stale cookies to afford it. It's staying up until after the senior prom next Friday night."

"They want this thing at the prom? What's their theme, nightmares come to life?" Not really expecting an answer, I scanned the room. "No one's wearing hunting camouflage. Looks like I owe Dad five dollars."

Stevie pointed to a red-faced, pudgy, blond man in a wrinkled brown suit, drinking from a plastic party cup. "Nope, Barry Townsend is wearing a mossy oak tie. Remember him? He played football with Big Andy, inside linebacker. He owns the car dealership now."

When Barry lowered his cup, liquid dribbled onto his shirt. "It's not even seven o'clock yet and he looks completely trashed," I remarked.

"He married Holly Gardiner," she said by way of an explanation, gesturing to the brunette woman dancing next to him. "There's the rest of the Pageant Minions: Rebecca Carson, Julie Kramer, and Amanda Fleming."

Not that I needed a reminder. All four women were practically clones, same as they had been in high school. They were each wearing a pink dress, but in different shades, and their hair was styled in the same glossy beach waves.

"Holly owns the beauty salon in town, the Siren's Sound," said Stevie. "She, Becca, and Julie are the hairstylists, and Amanda does waxing and nails."

I wanted to discuss those women as much as I did back in high school, which was not at all.

"Just be sure to give me a heads-up if you see the Harbour Queen." I raised my chin and extended my pinky finger. "Her Royal Highness, Jolene Dexter," I said in an absurdly regal accent.

"Don't worry, I'm sure the crown will be easy to spot," joked Stevie.

"Not to mention the sash."

Suddenly, Stevie froze like a deer in the headlights. The all too familiar sting of humiliation broke out on the back of my neck. Slowly, I turned around and saw a petite woman with blond hair standing right behind me.

"Silly me," trilled Jolene. "I seem to have forgotten them both at home."

Chapter Two

Jolene Dexter, class president, winner of both the Miss Junior Harbour Queen and Miss Harbour Queen pageants, class valedictorian, and the bane of my high school existence. She eyed Stevie and me expectantly, waiting for one of us to speak.

Stevie recovered first. "Hi, Jolene." She nodded to the handsome, bored-looking man with dark hair whom I recognized as Lawrence Dexter, Jolene's husband. "Hey, Trawler." Apparently, he still preferred to go by his nickname, which he got while working on his father's commercial fishing boat.

Stevie gestured toward their outfits. "Both wearing the school colors, I see."

Jolene wore a blue dress and white cardigan, a gold scarf tied around her neck. Trawler was dressed in casual tan slacks, white polo shirt, and blue blazer.

"Naturally," said Jolene, putting a hand on her waist in a playful pose. I recognized the same polite, vacant smile from her pageant days. She pointed to Stevie's head. "I love your hair. Did you dye it for the reunion?"

"Nope," said Stevie brightly. "My mother was nagging me to cover up my gray hairs, so I took the passive-aggressive route."

Jolene laughed before turning to me. "I wasn't expecting to see you tonight, Belinda," she said, eyebrows raised.

Immediately, my shoulders tensed. "Why is that?"

Her pageant smile became a smirk. "You swore after graduation you would never step foot in Little Blue Harbour again. You even defaced the town's welcome sign before you left."

Not my greatest moment, I'll admit. "In my defense, it was obvious what those clouds could be altered to look like."

"It was pretty funny," said Trawler, chuckling.

Jolene cut her eyes in his direction, and he quickly averted his gaze. "No harm, no foul, I suppose," she said. "The mayor presented me with a community recognition plaque for cleaning the sign."

"Wow, that's quite an achievement," I said with mock enthusiasm.

"It wasn't a big deal," she said, playing at modesty.

"Sure, it is. How often do you get the chance to be publicly recognized by the guy who embezzled all that money from the boardwalk restoration project?"

Other than a slight flaring of her nostrils, Jolene gave no reaction to the barb, but Stevie's eyes narrowed in warning.

I decided to dial it back a bit. I folded my arms tightly across my chest. "How have you both been? Still together, obviously."

She nodded, slipping her arm around Trawler's waist. "Married for fourteen years this September," she said smugly.

Of course, why take the time to learn how to be independent when you can just get married straight out of high school? No wonder she was clinging to him like an orphaned gorilla.

"Trawler owns and operates his dad's fishing boat now," Jolene continued. "I work part-time in the high school administration office. And I just heard this week from Principal Acker that our daughter, Sadie, is going to be skipped ahead in the fall. She'll be going from grade seven to grade nine. Can you believe it? But enough about me," she chirped. "How are things with *you*, Belinda? I heard you were working as a columnist for some big-city newspaper in Ottawa."

Well played, Harbour Queen. A classic Jolene move. Make me sound more successful than I really was so if I didn't correct her, she could immediately expose me as a liar in front of everyone.

I'd rather cut off my bun and eat it before I let that happen. "I covered weekend events for a community newspaper," I said shortly. It was 90 percent swap meets, and we both knew it.

"Oh, that's right, your mother told me all about it," she gushed, but I could hear the sarcasm behind her enthusiasm. "It's called the *Bytown Freebie*, isn't it? Are you still writing for them?"

"No, it folded six months ago." *Like she didn't already know that.*

"That's a shame," she said, pushing out her bottom lip in an exaggerated pout. "Are you here with your boyfriend? What did your mother say his name was?" she asked, snapping her fingers as if struggling to remember.

"Craig," I supplied tersely. "And, no. We broke up."

"I'm so sorry to hear that," she said, putting a hand theatrically to her chest. *Again, like she didn't already know.*

I decided the only way I was getting out of this conversation was to do what I did best, make things awkward.

"It happens," I said, with a breezy confidence I didn't feel. "Especially when you come home early and catch him with the same coffee shop barista who never gets your order right."

Both Jolene's and Trawler's eyes widened in horror. I guess my mother failed to share *that* particular detail.

I waved aside their shocked expressions. "It's okay, I never tipped her."

Stevie shot me the same exasperated glare as my parents when I was being deliberately difficult as a teenager.

"Well," said Trawler, after a short pause, "we should probably go say hello to a few people. We'll let you two get back to mingling." He gave us a polite nod before leading his wife over to their friends at the edge of the dance floor.

"Wow," said Stevie, her eyebrows raised as she watched them walk away.

"Ugh, I know," I said as I watched Jolene and the Pageant Minions air-kiss. "She's the worst."

"That was directed at both of you," said Stevie.

"What did *I* do?"

"You mean, besides unloading a decade's worth of animosity onto each other in under five minutes?" she asked, equally incredulous.

"Sorry," I said grudgingly. "I can't help it. Her whole 'Golden Child of Little Blue Harbour' act. Everyone in town thinks she's so perfect. It drives me nuts."

I could tell Stevie wanted to roll her eyes at me, but thankfully, she restrained herself. As teens, Stevie dutifully hated Jolene on my behalf, but I could tell her heart was never really in it.

"You can't still be holding a grudge because she won the English literature bursary award instead of you," she said.

"Of course not." She raised her eyebrows skeptically, and my cool facade crumbled. "Achieving the highest grade in the class doesn't mean she understood the subject matter more than everyone else," I said in a rush of renewed resentment.

She shook her head ruefully. "One of these days, you're going to have to tell me what *really* went down between you two."

My stomach clenched at the thought.

"Besides, you're wrong," continued Stevie. "Not everyone in town thinks Jolene is perfect."

Instantly, I perked up. "Really? What have you heard?"

Stevie hesitated. "There's just a dumb rumor going around. Maybe I shouldn't have said anything."

"Nuh-uh. I need this. Spill."

Her smile turned mischievous, further heightening my intrigue. We huddled closely together, even though there was no way anyone could have heard us over the music. "Word around town is that the queen has found a new king," she said. "Donna Dickie told me Jo always flirts with Andy whenever he stops by the admin office, and they usually eat lunch together."

I rolled my eyes, disappointed. "Boo," I said, drawing it out. "Your source is Donna Dickie? I thought you heard a real rumor."

"She's a credible source," said Stevie. "She's more up in other people's business than your mother. She works at the high school too. She's the office manager, Jo's boss."

"This is my nemesis, Stevie. I'm going to need something a little juicier than Jolene sharing a sandwich with another man."

"Oh, you want juicy?" she asked.

"Yes, please."

Stevie rolled her shoulders and stretched her neck as though preparing for a feat of strength. She leaned in. "The senior class held a dance-a-thon as a fundraiser for prom. Both Jo and Andy were chaperones. They disappeared together for over an hour, and when they came back, they were disheveled and Jo was wearing his hoodie." She raised her hands to mime her head exploding.

I looked back at Jolene with renewed interest. "Really?"

"It's not like Andy ever let something like marriage vows stop him," continued Stevie. "He married Fiona Mahoney after high school."

"My parents went to the wedding," I said, remembering. "Mum helped Fiona get her real estate license."

"They only lasted five years before Fiona left him," said Stevie. "She caught him with one of her friends from her book club. That was after she'd already forgiven a previous affair. I heard he and Holly used to be a thing too."

Of course, the head of the Pageant Minions. I could totally see her being Andy's type. "What, is he just going through our old yearbook?" I joked.

Suddenly, Stevie nudged me in the ribs with her elbow. "Look at Trawler!"

I followed her gaze and saw Andy now standing next to Jolene, leaning in to give her a quick kiss on the cheek. Trawler's expression soured as he watched the two of them. To my surprise, Holly, who was standing just behind them, had the same look on her face.

Maybe there is something to the rumor. That possibility didn't make me as happy as I thought it would, for some reason.

Stevie seemed to notice. "Come on, let's go get a drink."

I nodded. "Lead the way."

Together, we made our way across the gym toward the makeshift bar near the stage. A few people called out greetings to Stevie as we passed, and she kept up her running commentary on the current status of our old classmates.

I scanned the dance floor and realized who was missing. "Hey, do you know if Kevin Barclay is coming to this thing?" I asked her.

She shook her head. "I doubt it. He and his wife, Madeline, are probably working tonight. They run the convenience store on Harbourview Drive."

"Wait, *Kevin* bought Gull's Quick Stop? I thought he would be on his way to becoming the next Bill Gates by now."

"He was studying computer engineering in Vancouver, but he dropped out before he graduated," she said.

I stopped dead in my tracks. "Why? Kevin was a tech genius. He built a desktop computer from scratch using old parts for the science fair. Why would he drop out of school?"

Stevie shrugged. "No idea. I know his father has medical issues. I assumed Kevin moved back to Little Blue Harbour to help his family. He and Maddie bought the store after Mr. Gullberg retired. It's exactly the same, though. They kept the pool tables, pizza counter, and arcade games in the back."

"The Quick Stop is practically a landmark in this town," I said, laughing fondly. "They had the best pizza."

"They still do," said Stevie, laughing too. "Kevin had Gullberg's sauce recipe included in the sale."

"We should stop there after this," I said. "I always liked Kevin. Before you moved here, he used to let me sit with him and his friends whenever they played *Quest of the Mages* in the library during lunch."

But the less said about my fantasy role-playing games era, the better.

As we approached the bar, Stevie broke into a devious smile. "I think I've just spotted someone else you'll be happy to see."

Confused, I craned my neck in the same direction to see over the crowd. My brain registered the sight of chocolate brown hair and a fiery red beard. Suddenly, my stomach filled with thousands of butterflies, all fighting to get out.

"Did I forget to mention who was tending bar for the reunion?" asked Stevie, her tone overly innocent.

I gave her my best scowl. "Yes, you did."

She dragged me over to the bar and flagged down the bartender. "Hey, Jinx. Two rum and Cokes, please."

The bartender looked up from the red plastic cups he was filling with ice, breaking into a wide, friendly grin when he saw her. "Here comes trouble," he said fondly.

"You got that right," she said, shoving me to the front.

My entire body burned with humiliation. *Yeesh, be a little more obvious, Stevie.*

Ethan Sutherland tossed a striped dish towel over his shoulder and leaned against the tabletop, a classic bartender pose. He was just as achingly beautiful as he was at eighteen. "Belinda Bishop," he said, his eyes alight with surprise.

A shiver of pure pleasure ran down my spine. I didn't have to remind him. "Hi, Jinx. It's good to see you."

Every small town has its own superstitions, and Little Blue Harbour was no exception. Locals loved to tell the story of Wailing Martha, the ghost of a young widow who wanders the shoreline near the boardwalk, still waiting for her husband to return from the sea. It was believed her cries of despair meant a storm was approaching. And no fishing boat would ever leave port before tossing an ice cube over to the side to ensure a big catch.

The most persistent superstition was the Curse of the Sutherland Beard. Back when Little Blue Harbour was first founded,

Ethan's great, great, great, etc. grandfather was betrothed to the daughter of a midwife. When her daughter was jilted at the altar, the midwife swore that any Sutherland man who inherited the groom's brown hair and copper-red beard would bring misfortune to the people of Little Blue Harbour.

According to my grandfather, Jinx's great-uncle Arthur Sutherland had the red beard and an unlucky handshake. Anyone who shook his hand would lose a significant amount of money the same day. My own parents refused to say hello to William Sutherland because anyone who greeted him would receive bad news before the next sunrise.

When Ethan came back to school at the beginning of grade eight with red whiskers on his chin, the entire class waited to see what would be his "curse." Later that afternoon, the social studies teacher Mrs. Mitchell tripped and fell in the hallway, breaking her wrist. Her sole interaction with Ethan had been to call out his full name during morning attendance. It took a few more weeks to be sure, but eventually, any student who experienced bad luck, be it failing a test in their best subject, spilling chocolate milk on their new pair of white pants, or setting their braid on fire during science lab, swore they'd said his full name earlier the same day.

"You're a bartender now?" I asked Jinx. I couldn't help noticing the broad pectoral muscles pressing against his blue long-sleeved shirt.

"Pub owner," he clarified as he made our drinks. "The Right Foot restaurant and pub on the boardwalk. We converted the old general store."

"We?" *Please don't tell me he's married.*

"Me and my ex, Rosie."

"I'm sorry to hear that," I said, while internally cheering.

He shrugged. "It happens. Turns out living in a small town wasn't for her."

"You're divorced?"

"No, but we lived together for four years." He laughed. "Can't really have a wedding when the officiant is terrified of having to say your name. Makes the vows a little awkward."

I matched his easy laugh. "I can't believe people still buy into that."

Not that the so-called family curse had any effect on his popularity. A social chameleon, Jinx moved between cliques throughout high school with ease. One day he'd be tossing the football around with Big Andy and the other jocks, and the next you'd find him trading *X-Files* fan theories with Kevin Barclay and his friends. He took part in school plays and poetry slam nights with the drama kids, but he also headed up the school's debate team. It didn't matter where kids fell on the social hierarchy, Jinx had a smile and a greeting for everyone. It was one of the reasons he made my pulse race whenever we passed in the hallways.

And one of the many reasons I'd always felt he was miles out of my league.

Jinx slid my drink toward me, his fingers brushing mine as I accepted it. "Have *you* ever said my full name?"

I hesitated. "Sure. I mean, we went to elementary school together."

He gave me a cheeky grin. "What about after I grew the beard?"

Stevie cleared her throat suddenly, shaking her head slightly in a not-so-subtle warning. I ignored her, though. "Okay, no," I admitted, "but that's only because everyone else started calling you Jinx. It's not because I think your name is cursed."

"Of course not," he said, clearly enjoying this.

To my surprise, I realized I was enjoying it too. "You think I won't say it?"

"Oh, I know you won't say it," he said, his clever green eyes sparkling with the challenge.

We locked eyes and I struggled to keep a straight face. It was like we were playing a game of verbal chicken, each daring the other to back down first.

Unfortunately, Stevie jumped in between us. "Maybe that's not such a great idea."

Jinx laughed, and I was treated to a brief glimpse of the dimples hidden under his beard. "Relax, Stevie, I'm just messing with her." He moved down the bar to take another person's drink order. "It was great seeing you again, Belinda. Enjoy the reunion."

My spirits dipped, a little disappointed to have our banter cut short. "If you have a break later, come find us. We'll catch up."

He gave me a look that made my cheeks tingle with heat. "I'd like that."

"Great." I took a quick sip for nerves. "See you later, Ethan Sutherland."

Stevie grabbed my arm and steered me away from the bar. "What is the matter with you?" she hissed in my ear. "Why did you do that?"

"He used my full name, it's only polite to do the same for him." I grinned. "Besides, it was just a little harmless flirting."

"That was not flirting," she insisted. "That was tempting fate."

I giggled at her dire expression. "Come on, Stevie. It's just a local superstition."

"Tell that to Trudy Spencer," she snapped. "Remember when her parents went to Jamaica, and she threw that house party? She introduced Jinx to her cousin using his real name.

Later that night, Trudy walked into a tree and cut her forehead. She ended up with ten stitches right before school pictures."

"Trudy was doing tequila shots all night. She would have walked into that tree no matter what she called him."

Stevie let out a short, irritable breath. "This is payback for springing Jinx on you, isn't it?"

"Maybe," I answered smugly.

I wrapped one arm around her shoulder and gave her a bracing side hug. "The only thing you have to worry about is calling me tomorrow morning to admit that I was right, and there is no such thing as a cursed name."

"No, I'll be calling to say *I told you so*," she countered.

"Wanna bet?"

"Loser buys coffee and doughnuts," she said.

"You're on." I stuck out my hand and she shook it.

"This will be the easiest Boston cream I've ever won," she said.

Chapter Three

Three and a half hours later, Stevie and I were still at the reunion. If you didn't count the excruciating small talk and seemingly endless parade of baby pictures, things were actually going quite well. I even managed to swallow my pride and accept Jolene's invitation to sit with her and Trawler during the awards ceremony.

Unfortunately, the Pageant Minions were also sitting with them. Holly made a few snarky comments about my writing career, but it wasn't as bad as I anticipated.

As Stevie predicted, most of the awards went to the old popular crowd. Jason Zhou, whose parents owned the Sea Dragon Palace restaurant, now lived in Australia and won the award for Farthest Traveled. Most Interesting Job went to Nina Gould, who was now a performer with Cirque du Soleil in Montreal. Andy took to the stage amid thunderous applause and laughter to accept his Class Flirt award. I even managed to keep the eye rolling to a minimum when Jolene won Community Helper. The only unpopular person to win something was Donna Dickie, who won Teacher's Pet, which came as a surprise to no one.

"Ugh, she is still such a try-hard," complained Rebecca. "Always chasing after us, trying to be part of the group."

Holly turned to her, smirking. "And still raiding her grandmother's closet."

Most of the table's occupants snickered in return, but Stevie and I shared a disapproving glance. It was a well-known fact amongst our class that the Dickies weren't rich by any means, and Donna had been forced to wear her grandmother's old clothes growing up, which had mostly consisted of 1960s housedresses and smocked shifts. As a result, she was ostracized by the Pageant Minions even worse than I was, but it didn't stop Donna from hovering on the sidelines, always looking for an opportunity to join them.

Donna descended from the stage, her head oscillating back and forth, surveying the crowd. Even from across the gym, her bright red lipstick and expertly applied cat-eye makeup were visible. She seemed to have decided to fully lean into the vintage look as an adult. Her chestnut hair was half up with victory rolls styled in the front. Her dark green cocktail dress was paired with a white lace shawl and matching pair of evening gloves that I would have gladly sold my immortal soul to possess.

"Please don't come over here," groaned Amanda as we watched Donna scan the tables.

Donna's gaze landed on us, and her smile widened. She made a beeline for us, waving enthusiastically.

The Pageant Minions breathed a collective sigh of disappointment. "You'd think after a decade of rejection, she'd take the hint," Julie muttered. "Remember when she tried to worm her way into our limo for prom?"

Holly laughed. "What was it you said, Andy? 'Not even if it cured cancer.'"

He shifted in his seat, looking uncomfortable. "That was a long time ago, guys. Let's give her a break. Jolene and I still have to work with her."

As she approached, the entire table spread out in an attempt to claim every available inch of space. Unfortunately, it didn't stop Donna from barreling up to us.

"Hello, everyone," she cooed, clutching her trophy like it was an Academy Award. "Don't we all look wonderful tonight?" Without invitation, she grabbed an empty chair from a nearby table and wedged it in between Jolene and Andy. She turned to him with a bright smile. "Congratulations on your win, Big Andy."

He shifted his chair away from hers, avoiding her expectant gaze. "Yes, it was a very proud moment."

The entire table fell into an awkward silence while Donna surveyed us, clearly waiting for someone to send more praise in her direction.

Thankfully, Nina Gould decided to take the bullet for the rest of us. "I love your gloves, Donna," she said, her smile strained. "Where did you get them?"

Donna leapt on the compliment like it was Chris Evans covered in chocolate. "Thank you," she said, modeling them for the entire table. "They're Chanel."

"Really?" blurted out Julie. Her cheeks turned an impressive shade of maroon. I suspected she hadn't meant to sound so impressed.

Donna shrugged modestly, but her eyes narrowed smugly. "I belong to an online forum for vintage fashion collectors. A *very* exclusive group."

Fortunately, the hired photographer chose that moment to approach our table with his camera raised. Almost in unison, everyone at the table leaned in closer together for the picture. After the camera flashed, we all shifted back to our original positions.

Donna adjusted her shawl and folded her hands in front of her on the table, ensuring her gloves were still visible. "What were you all discussing before I got here?" There was an edge to her voice, as though we'd promised to save her a seat and then ditched her.

I was tempted to lie and say we were planning to prank the DJ, just to see if she'd still rat us out.

"Nothing much," sighed Jolene. "Just catching up."

Donna laughed. "A short conversation, I'm sure. Not much ever happens in Little Blue Harbour. Jolene knows that better than anyone. She hasn't left town in years, " she said, casting a sideward glance at Andy.

Maybe it was the two rum and Cokes, or some residual sense of childhood loyalty, but my hackles perked up at Donna's obvious scorn. I waited for Holly and the Pageant Minions to shut her down, but they seemed content to let Jolene fend for herself.

So much for sisterhood. "Congratulations on your big win, Donna," I said, taking care to match her supercilious tone "It must be so satisfying to know you're still sucking up to all the right people."

My sarcasm didn't faze her. "Yes, it's too bad you never learned, Belinda. You might be further along in life."

I heaved a dramatic sigh. "Yeah, that's one of my biggest regrets; a lack of cheap, plastic trophies."

"They are *not* plastic," objected Jolene. "I ordered them from an online store that does corporate award statues. They're made from real crystal."

I glared at her. Even when I was trying to defend her, she couldn't help showing off.

Stevie reached over and picked up Donna's award, a clear rectangular slab with the words *Teacher's Pet* etched into the crystal, affixed to a dark wooden base. "Oof, that's heavy," she said. "Definitely not plastic."

Donna gently retrieved it as if Stevie's hands would contaminate it. "You know Jolene. Nothing but the best for her."

The Pageant Minions seemed to have reached the end of their patience with Donna. Holly and Julie jumped to their feet. "I love this song," exclaimed Holly, cutting off whatever unsolicited opinion Donna was about to share. "Let's all go dance."

She pulled Barry roughly to his feet, dotting the tablecloth with specks of brown liquor from his cup in the process. The rest of the Pageant Minions followed suit and dragged their respective partners onto the dance floor. Jolene, Trawler, and Andy joined them, with Nina and her husband hot on their heels, leaving just me and Stevie at the table with Donna. For a split second, I wished I'd joined them.

Fortunately, Donna's eyes remained focused on the dance floor as though on the lookout for couples dancing too closely, which left Stevie and me free to chat. Stevie was just telling me about a well-known Canadian actor who had apparently bought a cottage in the area when I heard angry shouting over the music. Trawler was now standing in front of Andy, their faces only inches apart, while Jolene tried to separate them. Without hesitating, I left the table and joined the growing crowd, Stevie close behind me.

Trawler shoved Andy away from Jolene. "Keep your hands off my wife," he snarled.

Andy raised both hands up in surrender. "Whoa, Trawler, relax. What's your problem?"

"Trawler, stop!" Jolene tried to insert herself between the two men, but Trawler blocked her.

"He's been following you around all night. It's pathetic," said Trawler.

"He's not following me. We're friends. I'm allowed to talk to other men," cried Jolene.

"It's pretty obvious he's looking to do more than talk," retorted Trawler.

Andy shook his head. "I don't know what you think is going on here, but you're wrong."

A red-haired woman in a mint green pantsuit laughed. I recognized her as Fiona Mahoney, Andy's ex-wife. "Probably the same thing that was going on between you and Rhonda Wilson," she said bitterly.

Andy glared at her. "For Pete's sake, Fi, we got married when we were only nineteen years old. I was just a young, dumb kid. You need to let it go."

"Maybe I could if I hadn't *also* caught you with Sissy Donahue," Fiona fired back.

Andy's eyes narrowed. "Are you sure you want to start airing dirty laundry in public? Your hamper's not exactly empty either."

Fiona's smirk quickly flattened into a furious scowl. "Trawler's right; you're pathetic." She turned away but suddenly spun back around to face him again. "A more appropriate nickname for you would be Little Andy." She stuck her nose in the air and retreated, headed for the bar.

"Nice seeing you too, Fi," he called after her. "Classy as always."

"You see?" Trawler said to Jolene. "The guy is a total dog. He's just using you."

Andy glared at him. "Just because you can't be bothered to show her any attention doesn't mean no one else can."

"What the hell is that supposed to mean?" asked Trawler.

Jolene looked like she was close to tears. "Andy, please don't," she pleaded.

"No, he needs to hear it," said Andy. He turned back to Trawler. "You take Jolene for granted. You bailed on the silent auction fundraiser for the town library she helped organize last month. You went to Halifax to watch the Mooseheads play the same weekend as her community play. I'll bet she had to practically drag you here tonight."

Trawler's face paled under the spinning lights, and he rounded on his wife. "What do you do, go running to him every time we have a disagreement?" he accused Jolene.

"It wasn't like that," she cried. "We're friends, we talk to each other."

"Maybe you should try it sometime," Andy spat at Trawler. "You haven't shown a genuine interest in Jolene for years, so you don't have any right to get jealous when someone else does."

Trawler gaped at the two of them, his jaw slack with shock. The rest of the crowd watched, waiting for the verbal grenade Andy just lobbed to explode. But Trawler just shook his head after a moment and stormed off toward the interior of the school.

"Where are you going?" cried Jolene. "Trawler, wait!"

She started to go after him, but Andy grabbed her elbow. "Let go of me," she snarled, pulling against his grip.

"Why are you chasing after him? He doesn't deserve you," said Andy.

Jolene ripped free of his grasp and shoved him away from her, hard enough to make the former football player stumble. "You had no right to speak for me, Andy."

She banged into my shoulder as she rushed past me to follow her husband. Everyone on the dance floor immediately broke into their respective groups to discuss what just happened.

I whistled softly. "Looks like there's some merit to that rumor after all," I told Stevie.

Holly, Julie, Rebecca, and Amanda huddled together while Barry stood off to the side of them, his chin periodically dipping down to his chest. With the amount of alcohol he had consumed, I was surprised he wasn't passed out under a table.

"Trust Jolene to make tonight all about her," I overheard Holly say contemptuously.

"I would be so embarrassed," said Julie.

"Poor Andy," added Rebecca. "Getting dragged into the middle of their marital problems."

"Poor Andy?" Barry snorted so hard, he almost tipped over. "It's his own fault. Andy messed around and found out."

Holly gave her husband a look sharp enough to draw blood. "She should have kept their problems private. Making a scene in public is so tacky."

Barry chuckled as he took another drunken sip. "Cheating on your spouse is tackier."

Even in the low lights of the gymnasium, I could see Holly's cheeks burn bright red. She began to retaliate but seemed to reconsider.

"Yeah, that's what I thought." Barry drained his plastic cup and dropped it on the floor. "Screw this," he slurred. He lumbered toward the doors and out into the school lobby.

Holly watched him leave, her mouth set in a twisted scowl. She caught me staring. "What are you looking at?"

Without waiting for my response, she grabbed both Amanda and Julie by their elbows and pulled them out of earshot.

I turned back to Stevie. "Can't this town make it through one dance without a fistfight?"

"Of course not," she said. "How else would we know when it's time to leave?"

I rubbed my hands together in anticipation. "Gull's pizza?"

"Ooh, yes, please." She slipped her purse strap over her head and across her body. "Let me just go say goodbye to a few people first."

I sat down at the now empty table to wait for her to return. I wasn't sure where Donna had disappeared to, and I didn't really care. She was probably smelling the bathrooms for marijuana smoke. Across the gym, Jinx was busing tables, gathering up dirty paper plates and empty plastic cups. It occurred to me that he might like some pizza too.

As I made my way over to him, I noticed Andy standing on his own in a dark corner, looking down at his award. I hesitated for a second, and then changed course. "Hey," I said as I approached him. "Are you okay?"

Andy looked up at me, surprised. "Yeah, I'm good." He gazed past me at the others still huddled together. "Fourteen years later and we all just slide right back into the same roles, huh?"

"Yeah, I guess," I said awkwardly.

"The maladaptive behaviors we formed in adolescence tend to come back whenever we're around the places or people we knew as children." He smiled at my bewildered expression. "You'd be surprised what you can learn about yourself in therapy."

"Well, no judgment from me," I said. "I could probably use some myself."

"No one ever comes back to Little Blue Harbour for good reasons, do they?" Andy looked down at the award again. "You were right to get out of town when you did, Belinda. It's like no one around here wants you to actually grow or change."

A less generous person would have pointed out the best way to fix a bad reputation is to stop doing the things that caused it in the first place.

"I know I shouldn't have pushed Trawler's buttons," he said grimly, "but I can't stand how he treats Jo. How everyone in this town treats her. She does so much for others, and no one ever seems to appreciate it."

I tried to hold back, but a skeptical snort escaped me. "What are you talking about? The town loves her. Everyone thinks she's perfect."

Andy sighed. "Anything looks perfect if you stand far enough away."

His words settled in the center of my stomach like a stone. What was he trying to tell me? Was Jolene's life actually like the ocean, a stunning vista from the shore but a choppy mess at the center?

Andy ran his thumb over the engraved words, bitterness lining his grim frown. "I know I've made mistakes, but I'm trying to do better, you know? I'm thirty-two years old. I thought by now I'd be able to win an award for something a little more significant than Class Flirt."

"I'm sorry about your knee," I said.

He shrugged. "It's not all bad. I love teaching. I love coaching. As far as new goals go, I could have done worse. Maybe it won't be so bad for you either."

I stared at him, impressed. "I don't remember you being this perceptive when we were in high school."

He rolled his eyes comically. "Seriously, Belinda. So much therapy."

I giggled. "Stevie and I are going to stop in to see Kevin Barclay and grab some pizza. You're welcome to tag along."

He shook his head, his expression suddenly sour. "No, thanks. I think I'm just going to head home."

After he left, I turned in the direction of the table Jinx was clearing, but he was gone. I sat back down at the table with a sigh and continued waiting for Stevie. I got bored with crowd-watching after a while and began folding origami animals out of cocktail napkins. Five bullfrogs later, my desire for Gull's pizza won out over my patience. I checked the time on my phone. We only had thirty minutes until Gull's closed for the night. I decided to go look for Stevie.

I spotted her standing near the inflatable mascot, talking to a woman I didn't recognize. The woman was dressed in a white T-shirt and olive-green cargo pants with sneakers, and her auburn hair was swept back in a no-nonsense ponytail. The woman looked agitated, but she and Stevie didn't appear to be arguing. Before I could get close enough to hear what they were saying, the woman walked away from Stevie, brushing past me as she left the gymnasium.

"Who was that?" I asked Stevie.

"Madeline Barclay," she said. "Kevin's wife."

"I thought they weren't coming to the reunion." I stood on my tiptoes, searching the crowd for Kevin.

"They're not," said Stevie, looking worried. "Maddie was looking for Andy."

"Are you kidding me? Andy just made this long, insightful speech about becoming a better person." I flashed a pair of sarcastic finger quotes as I finished.

Stevie hesitated. "It was kind of strange. Maddie said she was here to collect an outstanding debt from Andy, but Kevin stopped keeping tabs when he took over the store."

We headed for the lobby. As we reached the doors, Jolene came barreling through them, her eyes red and puffy. Her glossy hair was disheveled. I stepped out of her way just in time to avoid a collision.

"Watch where you're going," Jolene snapped, her normally polished demeanor slipping.

"My apologies, Your Majesty," I said, bowing to her.

Stevie shook her head as Jolene stormed off. "Very mature, Bishop," she told me.

We continued into the lobby, and I noticed one of the doors leading to the second-floor corridor was ajar. A mischievous thought occurred to me. "Does Mr. Blenkhorn still work for the school?"

Stevie tilted her head to the side, suddenly suspicious. "Yeah, why?"

I grinned. "Does he still have that whiteboard hanging on the wall outside of his office?"

Stevie glanced between me and the door. "Uh-uh, no way," she said. "I know what you're thinking, Belinda, and count me out."

"Come on," I pleaded, pulling her into the hallway before anyone spotted us. "What's he going to do, give us detention again?"

She groaned in protest but did nothing to keep me from dragging her forward. "Okay, fine," she relented. "One quick cartoon and then pizza."

Giggling, we hurried up the stairs toward Mr. Blenkhorn's office.

During our senior year, Stevie and I began drawing cartoons featuring Manny the Muskrat in a variety of silly situations on the whiteboard outside of the vice-principal's office. Even though we never drew anything vulgar or rude, our vice-principal Mr. Blenkhorn seemed to take personal offense to the drawings, beginning a one-man crusade to catch the miscreants.

Which, of course, only made us draw more.

Naturally, Donna Dickie took it upon herself to snoop around his office after school and caught us. She immediately told Mr. Blenkhorn, who gave us a week's worth of detentions.

Still worth it, if you ask me.

We found Mr. Blenkhorn's office across from the school's music room, exactly as I remembered it. Even the same motivational poster hung on his door, a beach at sunset with the caption claiming every tomorrow was a promise of new beginnings.

I picked up the blue erasable marker and considered the blank whiteboard. "What should we draw? How about that giant inflatable mascot coming to life and terrorizing the reunion?"

"I love it," said Stevie, playing lookout. "Don't forget to add Mr. Blenkhorn."

The tip of the marker squeaked as I sketched the scene. "Don't worry, I've got him in the corner telling everyone to keep the noise down."

"Ah, his favorite lecture," said Stevie.

I finished the drawing and snapped the cap back onto the marker with a flourish. "Done."

"Great, now let's get out of here." I headed in the direction of the front lobby, but Stevie called me back. "No, let's leave through the west exit. It leads to the parking lot, and Gull's is right across the street," she said.

We scurried past the administration office and down a dark staircase with as much speed as our heels would allow. Suddenly, Stevie let out a sharp gasp, stopping dead in her tracks. The pointed toe of my shoe caught on something soft, pulling my feet out from under me, and I landed face first onto the linoleum floor.

I twisted around to see what tripped me. It took my eyes a moment to focus in the dark before I recoiled in horror.

Andrew "Big Andy" Perch, his normally flirtatious gaze now blank, lay sprawled in the hallway. A dark puddle of blood pooled by his head, staining the flecked linoleum floor crimson.

Tentatively, I reached out and touched his neck, feeling for a pulse. My stomach lurched into my throat. "He's dead."

Chapter Four

The next morning, I followed Stevie downstairs from her tiny apartment over the tearoom to help her and Diane get ready to open. Although, to be honest, my help mostly consisted of sitting at the back table and eating homemade tea biscuits with wild blueberry jam while we discussed the previous night's events. Stevie had insisted I crash at her place last night, but I'd barely slept. I'd spent most of the night tossing and turning, unable to get the image of poor Andy's slumped body out of my head.

After we found Andy's body, Stevie and I immediately called 911. Two officers I didn't recognize were the first to arrive. They secured the scene before walking us both back to the gymnasium. The police did their standard speech about having to speak to everyone present and nobody being allowed to leave before they had everyone's initial statements. It was after midnight by the time they finished, instructing us to make ourselves available for further questioning, if needed.

Knowing Stevie and Diane had a busy morning ahead of them, and not waiting to overstay my welcome, I left shortly before eight o'clock, promising to check in with Stevie later. I slumped down the front steps of the Osprey, still groggy, and made my way through the garden to the white picket fence that separated the tearoom from the rest of the boardwalk. Like the Osprey itself, the garden was designed to reflect a typical, Loyalist-era estate. The flower beds were bursting with white and purple peonies, yarrow, irises, and marigolds. Pink, purple and blue lupines lined the granite rock foundation. The building's wooden siding was painted a pale yellow and its glass bottle bottom windows were lined with white shutters. The only contemporary feature of the property, in addition to its modern appliances and indoor plumbing, was a small patio near the kitchen where tearoom patrons could enjoy their meal with a stunning view of the harbor.

I lifted the iron latch to the gate and was careful to not slam it closed behind me. The rest of the boardwalk was slowly coming to life as I walked down the promenade. I decided to take the scenic route home and continued in the direction of the old railroad tracks the town converted into a walking trail, near the picnic area that doubled as the Loyalist reenactment camp in the summer. The trail went right past my parents' house and Topsail Cottages and Campground.

Seagulls circled overhead, their lilting calls mingling with the waves breaking against the rocks that lined the edge of the promenade. Wailing Martha was silent today, so the sun likely wasn't going anywhere. The McGrey Island ferry was making its first pass of the day, shuttling tourists and residents alike from the island, which was home to both the town's lighthouse and wealthier inhabitants, across the harbor to the boardwalk. The soles of my shoes thumped reassuringly against the wooden walkway as I passed the Right Foot restaurant and pub, eyeing it with more interest now that I knew who owned it. I continued past the town's old shipyard, which was now the Hallett Performing Arts Center, followed by the Little Blue Harbour Museum and Historical Society, and Salty Sal's ice cream and sandwich shack.

As I approached Sand Dollar Pastries, the only bakery on the boardwalk, a middle-aged woman stood next to the entrance, watering the pots of purple and blue petunias hanging from the awning. Like the rest of the brightly painted shops that lined the boardwalk, the bakery reminded me of saltwater taffy with its bright pink exterior and white trim. Large ceramic seashells sat on either end of the front step like sentries, leading to a narrow porch with a bistro set fashioned from old lobster traps for the table and chairs.

"Morning, Vi," I called out to the woman.

Vivien Cox stopped and squinted at me, shielding her eyes from the sun. "Good morning, sweetie," she replied. "Surprised to see you out and about at this hour."

I stopped and joined her by the flowers. "I had a bit of a long night."

Vivien hesitated, tucking a thin black braid from her twisted bun behind her ear. "So I've heard."

"Ah," I said ruefully, "you must mean Andy Perch."

Vivien nodded. "You could've knocked me over with a feather when I heard," she said. "I popped into the Beanery for my morning coffee, and it was all anyone was talking about." She dropped her voice to a murmur. "Is it true you were the one who found him?"

My chest tightened at the memory of Andy's blank eyes. Unable to get the words out, I simply nodded in reply.

Vivien rested the watering can against her hip, clucking her tongue. "Terrible shame. Irene and I were close with his parents before they passed." She shook her head fondly. "You know, he still stopped in once a week for a box of butter tarts for the staff room at the school. He was a sweetie, that one."

I made a noncommittal noise. I didn't want to speak ill of the dead, but I could think of a few individuals who would disagree with her.

Vivien motioned me forward and I obliged by walking a few steps closer. "Is it true what everyone's saying?" she murmured, glancing up and down the boardwalk as though checking for eavesdroppers. "Big Andy was murdered?"

My mouth dropped open. "I thought he fell and hit his head."

She shook her head. "Not according to what I overheard in the Beanery. The police are treating it as a homicide. They're even bringing in some big shot from the Major Crimes Unit in Halifax to head up the investigation." She glanced around again before continuing. "You'll never believe who they think did it."

"Who?" I asked eagerly.

"Jolene Dexter."

My arms went slack with shock, my purse almost slipping from my hands. "Are you serious?" *Little Miss Beloved By All?*

Vivien nodded significantly. "Last night, Andy exposed their affair in front of everyone, including her husband."

"Yeah, I was there for that," I said softly, thinking back to the scene on the dance floor. "The cops think she—what? Pushed Andy down the stairs in retaliation?"

She shrugged, water sloshing in the watering can. "I guess. I mean, if they're looking at her, they've got to have *some* evidence she did it."

I chewed the inside of my cheek. On the surface, Jolene as the most likely suspect made sense; she and Andy fought shortly before he died, and she wasn't in the gym at the time of his death. But this was also the same woman who, as a child, insisted on releasing spiders outside instead of squishing them.

Vivien finished watering her flowers and started to head back inside her bakery. "You take it easy today, sweetie," she said over her shoulder. "If you're feeling brave later, Irene's working on a new scone recipe today."

As if on cue, her wife appeared in the doorway, her thin frame covered by an apron made from the Nova Scotian tartan. Her strawberry blond ringlets were dusted with flour. "Earl Grey tea, marmalade, and ginger," said Irene. "There's nothing brave about it. We'll sell out before noon, you just wait and see."

Vivien patted Irene's shoulder affectionately. "I'm sure it will be delicious, hon."

Irene looked over at me. "You'll try one, won't you, pet?"

"Of course," I said vaguely. Normally, the scent of sugar and vanilla that was currently drifting through the bakery's open door would have me already climbing their steps, but my mind was occupied with this new development surrounding Andy's death.

I gave Vivian money to set aside a scone for me and continued toward home, mulling over what I had just learned. By the time my parents' property came into view, I was fiercely regretting my decision to hoof it home in heels.

Shelly, my parents' Nova Scotia Duck Tolling Retriever, sprang up from her flannel dog bed outside of my father's workshop, barking wildly as she bounded toward me, her tail whirling behind her like a boat propeller. I squatted down to greet her, planting a quick kiss on her reddish-brown and white snout. As usual, Shelly took this as an invitation to cover my chin and cheeks with dog slobber.

I straightened, wiping my face with the sleeve of my blazer. "Ugh, missed you too."

Shelly barked once more, and then took off running for the rental cottages. I had the day off (as a further incentive for me to attend the reunion last night), so I was in no rush as I followed her up the lilac-lined driveway.

If I had to pick one benefit of the implosion that was my life in Ottawa, it was being back at my parents' nineteenth-century seaside cottage. I adored every detail of my childhood home: the square frame and mansard roof, its gray cedar shake siding, large dormer windows with bright red trim, and especially the widow's walk. The staircase had long since been removed due to dry rot, but as a kid, I spent hours on the widow's walk pretending to be Wailing Martha, crying out for my lost husband until my folks yelled for me to give it a rest.

After I left for Ottawa, my parents decided to finally make their retirement dream of renting summer cottages a reality. My father built four three-hundred-square-foot cottages, each modeled after the main house; three single bedrooms and one double with bunk beds. Each of the cottages had a tiny three-piece bathroom and kitchenette, making them almost entirely self-sufficient for guests. When the property next door was for sale a few years ago, my parents decided to expand their business to include six RV stalls. Topsail Cottages and Campground wasn't exactly a gold mine as far as money went, but its proximity to the boardwalk brought in enough revenue to supplement my folks' savings nicely, and kept them busy in the summer months.

When I reached the end of the driveway, I kicked off my heels and carried them with me up the stone path. Old wooden lobster buoys hung along the length of the narrow veranda, with traps piled up on either side of the steps. A large, blue porcelain starfish hung on the bright red door to the back porch. I went inside, dropping my shoes on the coir bristle doormat in front of the kitchen door. I continued into the kitchen, but it was empty, as was the living room. An impressive collection of antique furniture, handmade crocheted doilies, and vintage tea sets filled the dwelling without making the space feel cramped. The floors and overhead beams were restored to their original hardwood, and every available wall space was used to display local artists' works.

I went to the staircase and leaned against the banister. "Hey, I'm home," I called upstairs.

No response. My mother was most likely down at the cottages, changing linens or chatting with guests, and my father locked away in his workshop, tinkering. I took a quick shower and threw on a pair of cutoff shorts and my old Evanescence concert T-shirt. As I hung my wet towel on the hook outside my closet, I noticed my old high school yearbook sitting on my desk.

I flipped through the pages until I found Jolene's graduation portrait. Someone had drawn two devil horns with a black marker on the top of her head and blacked out three of her teeth. A thin, curly mustache over her smile completed the effect.

Eighteen was not the height of my emotional maturity.

I stared at her portrait, a strange, hollow feeling in my stomach. The list of extracurricular activities next to her portrait was twice as long as any of the other graduates. Underneath my scribbles, Jolene's blond hair was sleek, and her teeth were perfectly straight. Jolene's mother, Peggy Guay, could be intense when it came to the appearance and behavior she expected from her only daughter. Like the Sutherlands, the Guays were considered one of the so-called founding families of Little Blue Harbour, something Peggy never failed to mention, even in casual conversation. I could still remember when I convinced Jolene to explore the woods behind her parents' house in search of unicorns when we were eight. When we returned covered in mud and bug bites, Peggy was livid with me for dragging Jolene on such an "unladylike" excursion.

Next, I turned to Andy's graduation portrait. The same suave smile I'd seen last night beamed up at me from the page. I still couldn't believe I'd stumbled across his body. Or that one of the most beloved people in town was now the prime suspect for his death.

Before I could stop myself, an imaginary news ticker scrolled through my brain: *Oh, What a Night! Former beauty queen murders secret lover during their high school reunion.* I'd reached out to the *Foghorn*, the weekly newspaper in town, about a job. Unfortunately, Harvey Snow, the editor-in-chief, made it very clear the paper was fully staffed and to please stop calling.

They're not the only newspaper you could contact, whispered the stubborn voice in my brain. *What about one of the bigger outlets in Toronto?* Big cities loved reporting on gruesome small-town crimes. The quainter the town, the bigger the story.

I shook away the thought. Andy wasn't murdered. He couldn't have been. This was Little Blue Harbour, for Pete's sake. The biggest arrest to ever happen here was when my father caught the raccoon living in the town's only bank machine. This was simply the result of this town having more busybodies than seagulls, yet another reason I couldn't wait to get out of this town when I was younger.

I closed the yearbook with a snap and shoved it under my bed, determined to put the whole thing out of my head. I went back downstairs and outside again. I found my parents and Shelly in the reception hut, a tiny structure next to the guest parking lot. My mother was seated behind the desk, counting postcards of local landmarks, while my father helped himself to the complimentary coffee we kept out for guests. Shelly was curled up in the corner on yet another dog bed.

Despite the growing heat, my mother, Elizabeth Bishop, wore a full face of makeup, with her salt-and-pepper hair swept back in her signature French twist. When she worked as a real estate agent, my mother considered her appearance to be her most important marketing tool. And, even though she'd quit real estate to open Topsail Cottages, she still refused to step outside of the house looking anything less than perfectly polished.

The real surprise was that my father was with her. Since retirement, local sightings of Kenneth Bishop in Little Blue Harbour were rare. He was like Bigfoot, except with silver curls, half-moon reading glasses, and a faded green Alexander Keith baseball cap. He mostly handled the behind-the-scenes work for the cottages, like doing the landscaping or fixing clogged toilets. My mother was the face of the business. And now me, I supposed.

The seashell windchime over the door jingled as I entered. My mother looked up at the sound. "Oh, Belinda, it's you. I thought you were the Haliburtons, they requested an early checkout time and it's almost nine. I'm glad you're home. We were starting to get worried."

I joined my father at the coffee station and poured myself a cup. "I texted you last night to let you know where I was."

"You also found a dead body." She surveyed me closely, her brow furrowed with concern. "How are you feeling?"

"I'm okay. Much better than Andy." I snorted. "You won't believe the rumors that have already started. Vivien told me this morning that people actually think Andy was murdered and Jolene Dexter did it."

There was a long pause while my parents shared a knowing glance.

I almost choked on my coffee. "Wait, is that true? Do the cops really think his death is a homicide?"

My mother stood and busied herself with restocking the postcard rack. "Honestly, Belinda, how on earth would we know anything about it?"

"There hasn't been an official statement made yet," added my father, averting his gaze.

I sighed. If that's how they wanted to play this, fine. "Mum, your personal motto as a real estate agent was, 'Knowing everyone else's business is good for business.'"

"It's true," she insisted. "It's how I convinced the Johnsons to upgrade to a three-bedroom rancher. Everyone else just thought she developed an allergy to dairy, but I knew it was morning sickness. And being the first to know about the MacAllisters' impending divorce was how I got the listing for their five-bedroom farmhouse."

I turned to my father. "I know Saturday is your day to have breakfast with Huey and Randy at the Little Blue Beanery, Dad."

Randall Perry, my father's old partner, and Hubert Cox, the local GP, were two of my father's closest friends. If anyone knew what was really happening with the investigation into Andy's death, it would be those two men.

When he didn't respond, I crossed my arms and gave him my best stern glare. "I can either hear the correct version from you or the purple-monkey-dishwasher version the town is going to come up with."

My father pursed his lips, but I knew he was about to cave. "Obviously, I expect you not to repeat anything that I tell you." He raised his bushy eyebrows at me pointedly. "And for the information to be treated with the utmost discretion."

"Of course," I said, my face intentionally neutral.

His furrowed brow suggested he wasn't quite buying my innocent act, but it didn't stop him from continuing. "Huey performed the initial examination of the body. According to him, the cause of death was head trauma."

I tried not to roll my eyes, but I couldn't help it. "I figured that much out for myself, oddly enough."

My parents exchanged another furtive glance. "The thing is, while the bruising on the body was consistent with an accidental fall, the head injury was not," admitted Dad. "Huey thought it was more in line with being struck with a blunt object."

My mouth dropped open as my mind flashed back to the scene at the foot of the stairs. "His award trophy. Andy had it with him when he left the gym, but I don't remember seeing it in the hallway when we found him. That must have been the murder weapon."

My father nodded. "Randy said they searched the entire school but came up empty."

My mother took my hand and gave it a comforting squeeze. "It's a terrible thing to have happened," she murmured, echoing Vivian's earlier sentiment. "He was such a lovely boy."

I clutched the mug to my chest and began to pace. Movement always helped me think. "Does that mean it was a crime of passion," I asked thoughtfully, "or a crime of opportunity?"

"It's an open investigation, Belinda," said my father. "I really shouldn't have said anything."

I spun back to face him. "Why are the police so convinced Jolene is their culprit?"

My mother made a soft, disdainful noise. "It's ridiculous, if you ask me. Jolene is one of the sweetest, most caring people in town. She could never do something so awful."

"You'd be surprised, Ellie," offered my father. "If there's one thing I learned from my years on the force, it's that you never really know what someone is capable of. A woman's scarf was found under the victim's body. Constables MacDougall and Bower interviewed Jolene last night, and she admitted it belonged to her."

Internally, I shuddered. *The victim.* Less than twenty-four hours ago, he was just Andy. "But I spoke to Jolene on my way out of the gym. She was still wearing her gold scarf."

My father shook his head. "No, a different scarf. One with a blue floral pattern, according to Randy," he said. "They think it may have fallen out of her purse during a struggle."

"Andy was twice her size; it wouldn't have been much of a struggle." I set my coffee mug down on the counter. "I'm going to step outside and give Stevie a quick call."

My father gave me an aggravated look. "You promised you would be discreet, Belinda."

"I am. I mean, I will be. I just want to check in with her, make sure she's doing okay."

Shelly followed me outside as I dialed Stevie. She answered after the first ring. "It's about time," she said, skipping any pleasantries. "Do you know what everyone in town is saying?" She relayed more or less the same information as Vivien and my parents.

Well, that was fast. Even for Little Blue Harbour. "I know," I said, careful to keep my voice low. "Dad had breakfast with Huey and Randy this morning."

"This is unbelievable," said Stevie, sounding furious. "You should have heard what those snide women from the Rotary Club were saying about Jolene in the Osprey this morning. After all the money she helped raise for their fundraiser last month. We have to do something to help her."

I hesitated. "Do we, though?"

"Belinda, I know you two aren't friends anymore, but you can't possibly think Jo would actually murder someone."

"No," I admitted, "but what are we supposed to do about it?"

"I don't know," she said irritably. "We could visit her and let her know she has our support."

"Hard pass."

"This could be a chance for you and Jolene to finally bury the hatchet," said Stevie.

"Rock-hard pass."

She went quiet and I knew she was struggling to think of a strong enough argument to win me over. "I'm surprised I even have to ask you to get involved," she finally said. "I would have thought a talented journalist like you would be chomping at the bit over a story like this."

I rolled my eyes toward the clear blue sky overhead. "Flattery? Really, Stevie?"

"I'm just saying, the town football star found dead, the former Harbour Queen accused of the crime. Sounds like a pretty good news story if you ask me." Despite my best efforts, I hesitated, and Stevie swooped in for the kill. "Just ask yourself this, Bel: what would Keith Morrison do?"

I thought back to my yearbook and Jolene's bright (slightly marred) smile.

I sighed. "Fine, you win," I told Stevie, walking back to the reception hut. "Meet me outside the Osprey in fifteen minutes."

"You want to go now?" she asked, sounding surprised.

"Yes, before I come to my senses. Can Diane handle the tearoom on her own for a bit?"

"I think so. She's been trying to convince me to take the day off all morning, and our cook Malcolm is here if she gets desperate."

I stuck my head into the reception office, jammed my phone between my shoulder and ear, and mimed turning a steering wheel back and forth. My father nodded and tossed me the keys to their Honda Civic. I gave my parents a quick wave goodbye and headed back outside.

"Not that I'm trying to talk you out of this," asked Stevie as I unlocked the Civic and slipped in behind the wheel, "but what made you change your mind? I was only kidding about Keith Morrison."

"The Jolene Dexter I remember is way too Type A to push someone down the stairs and leave behind evidence directly tying her to the crime," I told her. "Trust me, any murder she commits would involve multiple to-do lists and at least one storyboard."

Chapter Five

"This is never going to work," I said as I drove in the direction of Jolene's house.

Stevie sat next to me in the passenger seat, a pastry box filled with Sand Dollar treats balanced on her lap. She was still dressed in her Loyalist server costume, a blue cotton skirt, brightly colored floral smock with white linen apron and matching shawl. "It will work," she said as she adjusted the mobcap covering her bright blue locks. "Who doesn't like free pastries?"

I shook my head. "You're banking on Jolene's love for sweets being stronger than her hatred for me, and that's a dangerous assumption to make."

We drove past a group of town workers hanging pole banners with the Nova Scotia tartan and the town's coat of arms (a lighthouse, a dory boat and a moose surrounded by mayflowers with the motto "From the Sea to Our Hearts") from the streetlamps to advertise the upcoming Harbour Days Festival in August. It was one of the biggest festivals in Nova Scotia thanks to our annual Harbour Days pageant, and almost as popular as the Festival acadien de Clare or Annapolis Valley Apple Blossom Festival. The sidewalks were lined with granite stone planters bursting with red and white petunias. I could smell the nearby harbor through my rolled down window. I inhaled deeply, enjoying the heat of the sun on my skin and the tickle of salt in my nose.

"There's Jo and Trawler's place," said Stevie, pointing.

We pulled up to the curb and got out of the car. The large Cape Cod–style house sat on a double lot at the end of the street. Its siding was the same shade of gray as driftwood, accented with white trim. An enclosed deck wrapped around the side of the house, continuing into the backyard, where I caught a glimpse of an impressive fire pit. The yard was beautifully landscaped with flower beds, decorative granite boulders, ornamental apple trees, and what looked like an herb garden. A black pickup truck and sporty SUV were parked in the gravel driveway lined with beach rocks.

Parked behind them was an RCMP cruiser.

"That can't be good," murmured Stevie, eyeing it.

As we continued up the walkway, the front door opened and Corporal Randall Perry appeared, followed by a younger, plain-clothes officer. Although I hadn't seen Randy since I was a teen-ager, he looked exactly the same. Same round babyface, walrus mustache, and aviator frames as I remembered. His uniform was a little tighter now, and his ginger hair looked to be a little thin-ner, but he still had the same jovial smile and friendly bounce to his step.

Randy's face lit up when he caught sight of us. "Stevie! And Belinda, my girl!" he boomed. "We were just on our way out to see you. Give us a hug, stranger!" He threw his arms around me and squeezed, almost lifting me from the walkway.

I wasn't sure if my shortness of breath was due to Randy's vice grip on my rib cage or the absolute Adonis standing next to him. The man was clean-shaven with a jawline that looked strong enough to crack lobster shells. His crisp white shirt and black tweed jacket hung off his muscular frame as though it'd been tailored specifically for him, and his charcoal gray pants were tight in all the right places. His dirty blond hair was slicked back into a widow's peak with not a strand out of place, and his eyes were the color of the harbor after a storm. I only got to enjoy them for a moment before he slipped a pair of sunglasses from the interior of his coat and slid them onto his wide-brimmed nose. There was an air of authority to him that was both intimidating and intriguing.

The unfamiliar officer cleared his throat sharply. "We are here in a professional capacity, Corporal Perry."

Randy dropped his arms, his round face suitably chagrined. "Oh, yeah. Sorry about that." He gave me a quick wink. "We'll catch up later." He seemed to remember his manners. "Oh, this is Sergeant Brady Finlayson," he said, gesturing to the man beside him. "He's on loan from the Major Crimes Unit in Halifax."

I looked down at Randy's hand and realized he was holding an evidence bag. "Why do you need to speak to me again? You already have my statement."

Randy chuckled. "It's just a follow-up interview. Nothing to worry about. You haven't lived in Little Blue Harbour for years, and it's not like you had any kind of personal history with Big Andy when you did."

Which was a polite way of saying I was too much of a loser for Andy to bother with me, but I appreciated the sentiment all the same.

"If I may interrupt, Corporal Perry," said Sergeant Finlayson. His tone was pointed, as though Randy had hijacked the conversation from him. "We need to speak with Stephanie Hart and Belinda Bishop next."

Stevie and I both raised our hands. "That's us," I said.

The sergeant frowned at Stevie. "Corporal Perry just called you Stevie."

She shrugged. "It's a nickname."

The sergeant's nostrils flared, and he let out a short puff of air. "Doesn't anyone in this town use their legal name?"

"You're not originally from Nova Scotia, are you?" I asked him.

He raised his chin slightly, challenging me. "Saskatchewan, actually."

I eyed his toned physique. It made sense. He looked like he wouldn't have any problems tossing a few hay bales. Among other things. Too bad he came across as such a pompous jerk.

Sergeant Finlayson shook each of our hands in turn. "I was hoping to conduct a follow-up interview with you and Miss Hart this afternoon." He gestured behind him toward Jolene's front door. "Are you two friends of Mrs. Dexter?"

"Not really," I admitted.

Stevie held up the pastry box. "We wanted to drop off some emotional support pastries."

Sergeant Finlayson reached back into his blazer and withdrew a pen and spiral notebook, which he immediately flipped open with the kind of speed and precision that made me suspect he'd practiced the move more than once in front of the mirror. He clicked his pen and held it to the page, ready. "How would you describe the relationship between Mrs. Dexter and Mr. Perch? Would you say it was romantic? Were both of you present for the physical altercation on the dance floor shortly before the victim's death?" He fired off his questions one after another without giving me a chance to respond in between.

Unfortunately for him, I knew this trick. It was a Kenneth Bishop favorite. The rapid-fire questioning was intended to overwhelm your subject and make them more likely to blurt out a response.

"I have no idea," I said. "Before last night, I hadn't seen either of them for more than a decade. And Andy put his hands on Jolene first."

"I see," he said, jotting down my reply.

"All of which was covered in my initial statement last night," I added pointedly.

I felt a dart of victory at his irritated frown. *I was raised by a cop, dude. You're going to have to do better than impeccable hair and a fancy notebook flip.*

Randy cleared his throat awkwardly. "We won't keep you girls. How about we swing by the cottages this afternoon, just to go over some more questions we have?"

"Today's not good for me," I said. Granted, my calendar was as full as a pessimist's glass, but I wasn't feeling particularly accommodating toward Sergeant Finlayson at the moment.

"I would prefer to speak with you at the station." He slipped the notebook back into his jacket and produced a business card. "Monday at one o'clock," he said.

It wasn't a request.

He scribbled the time and date on the card before handing it to me. With one last nod, he strode past me toward the cruiser. Randy gave me a friendly salute as he followed him.

Stevie and I continued up the walkway but waited until the cruiser pulled away from the curb before we knocked on the front door. It took a few moments before we heard approaching footsteps on the other side. It opened and Jolene stared at us. Even as a murder suspect, she was more composed than I ever was on an average day. Her blond hair was plaited in one of those purposely messy side braids I've never been able to master. Her lace camisole, knit cardigan, and linen pants were the perfect blend of comfort and elegance.

Her lip quivered and she shook her head. "I can't deal with you two, not today." She started to close the door.

I raised my arm, blocking it. "Okay, that's a fair reaction," I said, "but before you slam the door in our faces, there's something you should know." I inhaled deeply. "We think you're innocent."

"What a relief." Jolene knocked my arm aside and shut the door.

"We also have doughnuts," I called through the door hopefully.

Nothing.

I sighed. "That went as well as expected."

The door swung open and Jolene reappeared. "On second thought, screw it," she said, taking the box from Stevie. She walked back inside, leaving the door open. "Are you coming inside or not?"

We hurried inside in case she changed her mind. We found Jolene in her immaculate, almost blindingly white kitchen, sitting at a massive, marble countertop island. Her eyes were closed, cheeks puffed out like a chipmunk, as she devoured a powdered jelly doughnut.

She moaned softly. "Lemon-flavored, my favorite."

I'd remembered, but I didn't want to admit it.

She looked at us, her expression distraught. "Do you know how long it's been since I've eaten a doughnut? Three years. And that was during a knitting club meeting while Mama's back was turned."

Stevie and I joined her at the island, and each selected a pastry. "We ran into Randy and the new sergeant when we arrived," I said, biting into one of Irene's new scones. "What did they want?"

"Don't pretend like you haven't heard the rumors," she said ruefully. "The police think I killed Andy and want to test my clothes for blood."

"You just handed them over?" I asked, choking a little in alarm.

"What was I supposed to do?" she asked. "If I refused, that would have just made the sergeant even more convinced I was guilty."

Jolene opened her mouth to continue, but she quickly got to her feet as a thunder of footsteps came down the stairs. Moments later, a slender, dark-haired girl with purple glasses entered the kitchen. She had Trawler's coloring, but Jolene's delicate features. She opened the fridge, took out a bottle of flavored water, and headed back toward the staircase without acknowledging us.

"Sadie, sweetie," said Jolene, her tone bright but wavering. "You remember Stephanie, from the Osprey Tearoom. And this is Belinda Bishop, an old friend."

The girl stopped, surveying us both with cool disinterest. "Nice to meet you," said Sadie shortly. "Were you two secretly dating my teacher too?"

What little color was left in Jolene's face drained away, but she tried again. "Would you like a pastry, honey?"

"Not from you." With that, the girl spun on her heel and stomped back up the stairs.

Jolene collapsed back onto her stool and reached for a second doughnut. "That has been my entire morning. I can't even say I blame her. Sadie is thirteen, so she thinks I did all this deliberately to ruin her life."

"Where's Trawler?" I asked.

Her chin quivered. "Upstairs, also ignoring me."

Suddenly, Jolene's face crumbled, and fresh tears streamed down her cheeks as she rested her forehead on the countertop, her shoulders shaking. "Andy was the only person in my life who felt like a true friend, and now everyone thinks I had something to do with his death," she wailed. "I've already been blocked online by half my friends. My husband and child won't even look at me. Both of my brothers are ignoring my texts, and the only reason my mother called this morning was to berate me for what this scandal is going to do to the family."

A strange sensation spread throughout my chest as I listened to my former friend cry. What was this I was feeling? Pity? Was I actually feeling sorry for Jolene Dexter?

"I've spent my entire life trying to be a good wife and a good person," Jolene continued in between hiccups. "Did you know I was accepted to Dalhousie University after high school? I gave it up after I found out I was pregnant with Sadie. I do everything that's expected of me from Trawler, my mother, and everyone else in town. I join their charity committees, volunteer in the community, and help out with church functions. Because anything less would be unbecoming of a Guay."

Stevie scooted her stool closer to Jolene, making soothing noises as she wrapped her arms around her. I watched them for a moment. Should I do the same? Finally, I settled on awkwardly patting Jolene on her shoulder.

"Is that really the best you can do?" hissed Stevie.

"I'm not good with genuine displays of emotions," I hissed back.

"I can hear you," Jolene choked out through her sobs.

Fortunately, I was good at being blunt. "Okay, first of all, the Guays aren't exactly the Kennedys, so I'm sure your family will survive this. As far as Trawler and Sadie are concerned?" I trailed off a little at this point. "I don't actually have any advice on that. Interpersonal relationships aren't my strong suit."

My words of comfort only made her cry harder.

"Jo, where did you go when you left the gym last night?" asked Stevie gently.

She sat up, wiping the tears from her cheeks. "I was in the bathroom, crying like a middle schooler."

"Were you alone?" I asked. "Where was Trawler?"

"I don't know. I tried to follow him out of the gym, but I couldn't find him. He said he went for a walk to get some air and clear his head."

I exhaled softly in frustration. "Did anyone see you in the bathroom? Someone who could vouch for your whereabouts before Andy was killed?"

She shuddered. "No, thank goodness. I already wanted to throw myself into a black hole. The last thing I needed was for someone to see me in such a state."

"No, you're right," I said sarcastically. "Much better to have your image intact than a witness who could prove your innocence."

She glared at me. "Why are you really here, Belinda? Do you honestly believe I'm innocent, or are you just trying to score an exclusive interview as part of your writing comeback?"

"Don't be absurd." I hesitated. "Why? Has someone else already contacted you for an interview?"

Stevie gave me a swift kick in the shin, which I probably deserved.

"Of course, we believe you," she assured Jolene. "We know you would never do anything to hurt Andy. Once the police finish their investigation, everyone else will know it too."

Jolene's eyes spilled over with fresh tears. "But they found my scarf."

"It wasn't the scarf you were wearing last night," I pointed out.

She shook her head. "I don't even know how Andy ended up with it. I certainly didn't give it to him."

"Did you ever invite Andy over here for a visit?" I asked.

Jolene sighed. "We weren't having an affair."

Stevie and I shared another hesitant glance. "The thing is, according to Donna Dickie, you and Andy had a habit of disappearing together at school events," said Stevie delicately.

Jolene rolled her eyes. "We were doing the rounds during the dance-a-thon and caught some kids drinking in the science lab. One of the girls threw her beer all over me. After the parents picked them up, Andy gave me the extra hoodie he keeps in the teachers' lounge to wear." Her lips trembled. "Kept in the lounge. You can ask Vice-Principal Blenkhorn if you don't believe me. He's the one who notified the parents."

"What about what Andy said last night on the dance floor?" I asked. "About another man being interested in you?"

"He didn't mean it like *that*," she said. "Andy and I were just friends. When Trawler and I were first together, it was like we shared the same brain. If one of us was upset or unhappy, the other just knew. It felt like we were soulmates. We even made a time capsule together and buried it at the school during our senior prom."

"Really? That's so romantic," said Stevie.

Jolene closed her eyes and groaned. "Now, Trawler treats me like his roommate. Or worse, his mother. Not his wife. Andy listened when I talked. He was interested in my community projects or club events I was planning. When I landed a role in the Performing Arts Center's production of *Grease*, Andy bought tickets. My own husband couldn't even remember what character I was playing, and I was Rizzo."

"That's the best role," I said before I could stop myself. Nemeses or not, that was simply unacceptable from a spouse.

"I know," she exclaimed. "I should have just talked to Trawler about how I felt, but I was scared of nothing changing. I'd be lying if I said I didn't enjoy the attention from Andy."

"Especially since he wasn't exactly hard to look at," I added.

Jolene cradled her head in her hands. "Everything is a mess now. People think I'm a murderer, and even the ones that don't still think I'm a cheat. Either way, I'm screwed."

She reached for the pastry box again, but I flipped the lid closed. "No, you're not." Jolene shot me a deeply skeptical glance. "You've still got Stevie and me," I continued, undeterred. "We are going to help you prove your innocence."

She laughed humorlessly. "The idea of us teaming up together is as ridiculous as Snow White teaming up with the Evil Queen."

I shrugged. "I always thought that would've been a much more interesting story."

Chapter Six

Despite her protests, Stevie and I drove Jolene to the boardwalk and practically frog-marched her down to the Right Foot restaurant and pub.

"I can't be seen drinking here, it's not even four o'clock," she said, running her fingers nervously down her braid.

"Who cares?" I countered. "You've already eaten refined sugar today. I say, enjoy the spiral."

Both with a firm grip on each elbow, we dragged her over to the bar. While we waited for the honey-blond bartender, who Stevie introduced as Hannah Acker, to finish serving her other customers, I took the opportunity to do a quick scan of the restaurant. There are a lot of nautical-themed pubs in Nova Scotia, but I immediately decided that the Right Foot was my favorite. The glass-topped pub tables and chairs looked as though they'd been crafted from old whiskey barrels. Above us hung multiple ship wheel chandeliers, their Edison-style bulbs casting a warm light over the room. The pine walls were adorned with old black-and-white portraits of local fishing boats, including a small memorial dedicated to crew members lost at sea. The chalkboard hanging by the entrance promised an upcoming performance by the Albatross Boys.

The pub's main draw in the summer seemed to be its outdoor deck, which extended out over the water. After Hannah poured our drinks, gin and tonics for Stevie and Jolene, and an ice water with lemon for me since I was driving, we grabbed some menus and took our drinks outside to the deck.

Once we had selected a table, I plucked one of the cardboard drink coasters from the table and found a pen in my purse. "Okay, the first thing we need is a list of suspects."

"We're not cops," pointed out Jolene.

"What do you want to do?" I asked her, a little irritated. "Leave this up to the people who are already convinced you're guilty?"

"Of course not, but I also don't want to start running around town accusing people."

"Obviously, we wouldn't accuse someone without evidence," I said.

"Maybe that's what we should do first," interrupted Stevie. "We'll come up with a list of rules for our investigation."

I huffed. "Fine. Rule number one, no accusations without evidence."

"Seconded," said Stevie. "I say rule number two is we don't break the law. Sergeant Finlayson strikes me as a very *by the book* kind of guy."

"He definitely wouldn't approve," I agreed. "Rule number three is to always communicate with each other. I don't want to be one of those idiots who end up cornered or trapped by the real killer because they didn't think to tell anyone where they were going."

"Agreed," said Stevie. "I hate when they do that on shows."

Jinx came out of the restaurant and headed over to our table, carrying an order pad. I wasn't sure how, but he managed to look even cuter in a waist apron.

"Afternoon, ladies." He turned that 100-watt smile on me. "Hey, Belinda. I was worried that you might start to avoid me after last night."

"Of course not," I said, laughing just a little too loudly. I trailed off as I noticed the little flecks of hazel in his green eyes. Jinx stared at me expectantly. *Oh, right; it's still my turn to speak.* "Why would you think that?" I finished quickly.

Come on, Bishop, you know how the English language works.

He shrugged, looking embarrassed. "I was worried you would feel uncomfortable around me." He gestured vaguely toward his beard.

I waved away his concern. "I told you, I don't believe in superstitions."

He chuckled. "I'm happy to hear that. But just to be safe, maybe you should call me Jinx like everyone else."

"I'll call you whatever you want."

A hint of pink crept up his cheeks from under his copper beard. My own face began to burn as the implication of my words hit me. He rubbed the back of his neck, causing his shirt to lift just enough for me to catch a glimpse of his toned, flat stomach.

Breathe, Bishop. Remember to breathe.

Fortunately, Stevie gave my chair a swift kick under the table, jarring me back into reality.

Jinx cleared his throat softly. "Are you, uh, ready to order?" He held his pen to the pad, reminding me of Sergeant Finlayson.

"I think we need another minute," said Stevie sweetly. She waited until he was out of earshot before rounding on me. "What was that?"

I grabbed my icy drink and pressed the cool glass against my cheek, then down along my neck. "I don't know. There's hazel in the green now. His T-shirt rode up. It looks so smooth."

Jolene and Stevie stared at me like I'd grown a second head. "Do you think you're making sense right now?" asked Jolene.

Stevie rubbed my back. "Do you need to stick your head in the harbor?" she asked sympathetically.

I groaned. "More like throw myself into it."

"Why did Jinx think you would avoid him?" asked Jolene, frowning. "You obviously have no interest in that."

"Last night, Bel thought she would be cute and say his real name," said Stevie, the tattletale.

Jolene gaped at me, horrified. "You didn't."

I put down my glass, aggravated. "First of all, it was cute. And second of all, Andy did not die because I said Jinx's real name."

"No, but you were the one who found his body," said Jolene.

"And you're the one who is a suspect," I fired back.

She narrowed her eyes. "Ooh, cheap shot."

Stevie sat up in her chair. "He's coming back," she murmured. She pointed at me from across the table. "Keep it in your pants, Bishop."

"Very helpful, thanks," I snapped.

Jolene ordered the house salad with dressing on the side. Stevie opted for the Sailor's Delight, pan-fried scallops in alfredo sauce over linguine pasta. I managed to order the Pirate's Platter without melting into a puddle of amorous goo.

After Jinx left with our orders, I noticed Jolene's disapproving frown. "What?"

"When was the last time you ate a vegetable?" she asked.

I shrugged. "The platter comes with deep-fried mushrooms."

"I have no idea how you made it to adulthood."

"Stand down, you two," Stevie said, ever the peacemaker. "Back to our suspects list." She took the coaster and pen from me. "Who goes at the top?"

"Madeline Barclay," I said.

"Kevin's wife?" asked Jolene. "What motive could she have?"

"You mean besides the obvious?" I countered. "Andy had a preference for married women."

"I don't believe it was anything like that," said Stevie, "but Maddie did show up at the reunion looking for him."

I nodded. "And the cover story she gave you was an obvious lie. Plus, we only saw her leave the gymnasium, not the school." I snapped my fingers, a sudden thought occurring to me. "The west exit is right across from their store. That's why we went that way in the first place."

Stevie rolled her eyes. "Fine, she goes on the list, but it's a waste of perfectly good writing space. I'm telling you, there is no way Maddie could be a suspect."

As Stevie wrote Madeline's name on the coaster, Jinx reappeared on the deck, leading Holly, Rebecca, Julie, and Amanda to a table. He handed out the menus and gave me a quick grin before heading back inside. Holly twisted around in her seat, spotting us. She went rigid for a moment, staring at Jolene. I couldn't be sure, but underneath the perfectly applied makeup, Holly's face looked puffy, like she had spent the morning crying too. She nudged Julie and not-so-subtly gestured in our direction. The four of them immediately put their heads close together, their murmured conversation occasionally punctuated by low gasps.

"What about Holly as a suspect?" I asked, watching her closely. I quickly recapped for Jolene the conversation we'd overheard between Holly and Barry. "You should have seen Holly's face when you and Andy were dancing together," I added. "She was not impressed."

"Did Andy ever mention any of the women he was seeing?" Stevie asked her.

She frowned and shook her head. "Not by name, but I know his last relationship didn't end well. He said she refused to accept that it was over. She called him so many times, he eventually had to block her number."

"Sounds like Holly. Add her to the list," I told Stevie. "Barry too. Remember that remark he made about people who run around on a spouse? Maybe he knew about the affair. He left the gym before Andy was killed."

Before we could continue the discussion, Jinx returned with our food. Quick as a flash, Stevie slipped the coaster into her pocket. I decided the best strategy with Jinx was to just avoid eye contact, so that's exactly what I did. I still caught a glimpse of his smile from the corner of my eye as he set the larger-than-expected platter in front of me. The plate hadn't even left his hand before I jammed a couple of deep-fried shrimp into my mouth in an effort to prevent any more verbal mishaps.

He eyed my full cheeks with amusement. "Let me know if you need anything else."

I nodded and flashed him a thumbs-up. I waited until he disappeared back inside the pub before risking speech again. "Barry could have been hiding somewhere in the school, waiting for a chance to catch Andy alone. He's roughly the same size as Andy so it wouldn't have been too difficult for him to get the upper hand."

Jolene picked up her utensils and began eating. "You've really got a knack for this, Belinda," she said, somewhat grudgingly. "How did you end up working for an unknown newspaper like the *Bytown Freebie*?"

Stevie looked up from her own plate. "Yeah, I always thought you'd end up writing for the *Toronto Star* or the *Globe and Mail.*"

I took a short sip of my water, averting my gaze. "I don't know, life is just like that sometimes, isn't it?"

Stevie snorted. "You're the definition of tenacious. If you'd wanted to write for one of the big papers, you would've made it happen, no matter the obstacles."

I pushed a fried mushroom around my plate. "It's kind of embarrassing."

Jolene huffed as she speared a chunk of tomato with her fork. "Just tell us already. I'm spilling all of my deepest secrets."

She raised a good point. I lifted my hand and extended my pinky. "Three-way pinky promise?" I asked them. They obliged, albeit each with an eye roll. "Unfortunately, there is one obstacle that even I couldn't get around, and that's a criminal record."

Stevie froze in the midst of taking a sip of her gin and tonic. "What do you mean?"

Jolene looked as though her eyes were about to pop out of her skull, cartoon-style. "You have a criminal record?" she gasped loudly.

"Keep your voice down," I hissed at her. "After university, I landed a really great opportunity for an entry-level position as a fact-checker for the *Ottawa Sun.* I thought if I went into the interview with an amazing, exclusive story, it would show that I have initiative."

"What did you do?" asked Jolene.

I sighed. "You guys know who Suede Damon is, right?"

"The pop singer," said Jolene, nodding. "He has that song, *Gonna Make Space for Your Love.*"

"Oh, I love that song," said Stevie.

I grimaced. "He's notoriously standoffish with the media. He'll only grant interviews with the biggest names in Canadian entertainment. He was in Ottawa doing a benefit concert and it seemed like the perfect opportunity to prove myself."

Stevie shook her head. "I'm almost scared to ask."

I spun my glass of ice water in a circle, wishing it was something stronger. "I ended up sneaking into the backstage area."

Stevie shrugged. "That's not so bad."

"And into his dressing room," I finished with a wince.

"Belinda!" exclaimed Stevie.

"He wasn't returning my calls," I wailed. "Anyway, he freaked out."

"Understandably so," interjected Jolene.

"He called the cops and I was charged with trespassing. I ended up missing my interview altogether because of my court date. I was only sentenced with probation and two hundred hours of community service, but it still shows on a background check," I concluded morosely.

Stevie reached out and squeezed my hand. "I'm sorry, sweetie. That sucks."

Jolene braced one elbow on the table, her napkin dangling in front of her mouth. It took me a moment to realize she was trying to hide her laughter. "It's not funny," I snapped.

Jolene lowered the napkin, all pretenses gone. "It's a little funny." She snorted. "You, fresh out of journalism school, a complete nobody, broke into a celebrity's dressing room for an interview." Fortunately, she ran out of steam fairly quickly, her cheeks still pink with amusement. "I know we're not friends anymore, but sometimes I miss your brazen confidence."

I blinked at her, surprised. "Thank you?"

From the corner of my eye, I noticed Holly looking over as the last of Jolene's giggles died. Holly watched us for a moment, her angry gaze slowly becoming calculating. I could practically see a plan forming in her head. It was the same look she would get right before she humiliated an unsuspecting victim in high school. She got to her feet and walked over to us, a fake smile on her face.

"My, my, listen to you three over here. I just had to come see what was so funny," she said.

Jolene wiped her mouth with her napkin, crumpling it in her hand. "Oh, nothing. We were just goofing around."

"I can see that." Holly rearranged her expression into one of concern. "Is that really appropriate? Especially at a time like this?"

Jolene looked down at her plate, chastened.

Stevie frowned at Holly. "We thought we'd treat Jo to lunch to help take her mind off things for a while. You know, cheer her up."

"Yes, of course. Jo, you poor thing," Holly cooed, bending down to give an insincere hug. She straightened up and looked back at the others, who were still watching from their table. "First that embarrassing scene last night, and then police showing up at your door this morning." She clucked her tongue sympathetically.

None of us bothered to ask how she knew about that. "And more importantly, her close friend just passed away," said Stevie pointedly.

"Yes, I'm aware of that," snapped Holly, and for a second, she looked absolutely furious. But when she addressed Jolene, she was once again sweet as pie. "The girls and I just feel awful for you. I was going to call, but I assumed you wanted to use this time to focus on your family." She surveyed our table, her gaze lingering on the gin and tonic in front of Jolene. "Clearly, I was wrong."

"Give me a break," I muttered before I could stop myself.

"Excuse me?" demanded Holly.

"If you want to fake concern for someone, try being less condescending," I said.

Holly tilted her head. "Really? Life advice? From you, Belinda?"

I rolled my eyes. "Yes, I'm a total loser, the same insult you've been making since high school. Don't you think it's time to get some new material, Holly?"

"You always thought you were so much better than this town. But the truth is, you were never good enough for it." Holly turned to Jolene. "She wasn't good enough for a lot of things, was she, Jolene?"

Jolene swallowed nervously. "I don't know about that." She looked at me. "I mean, I never said anything like that."

Holly continued as though Jolene hadn't spoken. "But I, unlike you, have been Jolene's friend since she was thirteen. You've been back in town for, what? Five minutes? At least I didn't abandon her like you did."

I gripped the edge of the table. "That is not what happened, and you know it." I glared at Jolene expectantly, but she kept her gaze on her salad and remained silent.

"I'll let you get back to whatever this is," Holly said to Jolene, her tone dismissive.

I waited until Holly rejoined the rest of the Pageant Minions before speaking. "Gee, thanks for sticking up for us," I muttered to Jolene.

"I knew I shouldn't have come here," she whispered, her eyes filling with tears. "I told you people would take it the wrong way. The whole town is going to be talking about how I was out having drinks and laughing the day after Andy's death." She shook her head. "Mama is going to freak out when she hears about this."

"Is that really all you care about?" I asked angrily. "What a bunch of stuck-up snobs think about you?"

"Dial it back, Belinda," said Stevie gently. "This can't be easy for Jolene."

"You could have fooled me," I snapped, "considering how often she's thrown me under the bus for them."

"Okay, that's it." Stevie set down her drink and leaned back in her chair. "If we're going to do this together, we need to settle this *now*. What exactly happened between you two? Why did you stop being friends?"

Jolene shrugged. "No specific reason. Kids grow up and grow apart."

I stared at her, gobsmacked. "Are you serious?"

"Why, what do you think happened?" she asked defensively.

"You ignored me for almost the entire school year. When you finally did invite me to a sleepover with you and the Pageant Minions, they played a mean prank on me while you did nothing." To my immense pleasure, her nostrils flared at my use of the nickname.

"What prank?" Jolene and Stevie asked in unison. Stevie was curious while Jolene just sounded confused.

My stomach curdled at the memory. "They waited until I fell asleep, then tickled my arms and legs with a feather. Only instead of putting shaving cream in my hand, they used cheap self-tanning lotion. When I woke up in the morning, my sleeping bag was ruined, and I was covered in orange streaks."

Stevie gasped and rounded on Jolene, furious. "Why would you let them do that?"

"I wasn't even awake when they did it. And Belinda thought it was funny." Jolene twisted in her seat to face me. "You laughed even harder than Holly when you saw yourself in the mirror."

I scoffed at her, unable to believe someone could be so obtuse. "I couldn't let the Pageant Minions know how humiliated I felt. Otherwise, Holly would've never let me live it down."

"Well, why didn't you at least tell me how you really felt?" asked Jolene, her blue eyes wide with confusion.

"What would've been the point?" I asked, bitter. "You'd already made it clear you preferred them over me. After you won your first pageant, it was like I didn't even exist anymore. You ate lunch with the Pageant Minions, went to dances with them, and joined all the same clubs as them. I didn't abandon you; you abandoned me for them."

The other deck patrons fell silent, and I realized how loudly I was speaking. Holly and the others giggled, causing my cheeks to tingle. *Great. I'm still letting these women humiliate me.*

"I had no idea you felt that way," said Jolene softly.

I snorted. "How could you not know?"

Her cheeks flushed pink. "I invited you to eat lunch with us, didn't I? You always said no. I tried to get you to join the yearbook committee with me. Same thing. You acted like my signing up for the pageant was this huge betrayal toward feminism or something. Whenever I tried to talk to you about it, or any of my interests like clothes or makeup, you'd roll your eyes and change the subject. You made me feel like I was stupid or shallow for reading romance novels and watching *Friends*."

A small beat of guilt began to pulse in my chest. Jolene and I had been so close, just the two of us, for so long, I wasn't prepared to have to compete for Jolene's attention. Or with Jolene, for that matter. After she won her first crown, Jolene's popularity at school skyrocketed, while mine was still stuck on the tarmac. Suddenly, I found myself determined to prove myself to my former friend, by any means necessary.

"Okay, it's possible there is some truth to what you're saying," I admitted.

Jolene hesitated. "Also, my mother thought Holly, Julie, Becca, and Amanda would be more appropriate friends for me."

"What is that supposed to mean?" I asked.

Jolene looked like she would rather be swept out to sea than answer me. "She thought you were too much of a tomboy, and she's not a fan of your parents," she mumbled.

Something clicked in my brain. "This is about your Uncle Matt's speeding ticket, isn't it?" She nodded. "He was going twelve kilometers over the speed limit in a school zone."

"I know," she sighed, "but you know what Mama is like. It's like trying to stand up to a battering ram." She glanced over at Holly's table, where she and the Pageant Minions had their heads huddled together again, obviously discussing my outburst. "But you're right, that doesn't excuse my actions. I should have been honest with you back then and fought harder for our friendship." She looked me in the eyes. "I'm sorry."

I'm sorry too. But I was not ready to admit that out loud yet, so I just nodded. "Thank you. I accept your apology."

"Are you two good now? Truce?" asked Stevie.

I nodded, and Jolene said, "Truce."

"Very good," said Stevie, rapping her fork against her plate like a gavel.

The rest of our meal passed in relatively awkward silence, but strangely enough I felt like a huge weight had lifted from my chest. When Jinx brought over our check, Jolene insisted on paying. I knew she was only doing it out of guilt, but after six months of unemployment and a savings account that was running on fumes, I swallowed my pride.

We left the Right Foot and started walking back to my car. Foot traffic on the boardwalk had increased. It appeared as though all of Little Blue Harbour wanted to enjoy the sunshine and sea breeze before having to share it with the tourists. There was already a line of customers at Salty Saul's Ice Cream and Sub Shack.

I was just about to suggest we turn back for a couple of ice cream cones when a familiar police cruiser drove past the entrance to the boardwalk, slowed down, and made a U-turn. It pulled into the parking lot and Sergeant Finlayson jumped out, straightening his blazer as he marched toward us. Randy got out the passenger side and followed, but at a much slower pace and with an air of reluctance.

"What, these two again?" I muttered. "You said my interview wasn't until Monday," I said louder as Finlayson approached.

He ignored me. "Jolene Dexter, we would like you to come in for questioning in relation to the investigation of the death of Andrew Perch."

Chapter Seven

The three of us stared at him, too stunned to speak, as he prattled off the rest of her legal rights.

"You're not under arrest at this time," he continued curtly, "but we need you to come with us. You have the right to have a lawyer present for questioning if you wish."

"This is ridiculous," I blurted out before Jolene could respond.

"Do you want to call a lawyer, Mrs. Dexter?" he repeated, giving me a pointed glare.

Jolene's eyes widened, and she glanced between Finlayson and the boardwalk entrance as though contemplating making a run for it. "I don't have a lawyer," she finally squeaked.

A crowd began to gather at the entrance of the boardwalk as people came to a stop to watch. Sergeant Finlayson led Jolene away, his outstretched arm guiding her to the police cruiser without actually making contact.

I followed him. "Did you really have to do this here, in front of the entire town? You were just at her house this morning." I scooted in front of him, blocking his path. "What happened?" I asked, allowing my sarcasm to run free. "Did you suddenly discover an important piece of evidence?"

Finlayson edged around me and opened the back door to the cruiser. He eased Jolene into the back seat before turning back to face me. "As a matter of fact, we have," he said. "This afternoon, Mr. Perch's award statue was found buried in the football field behind the school. Traces of blood and hair were found on it, which will almost certainly come back as a match for the victim. We also found a set of fingerprints on the murder weapon we believe belong to Mrs. Dexter."

His statement brought me up short for a moment, but I shook off my surprise. "What a shock, Sherlock," I said scathingly. "Jolene is the one who bought the awards."

"Yeah, that's right," Stevie jumped in. "The award trophies were sitting out on a table all night. Everyone was picking them up and looking at them."

"But no one else's personal belongings were found with the body," said Finlayson as he closed the car door with a snap.

"How did you manage to match her fingerprints so quickly?" I demanded. I knew for a fact Little Blue Harbour did not have its own crime lab.

"Preliminary comparison," he said curtly.

I rolled my eyes. "You eyeballed it. Hardly official."

He stalked past me and got back in behind the steering wheel. "Let's go, Corporal Perry."

Randy took my arm in an attempt to lead me away from the police cruiser. "Please, Belinda, just let us do our jobs."

"This is ridiculous, and you know it," was my only response to that.

He pressed his lips flat but didn't contradict me. "Sergeant Finlayson was only transferred to Major Crimes last month. This is his first time leading an investigation. He's determined to impress his superiors. You don't want to get in his way."

Randy gave me another stern look as the cruiser pulled out into the street, driving in the direction of the police station.

I turned to Stevie, my jaw clenched. "Okay, Jolene's scarf at the scene and a murder weapon guaranteed to have her fingerprints on it. Are you thinking what I'm thinking?"

"Someone is trying to frame her," said Stevie grimly. "Someone with access to her belongings."

I nodded. "There's one more suspect we need to add to that list."

She sighed. "I know. I just didn't want to add it in front of her." She took the coaster out of her pocket and wrote down the name.

Trawler Dexter.

* * *

Stevie and I followed Randy and Finlayson in the Civic to the police station. We arrived in time to watch as Jolene was led through the door to the bullpen and into a back room. I tried to follow them, but the officer behind the glass partition instructed us to wait in the lobby. Stevie walked over to the row of plastic chairs lining the side wall and sat down while I paced in front of her. The minutes on the wall clock ticked by as we waited. The more I paced, the faster my thoughts spun inside my head.

Finally, I couldn't take it anymore. With a furtive glance at the officer in the window, I paused in front of Stevie and leaned forward to whisper, "Do you really think Trawler would set up his own wife?"

She shrugged. "If you asked me that last week, I would've said absolutely not. They always seemed like the ideal couple. We know that's not the case now."

I sat down next to her with a sigh. "Maybe last night's confrontation pushed him over the edge."

Stevie shook her head. "I've known Trawler for years. I don't know if I can picture him doing something like that."

"We both saw him leave the gym before Andy died," I reminded her.

She sighed. "He would have access to Jo's closet."

We were both silent as we pondered the implications of these facts. "It doesn't make sense," I said eventually. "If Andy's death was a crime of passion, why would Trawler already have the scarf to plant on his body?"

"That would mean Trawler attended the reunion with the intent to kill Andy and frame Jolene for it," Stevie said darkly.

My thoughts swirled around the possibility of Andy's death being premeditated. All the evidence so far suggested to me that Andy's murder was a spur-of-the-moment decision, born of impulse and opportunity. Why else would the killer strike in the middle of a crowded event? Unless Andy was lured to the back of the school for that very reason. Maybe the fight on the dance floor was orchestrated by Trawler to drive Andy out of the gym and away from any possible witnesses.

"What about the murder weapon?" asked Stevie. "Why would the killer bury it in the football field?"

A sudden thought occurred to me. "Andy said something to me before he died about how we tend to revert back to old tendencies and behaviors from our youth when stressed. Maybe the football field holds some kind of sentimental value to the killer."

Stevie groaned, letting her head fall to her chest. "That could be anyone on the team."

Great, more potential suspects. Our little coaster was filling up quickly.

I shook my head in an attempt to clear it. "We can't just focus on Trawler. Otherwise, we're no better than Sergeant Finlayson," I said, with an irate thumb jerk in the direction of the bullpen.

Stevie took out her phone. "Maybe there's something on the Pageant Minions' social media accounts. I already follow Holly." She glanced up in time to catch my disapproving grimace. "What? She posts really cool hair tutorials."

I took out my own phone and pulled up the app. "Barry's account is set to private," I said, disappointed. "I'll send him a follow request. Hopefully, he accepts it."

Since I already had the app open on my phone, I sent one to Jinx's profile too.

"We should check out the account for Holly's salon, the Siren's Sound, as well," said Stevie.

"I hate how clever the name is," I admitted as I searched for it.

The majority of the salon's posts were before and after photos of clients' hairstyles, announcements regarding a change in their hours of operations, and the odd hairstylist meme. Nothing suspicious, to my immense disappointment.

Stevie glanced at my phone, then suddenly grabbed my wrist. "Wait, scroll back up."

I slid the screen back up to the previous post, a photo of Holly posing with her employees in front of the salon. According to the caption below it, the salon was scheduled to be featured on a popular beauty blog.

"Look at what Holly is wearing," she insisted.

I used two fingers to zoom in on Holly. She was dressed in a pale blue peasant dress and a trendy-looking ripped denim jacket. There, tied around her neck, was a blue floral scarf.

The door to the bullpen opened, and Jolene appeared, looking anxious. I glanced up at the clock and realized almost an hour had passed since we'd arrived at the station.

Jolene dropped down into the chair next to me with a sigh. "Thanks for waiting," she said. "I just want to go home, crawl under the covers and never come out."

I knew I should say something supportive, but once again, I opted for time-efficient bluntness. "Why didn't you tell us you lent your blue scarf to Holly?"

Jolene blinked, clearly caught off guard. "What?"

Stevie took my phone from me and turned it so Jolene could view the screen. "We found this picture on the salon's Instagram page," she said.

Jolene peered at the phone for a moment before her eyes widened in recognition. "Oh, that. Holly was going to be interviewed by some beauty blogger from Toronto, and she wanted to wear it for the pictures."

I pressed one hand against my forehead as I willed myself to remain calm. "Jolene, you're being investigated for murder," I whispered, careful to keep my voice low so the officer in reception didn't hear. "Someone is obviously trying to frame you. Don't you think it would be helpful for us to know that you lent one of our suspects the main piece of evidence against you?"

"I forgot," she said, defensive.

I took a moment to compose myself with a deep cleansing breath. "Do you at least remember whether or not Holly returned the scarf?"

"Yes." Jolene trailed off, sounding less sure. "Although, now that I think about it, I can't say I remember specifically when that would have been." She tilted her head and bit her lip. "Do you think I should tell Sergeant Finlayson about this?"

"Yes," said Stevie, just as I cried, "No!"

Stevie gave me a bewildered stare. "Why on earth not?" she asked.

I matched her incredulous expression with one of my own. "What do you want her to do, march back inside and tell him, hey, you know that scarf that points directly to me as the killer? Well, I've just now conveniently remembered that I gave it to someone else."

Stevie raised her eyebrows. "Obviously not like that."

"Finlayson won't believe her. We need to talk to Holly first," I said. "See if we can get her to admit she still had the scarf in her possession at the time of Andy's death. What if we stop by her salon tomorrow morning?"

Stevie shook her head. "They're closed on Sundays. Besides, Holly owns the place. If she doesn't want to talk to us, she can just throw us out."

"You're right," I said. "We need to approach Holly somewhere she doesn't have any control over."

Stevie snapped her fingers in inspiration. "There's a fitness class every Sunday afternoon that Holly attends."

"That's right, Barbie Jamison's Boot Camp on the Boardwalk," said Jolene excitedly. "We can pay a drop-in fee and all go together. There should be enough spots available."

The three of us left the police station and headed for my car. I unlocked the doors to the Civic as a black pickup truck drove into the RCMP parking lot. Trawler jumped out and hurried forward, leaving his truck door wide open.

He ran up to Jolene, looking furious. "I leave the house for a couple of hours and when I get back, I find out you've been arrested. I thought you were just going to lunch."

"Gee, Trawler, thank you so much for your concern," she said hotly as she opened the front passenger door of the Civic. "How did you even know I was here? None of us called you." She looked to me and Stevie for confirmation, which we gave with mutual head shakes.

Jolene got into the car and moved to shut the door, but Trawler braced it open with his arms. "Sadie told me," he said.

"How did she hear?" asked Jolene.

"One of her friends saw you being put into a police cruiser on the boardwalk," he said angrily. "I found her in her bedroom, crying her eyes out because she thinks her mother is going to jail."

Jolene rested her head against the dashboard, groaning. "Great." She looked up, her eyes narrowed, as though just noticing his disheveled appearance. "Where were you? Why are you all sweaty?"

I realized she was right. Trawler's dark hair was plastered across his forehead, and his T-shirt appeared damp with perspiration. "It's not important," he sputtered.

"Right," she scoffed. "Maybe our daughter would have been less upset if her father was actually there to comfort her instead of running around town, doing who knows what." When he didn't respond, she pulled the door shut, narrowly missing his arm.

He jumped back, cursing. "It's not like I knew I'd have to come pick you up from the police station of all places."

"Well, you don't have to worry about that anymore, do you?" she said through the rolled-up window. "Belinda already offered to drive me home."

He glanced sideways at Stevie and me. "These two?"

I understood his confusion, but still. *Rude.*

Jolene lowered the window. "Frankly, I'd rather be with them right now."

"I'm here now," he snapped.

Jolene gave him a look so fierce, I almost took a step back myself. "You're too late, Trawler. As usual."

Trawler threw up his hands. "Fine. Have it your way. As usual," he added mockingly.

He climbed back into the cab of his truck and slammed the door behind him. He revved the engine and reversed into traffic without even looking. As he sped off down the street, I couldn't help but notice the muddy shovel in the bed of the truck.

Chapter Eight

The next morning, Stevie was already waiting at the boardwalk entrance when I parked the Civic. The fitness class was scheduled to start at noon, but Stevie insisted we arrive fifteen minutes earlier for warm-up stretches.

I grabbed my water bottle and exited the car. "I think I'm a little underdressed," I said, eyeing her sporty outfit.

Stevie and I looked like the before and after pictures for a fitness program. Her, trim and strong, dressed in a blue fitted hoodie, black leggings with stripes running up the legs, and high-traction sneakers, all perfectly matched with her bright blue hair. I, on the other hand, barely managed to roll out of bed on time, throwing on a baggy gray T-shirt, black gym shorts, and my worn Adidas sneakers before rushing out of the door.

We began walking toward the picnic area at the other end of the boardwalk. "Where is Jolene?" I asked.

"She texted me this morning. She's not coming. Trawler disappeared again, and she doesn't think it would be a good idea to leave Sadie on her own. Not after how upset she was yesterday." Stevie shot me a cautious side glance. "Are we both still on board with not saying anything about Trawler? Or the muddy shovel you saw in the truck? 'Cuz I have to say, I'm not loving this plan."

I peered at Stevie over the top of my glasses. "Do you really think Jolene's going to be happy to hear we suspect her husband?"

"Okay, probably not," she admitted. "But rule number three; we promised we would communicate with each other. If Trawler really is a suspect, Jo deserves to know."

I sighed. "If we're going to investigate, we need Jolene to trust us. She's not going to do that if she thinks we might send her husband to jail. Besides, you said it yourself: Trawler doesn't seem like the kind of person to do something like this."

She frowned, her eyebrows lifting toward her hairline. "He also played wide receiver for the football team. And argued with Andy right before he died."

I waved aside her grim implication. "That was just a theory. We don't know for sure the killer is a former teammate." Trawler as the killer felt too easy, too obvious. Jealous husband was barely a plot twist, and definitely not one that would sell this story to the big news outlets.

We found the fitness class gathered on the grass just beyond the Right Foot pub. A petite woman with impressive muscle tone (the instructor, I presumed) was busy arranging exercise mats and workout stations, while the rest of the class stood by the picnic tables, stretching. There was a reassuring mix of ages and body types, leading me to hope I wouldn't be the only beginner in the group.

A woman bent down to tighten her shoelaces. When she stood up, I groaned. "You didn't tell me Donna Dickie would be here."

"I don't know how to break this to you, Belinda," said Stevie, "but it's a small town. It's the same people everywhere, all the time. Even the ones you find annoying."

"Is it just me or is it weird to see Donna in track pants?"

Stevie laughed. "What would you expect her to wear to a fitness class?"

"I don't know, a leotard and pearls?"

"People in ratty gym shorts should not throw stones," she teased.

I did a second scan of the class participants. "It doesn't look like Holly is coming to this thing."

"Maybe she's just running late," said Stevie. But she looked disappointed too.

Fiona Mahoney stood with the waiting crowd, stretching out her calf muscles. Her curly red hair was styled into two French braids and held in place with a bright headband that matched her pink exercise tank top and leggings.

The sight of her sparked a memory in my brain. "Stevie, do you remember seeing Fiona in the gymnasium before we left?"

She frowned as she raised one arm over her head, stretching. "I don't think so. Why?"

I remembered Fiona's furious expression on the dance floor that night. "She had a bad history with Andy too. He cheated on her multiple times while they were married."

Stevie inhaled sharply. "Remember what he said about dirty laundry? He definitely had something on her."

"Maybe she confronted him after he left the gym, and he threatened to reveal it."

Stevie squared her shoulders. "Since Holly didn't show, we might as well take the opportunity to question Fiona instead."

She moved as if to approach her, but I raised one arm to block her path. “Maybe we should wait until after class. The endorphins might make her a little more receptive.”

Stevie nodded. “You might be right.” She gave me a playful nudge with her elbow. “You’re so good at this.”

I watched Fiona as she chatted with the others. She certainly didn’t *look* like she was grieving.

The instructor approached us, her dark ponytail shining in the sunlight. “Hello there, newcomer,” she said, giving me a friendly smile. “Welcome to Boot Camp on the Boardwalk. I’m Barbie Jamison, and I am honored to be included in your fitness journey.”

“Oh, um, thanks,” I said, a little taken back by her enthusiasm.

“We’d like to do a drop-in session,” said Stevie.

“Absolutely,” Barbie exclaimed. “It’s great to see you back with us, Stevie.”

I leaned in and whispered, “Have you taken this class before?”

“Only once or twice,” Stevie assured me.

We handed over our money, and Barbie added it to her cash box. She turned back to us and clasped her hands together, pointing to me with both index fingers. “Before we begin, I’ll just quickly go over the program with you since this is your first time. We’re going to do my HIIT routine this morning, so that’s High Intensity Interval Training, alternating forty seconds of activity with twenty seconds of rest.” She did a polite but slightly critical scan of my body. “How would you describe your current fitness level?”

I glanced around at the rest of the women. Personally, I felt my level of fitness was on par with theirs. I liked taking walks along the shore, and it's not like I got winded taking the stairs or needed help bringing in the groceries.

"Moderate, I think," I said.

"Fantastic!" she gushed, which I suspected was her default setting. "You two find a spot while I finish setting up."

Stevie and I made our way to the back row of the mats. "Are you sure Barbie is a human and not a labrador retriever in yoga pants?" I asked her.

Stevie giggled. "I know, she's a little intense." She unzipped her hoodie and tied it around her waist, revealing a cute spandex crop top and abs that could grate cheese.

I stared at her six-pack, dumbfounded. "Who's your personal trainer, Sarah Connor?" I blurted out.

Stevie shrugged modestly. "I had a lot of free time, not to mention stress, during the shutdown, so I started doing exercise tutorials online."

I looked around the class again. New and disturbing details sprung into focus. I watched in horror as one woman bent over and placed both of her palms flat on the grass without bending her knees. Fiona's bicep muscles popped in a way that could only be described as *rippling*, while Donna briskly jogged in place, her knees almost coming up to her chest.

Barbie bounced to the front of the group and picked up her cell phone, plugging it into a pair of tiny speakers. Up-tempo dance music began to play as she spun around to face us, adjusting the mic on her wireless headset. "Okay, ladies," she boomed, "let's start off with some warm-up squats."

"Oh, this is going to be bad," I whispered.

Stevie patted my shoulder sympathetically. "Just remember to breathe and drink lots of water."

* * *

"Great job, everyone," cheered Barbie, as we finished the last set of exercises. She walked over to the picnic table and adjusted her playlist. The dance music transitioned into the tranquil sounds of panpipes. "Now we're going to slow it down and stretch it out. Sit down on your mats."

I collapsed onto my mat before she finished speaking. Every muscle in my body screamed at the slightest movement. My arms and legs were heavy with fatigue. It was like trying to move underwater, except the water was on fire. Why did I do this to my body? Why did Barbie do this to my body? I was wrong. She wasn't a harmless labrador retriever woman; she was a brutal assassin whose method of execution was deep lunges and squat thrusts.

"Okay, let's stretch out our triceps," said Barbie, her voice serene. "Starting with your left."

The other women copied her movements obediently while I focused all my remaining energy on continuing to breathe.

"And now the other arm. Um, hello? You there in the back?" I assumed by the level of concern in her voice she was speaking to me. "Are you still with us?"

"Barely," I managed to groan.

I heard a snort of laughter that sounded suspiciously like Stevie.

"You all did wonderfully this afternoon," continued Barbie in a soothing tone. "Focus on your breath. Feel the warmth of the sun on your skin. Listen to the crash of the waves against the rocks. The gentle call of the seagulls as they fly overhead. This moment is a gift."

I struggled to sit up. "My body wants to know how I can return it."

I completed the rest of the cool-down routine without succumbing to audible screams. As soon as Barbie told us to go with love and peace in our hearts, I resumed my sprawled position, spread-eagled on the exercise mat.

Stevie stood over me. "I hate to interrupt the coma, but Fiona is gathering up her stuff. If we want to question her, we'd better do it now."

"Go on without me," I moaned, closing my eyes, "and tell my family I loved them."

"Don't be so dramatic," she said, laughing. "Believe or not, Barbie took it easy on us today."

I cracked open one eye to glare up at her. "You lied to me. I agreed to an exercise class, not a torture session."

She nudged my thigh with the toe of her sneaker. "Let's go. Get up."

"I can't get up," I wailed. "I don't think I'll ever be able to get up again."

Stevie sighed, then suddenly smiled at someone off in the distance. "Oh, hiya, Jinx." she said, waving.

I sprang to my feet, biting back a howl as my muscles protested. But when I looked behind me, he was nowhere to be seen.

"There, see?" said Stevie proudly. "I knew you could do it."

"You are so dead," I growled, fighting the urge to sink back to the ground.

"You'll have to catch me first," she said, skipping out of reach toward Fiona.

I lurched after her, swinging my stiff legs forward like Frankenstein's monster. Fiona had almost reached the end of the picnic area by the time we caught up with her. We called out her name, but she didn't stop until we both cut in front of her, blocking her path.

"Oh, hey," said Fiona, removing her earbuds. "Great workout, huh?"

I grabbed the nearest picnic table to steady my sore legs. "Oh, yeah. I'm really feeling the burn."

Her expression was sympathetic. "Trust me, it will get easier. When you get home, run a warm bath."

Fiona started to walk away again, but Stevie stopped her. "We wanted to talk to you about Andy."

Fiona frowned, immediately on guard. "I heard you two were the ones who found him. Sorry you had to deal with that."

Okay, not exactly beside herself with grief, but not jumping for joy either. "How are you handling the news?" I asked.

She sighed and shifted her exercise bag a little higher on her shoulder. "I'm sorry someone killed him, but other than that, I'm fine. I know I'm supposed to be weepy or whatever, but Andy and I were over a long time ago."

"You didn't sound this blasé about your relationship on Friday night," I said.

Fiona shrugged. "Okay, you got me. I'd be lying if I said I've never felt the urge to kill him myself. Andy made a fool out of me for years, and I've never forgiven him for it."

"It sounds to me like he wasn't the only one in your marriage who stepped out of line," I said.

She looked more intrigued than offended by the suggestion. "Meaning?"

"We heard what Andy said to you on the dance floor," I told her.

"About your dirty laundry," said Stevie. "Maybe he knew something you didn't want anyone else to know."

"Something big," I added.

"Something you were desperate to keep hidden," Stevie finished.

Fiona looked between the two of us. "Do you two think you're Nancy Drew or something?" she asked, sounding amused. "Andy didn't have anything on me. At least, not anything that isn't already public knowledge."

Stevie appeared to be just as confused as I was. "What are you talking about?"

Fiona lowered her voice. "My settlement," she murmured. "About a year before we divorced, I was sued by the buyers in one of my real estate deals. The house passed inspection, but after the sale was finalized, the buyers learned the house had a few issues."

"What kind of issues?" asked Stevie.

Fiona sighed. "The foundation was sinking, the electrical system needed to be rewired, and the roof leaked."

"Those sound like pretty big issues for a home inspector to miss." Fiona suddenly looked shifty, and the truth dawned on me. "Unbelievable. You paid off the home inspector, didn't you?"

"We may have had an arrangement," she said grudgingly. "Fortunately, I managed to settle out of court for less than expected. I tried to keep it quiet, but you know how this town works. Word still got out."

"Wait, is this why you started your own real estate company?" I asked. I remembered how angry my mother was at the time, but I assumed it was because her former protégé was now her competition.

"Yes, your mother was furious with me. She said I risked the reputation of every other real estate agent at her firm, and if I didn't leave quietly, she would file a complaint against me."

"That sounds like Mum," I said proudly.

"I wouldn't kill Andy over something like that," insisted Fiona. "I was in the gymnasium the entire night until the cops told us we could leave."

"Can anyone verify that?" I asked.

"The bartender, Jinx. After my exchange with Andy on the dance floor, I ordered a glass of red wine and told him to keep them coming."

My shoulders drooped with disappointment. "I see."

I could tell from Stevie's crestfallen expression that she shared my assumption. "Thanks for your time," she mumbled to Fiona.

"My pleasure." Fiona put her earbuds back into her ears. "Later, Nancy," she said to Stevie, smirking. She pushed past me. "Later, Bess."

"Well, that was embarrassing," said Stevie as we both watched her leave.

"I know," I said. "It's pretty obvious I'm the Nancy."

"I meant questioning the wrong suspect."

"We'll still have to confirm her alibi with Jinx," I pointed out.

"It will check out," she said with a sigh. "Jinx is a stand-up guy. There's no way he'd lie for someone like Fiona. Remember when Andy and his friends got a hold of the biology midterm answer sheet and handed it out to the entire class? Jinx was the only one who refused to use it."

Of course, I remembered. That impressive act of integrity was what bumped a mild crush up to full-blown infatuation. "We should still talk to him," I said. "Just to check all of our boxes." If that meant I got to sneak another peek at those dimples, so be it.

"Don't bother," said someone behind me. Donna Dickie approached, now wearing a warm-up hoodie and vintage pearl necklace. "I was at the bar for the rest of the night too. Fiona was exactly where she said she was."

Well, I guess that settles that. If anyone was keeping track of people's movements that night, it was the Teacher's Pet. "You didn't happen to notice anyone missing from the gym before Andy was found, did you?" I asked Donna.

She arched her eyebrows. "You mean, besides Jolene? The evidence is stacking up against her pretty quickly, from what I've heard."

And have no doubt been repeating all over town. "Unsolicited opinion noted," I said, shooing her away irritably.

I watched Donna leave, frustration churning in my stomach. Unfortunately, the entire town seemed just as determined as Sergeant Finlayson to believe in Jolene's guilt. We had to clear her name, and quickly. I didn't agree with a lot of things Andy did, but he had been right about one thing.

Reputations were not easy to shed in Little Blue Harbour.

Chapter Nine

Slowly and painfully, Stevie helped me back to my car, my arm thrown over her shoulder for support as we discussed what we learned. Like her, I was disappointed our questioning of Fiona had not gone to plan, the plan being a quick and detailed confession. But, as my father used to say, sometimes your investigation is simply a process of elimination.

"It's fine," I said, as I limped down the boardwalk. "Don't you watch mystery shows? It's never the first suspect. Fiona was just a practice swing. You know, like a mulligan in golf."

"I suck at playing golf," she said. She looked down at my sneakers. "Are you even lifting your feet?"

"Sorry, but walking is a little more difficult now that my body has turned to stone."

"You are such a pain wuss." She stopped to readjust her grip on my waist before continuing our trek toward the car.

"We need to find out if Holly was the jealous ex-girlfriend. It would give her motive to kill Andy and frame Jolene."

Stevie's cell phone pinged, and she shifted me to the side as she wiggled her phone free from her pocket. "It's Jolene," she said, reading the text notification. "Trawler is home."

"Perfect. We can swing by and pick her up on our way to Holly's house."

"You want to question Holly right now?" she asked.

"Why not? We can talk to Barry while we're there too. We might as well strike while we've still got the momentum."

We finally reached my car, and she gently lowered me down onto one of the granite boulders that stretched the width of each parking stall.

"What momentum?" argued Stevie, straightening. "You can barely move. Also, don't take this the wrong way, but I am not going anywhere with you until you shower."

I started to protest, but just then the breeze picked up. Either it was low tide or a quick shower was definitely in order. "Okay, you win," I said. "Shower first; interrogations second."

"What makes you think Holly and Barry will even talk to us?" she asked.

"If Holly doesn't, Barry probably will. You saw him at the reunion. She obviously cheated on him with someone."

Stevie groaned softly. "Great, inserting ourselves into the breakdown of a marriage. I'm sure that won't blow up in our faces at all."

* * *

One hour later, after Stevie and I were both washed, rinsed, and dried, we pulled into Jolene's driveway. Pressing the gas pedal and using the turn signals were the extent of my range of motion, so Stevie ran inside to collect her. When Jolene got into the car, she pulled the door closed with more force than necessary.

"You don't need to slam it," I said, unintentionally channeling my father.

Jolene let out a sharp growl. "Trawler is driving me insane today. He still refuses to tell me where he keeps disappearing to or what he's doing," she griped.

Stevie and I exchanged an awkward glance. I felt a little guilty hiding our suspicions about Trawler from her, but on our way to interrogate Holly about her affair with Andy didn't feel like the right time. No reason to blow up *two* marriages if we didn't need to.

"How are things with Sadie?" asked Stevie instead.

"A little better, actually," said Jolene. "She's speaking to me again. Yesterday really scared her." She sighed. "I hate that I put her through that."

"Hey, *you* didn't put her through anything," I said firmly. "Whoever is trying to set you up for this did. And as soon as we find out who they are, we're going to make them regret it."

"Exactly," added Stevie.

"Which reminds me," said Jolene, rummaging through her large tote bag. "Since I missed the fitness class with you this morning, I wanted to do something to contribute to the case."

She pulled out three pleather-bound portfolio notebooks and passed the blue and black ones up front, keeping the pink one for herself.

"I've already compiled profiles for each of our suspects," she said, "and separated them by colored tabs. There's also a pen and notepad to take notes, as well as emergency contact numbers for each of us. I used your respective business numbers, but I can change them, if you'd prefer."

I stared at her, impressed. "You made us murder binders?"

"Investigation binders," she clarified.

"Murder binders," I whispered to Stevie.

Stevie slipped her fingers into one of the inside pockets and withdrew a plastic sandwich bag. "What are these for? Snacks?"

"I thought we could use those in case we find any evidence," said Jolene.

I flipped through the colored tabs. "How much did all of this cost?"

Jolene shrugged. "Nothing."

"Impossible," said Stevie. "The binders alone had to cost at least twenty dollars each."

Jolene's cheeks flushed pink. "I might have a thing for stationery stores," she mumbled.

"And by *thing*, do you mean addiction?" I asked.

"I think this is great," said Stevie. She held the blue binder next to her head. "Mine even matches my hair."

I picked up the black one and held it against my chest. "This one matches my soul."

Rolling her eyes, Jolene gave me directions to the Townsends' house. On the way there, Stevie and I brought her up to speed on what we found out from Fiona. When we pulled up to Holly and Barry's pale green Craftsman-style house, the driveway was blocked by a small moving van. Cardboard boxes were scattered on the lawn. Holly stood on her front steps, one arm tightly wrapped across her torso as she smoked a cigarette with her other hand. The front door was propped open, and Barry appeared, carrying more boxes. Holly glared at him as he walked past her. When she spotted us, her scowl intensified. She dropped her lit cigarette butt on the grass and ground it out under her shoe.

"What are you three doing here?" she barked at us from across the lawn.

Jolene exited the car. "What's going on? Are you guys moving?"

Barry rearranged a few boxes to make more room in the back of the van. "I am."

"Shut up, Barry," snapped Holly. "It's none of their business."

"I don't care whose business it is anymore." He turned back to us. "We're getting divorced," he said matter-of-factly.

I looked at Stevie. "See? And you thought we were going to make this awkward."

"Maybe this isn't the best time for an interrogation," Jolene murmured as she and Stevie lifted me from the driver's seat.

"Are you kidding? This is the perfect time," I said. "Heightened emotions, tempers flared; it's like they've both taken truth serum. If we can provoke them in the right way, they might say something they otherwise wouldn't."

"Or they might throw a moving box at our heads," argued Stevie.

"Fine, stand behind me," I said, shuffling up the driveway on my stiff legs. "My entire body is numb at this point, anyway."

Holly stormed across the lawn, coming to a stop in front of Jolene. "What do you want?"

Stevie and I looked at Jolene, silently handing over the controls to the conversation. She cleared her throat nervously. "You weren't at boot camp this morning," said Jolene.

"Obviously, something more important came up," snapped Holly.

"You looked pretty upset at the Right Foot yesterday, especially when we mentioned Andy. I just wanted to make sure you were okay."

Holly quickly blinked a few times before answering. "Of course I am," she said shortly. "Why wouldn't I be?"

"Hey, come on now, Holly," said Barry as he hopped down from the moving truck. "Is that anyway to talk about your ex-boyfriend?"

"Shut up, Barry," Holly forced through gritted teeth.

Well, that was easier than I expected. "So, you're the woman Andy broke up with before he died," I said to Holly.

She exhaled a short, angry puff of air from her flared nostrils. I noticed she didn't deny it. "Okay, fine," she said, throwing up her hands in the air. "I was seeing Andy, but he dumped me. Happy?"

Triumphant was more like it, but admitting that was hardly the best way to get Holly's cooperation. "Why'd Andy give you the boot?" I asked her.

To my surprise, Holly's eyes filled with tears. Despite her attitude, I regretted my choice of words. She'd clearly been hurt by Andy, and it felt unfair to make light of that. However much we disliked each other, I could relate to her pain.

"He said he wanted to be single for a while, so he could reevaluate his life and develop a sense of internal validation," said Holly. "Whatever that meant."

It seems like Andy really was trying to change his ways, I thought. It made his ultimate fate all the more upsetting.

Angrily, Holly wiped away the tears clinging to her eyelashes. "I kept calling him, trying to get him to change his mind. I told him I wanted him just the way he was, but he refused to listen."

"Then he blocked your number," said Stevie.

She laughed bitterly. "Yeah, the coward."

I tried to keep my expression neutral, but my eyebrows shot up toward my hairline before I could stop them. "You think not wanting to be harassed is cowardice?" Apparently, Holly hadn't lost her sense of entitlement over the years.

Holly glared at me, but she didn't refute my observation. "After he blocked me, I came clean to Barry about the affair. I apologized, but he won't forgive me." She gestured furiously toward the moving van where Barry had resumed stacking his boxes. "Now, I've lost them both."

Barry slid another box into the back of the van. "Holly, I'm sorry. I really am," he said shortly. "I thought I could stick it out until Rena and Shawn were older, but I just can't. It's not fair to any of us. Our kids deserve parents who don't actively hate each other."

"I don't hate you," insisted Holly. "Andy was a mistake; I know that now."

For a second, Barry almost looked as though he pitied her. "We don't love each other," he said. "We don't even like each other anymore. At least if I leave now, we have a better chance of being friends again someday."

Holly snorted rudely. "You want to be friends? What are you, twelve?"

His expression became harder, a little more impatient. "Can you honestly say if Andy hadn't called it off, you wouldn't be doing exactly what I'm doing right now?"

Her shoulders slumped and for a moment, Holly looked smaller and frailer than I had ever seen her. But it didn't last. "Fine," she spat. "I don't need you, Barry. Go! And take your stupid dwarf figurines with you."

For the first time since we arrived, Barry looked offended. "They're hobbits."

Holly turned to leave. I grasped for her sleeve, but the fabric slipped through my fingers. "You borrowed Jolene's blue scarf," I blurted out.

To my relief, it worked. Holly spun back around to face us. "Yeah, so?"

"The same scarf that was found with the body of your ex-lover," I clarified.

Holly threw back her shoulders and puffed out her chest like a rattlesnake preparing to strike. "You think I killed Andy?" she exploded.

"It's a pretty big coincidence, don't you think?" I asked. "You were the last person to wear it."

She turned her furious expression on Jolene. "Just wanted to check on me, huh? You are so full of it. Showing up unannounced, pretending to be my friend, and now trying to frame me?"

I leaned closer to Stevie and whispered, "I think Holly has Jolene confused with a mirror."

Fortunately, neither Holly nor Jolene heard me. Jolene reached for Holly's arm. "The police have been asking questions. You need to tell them the truth."

Holly jerked her arm free. "I don't need to do anything, least of all help you. I've heard the rumors. I know you're the reason Andy broke up with me."

Jolene shook her head, aghast. "No, that's not it at all."

Holly stalked up the driveway and into the house, slamming the door behind her. A moment later, it opened again. She reappeared, pointing at me, Stevie, and Jolene. "You three better get off my lawn within the next five minutes or I'm calling the police!"

"Are you sure you want us to go?" I yelled back to her. "I have some life advice on starting over in your thirties, if you're interested now."

Her only response was to slam the front door closed again. I couldn't help snickering. *I knew that would get her.*

Barry turned to us. "Sorry you had to see that."

"Where are Rena and Shawn?" asked Jolene, looking toward the house with her brow creased. I assumed those were Barry and Holly's kids. "They're not inside where they can overhear this, are they?"

"No, my mother came by and picked them up this morning," said Barry. "She took them to McGrey's Island for the day. I didn't want them here in case Holly, well, you know."

"Acted like Holly?" I guessed.

He nodded. "Exactly."

"Where are you staying?" asked Stevie.

"My mother has a spare room at her house," he said, picking up another box. "She said I could move in, just until I find somewhere bigger. I'm going to meet her and the kids for supper after I get everything unloaded on the other end, and try to explain things to them."

He fumbled with the box and Stevie hurried forward to help load it into the van. I surveyed the rest of the boxes still on the lawn. "You seem to be handling the breakup remarkably well," I told him.

"It's been a long time coming," he said.

I couldn't help thinking of my own move back to Little Blue Harbour, the intense feeling of failure as I packed up my adult life and loaded it into a similar truck. The shame of it all made my insides feel so tightly coiled, I feared I would snap. Did Barry feel the same way about the end of his marriage? Had it been enough to drive him to murder?

"But why leave now?" I asked him. "You've obviously known about Andy and Holly for a while."

"I guess that's a fair question." He looked back at the house. "Honestly, it was Andy dying that did it for me."

"How so?" asked Jolene.

He ran one large palm over his short hair. "I'm sure you three noticed how drunk I was at the reunion." We nodded solemnly. "That used to be a rare occurrence for me, but lately not so much. At first, I blamed Holly, but it wasn't fully her fault. We were unhappy long before Andy came into the picture. But he and I used to be buddies, you know? Teammates. Even though he ended things with her, every time I saw him, it just made me so angry."

"How angry?" I asked carefully. "Barry, where did you go when you left the gym that night?"

He blinked, surprised by the question. "Home," he said simply. "Iggy drove me."

Ignatius Saxton owned the only taxicab company in Little Blue Harbour. He and his son, Teddy, drove the vehicles while his wife, Lottie, handled dispatch. Iggy was in his early sixties, built roughly the size of a fishing shack, and could name every customer he'd ever driven.

"You didn't run into Andy before you left, did you?" asked Stevie.

Barry shook his head. "If I did, I don't remember," he said, looking embarrassed. "I couldn't even make it inside the house by myself, Iggy had to help me. When I heard what happened the next morning, I couldn't help thinking that could have been me. I was so drunk I could hardly walk. What if *I* had ended up dead at the bottom of a flight of stairs or something? That's not how I want to go out, trapped in a bad marriage, miserable with my life."

"Andy didn't fall," I reminded him. "Someone cracked him over the head with his own award."

"Yeah, but that wasn't me." His eyes darted in Jolene's direction.

"It wasn't me either," said Jolene, offended.

Barry's cheeks flushed. "No, of course not." He paused. "I heard the police found your scarf."

"A scarf Holly liked to borrow," I reminded him.

He shook his head. "Holly didn't kill Andy."

I crossed my arms. "What makes you so sure? She clearly doesn't respond well when she doesn't get what she wants."

"My marriage might be over, but I still know my wife. She really cared about Andy. I think she thought he was going to be her fresh start."

I shrugged. "Sometimes people lose control in ways we wouldn't expect."

"Talk to Julie, Becca, and Amanda if you don't believe me," he said. "Holly was with them all night."

I looked at Stevie and Jolene and shrugged, silently asking if they were satisfied with his answers. To my relief, they both nodded. My legs were ready to give out, and my lower back was screaming for a heating pad.

"I guess we'll let you get back to it," I said to Barry.

I extended both arms and Stevie and Jolene obediently each took one, helping me limp down the driveway toward the car. Whatever amusement Barry may have felt for my current state, he kept it to himself, thankfully.

"What do you guys think?" asked Stevie as she lowered me behind the steering wheel. "Personally, I'm leaning toward Holly as the guilty one. She's unpleasant enough under normal circumstances, never mind when she's been rejected."

"Crossing Barry off the suspect list should be easy enough," said Jolene, getting into the back seat. She took out her cell phone and dialed. "Hello, Lottie. This is Jolene Dexter. I'm calling about Barry Townsend. I heard Iggy drove him home from the reunion on Friday night, and he was in a bad state. I just wanted to apologize on behalf of the reunion committee."

Stevie whistled softly. "Oh, she's good."

"Mm-hmm," murmured Jolene, waving for us to be quiet. Her forehead creased as she listened to Lottie on the other end. "Oh, really?" She glanced up at us, her expression grim. "You don't remember a call coming in for Barry Townsend on Friday night?"

She fell silent again as we watched her with bated breath.

"You're sure? No, no, I just wanted to make sure you weren't owed a fare. Thanks so much, Lottie. Give my best to Iggy and Teddy." Jolene disconnected the call. "Sneaky little bugger."

"But definitely not clever," I said. "Everyone in town knows a Saxton never forgets when it comes to money."

Stevie nodded in agreement. "Why would he say Iggy drove him home when he didn't? It's such an easy lie to disprove."

Jolene opened her binder and turned to Barry's suspect profile. "Maybe he panicked," she said, making notes in the margins.

"Or he wasn't expecting us to confirm his alibi," I said.

"Which is fair, because why would we?" asked Stevie. "We're just three women from his wife's fitness class as far as he knows."

Jolene turned to Holly's profile. "What about Holly? Is she still in play as a suspect?"

"Oh, definitely," I said. "That woman practically goes unhinged when she doesn't get what she wants."

"That's true," she said thoughtfully.

"What?" asked Stevie, twisting in her seat to look behind her.

"I know Holly better than the two of you," she said. "It just doesn't feel calculating enough for her tastes. When Holly sets her sights on someone, she aims for complete destruction. Just killing Andy would've been too quick for her."

I had to admit, she had a point. The bully I remembered liked to play with her food.

"Maybe we should talk to the Pageant Minions," said Stevie. "See if their story matches what Barry said."

"Can we please call them by their real names?" asked Jolene from the back seat. "It's a little dehumanizing. Julie, Becca, and Amanda aren't bad people, really. They're just scared to stand up to Holly."

"If that's true, it just means they'll cover for her," I pointed out.

"Yeah, but let's be honest; they probably won't do a very good job," said Stevie. "Remember when Julie and Amanda were caught smoking in the school library? They tried to convince Mr. Blenkhorn that someone else had started a very tiny fire."

She raised a good point. Outside of inventive insults, the Pageant Minions hadn't been known for their intellectual prowess.

I glanced over at Stevie, considering her blue bob. "You know, Stevie, I think your hair color is looking a little faded."

She smirked. "No, it isn't. I'm not forking out more than a hundred bucks just to have an excuse to book an appointment at the salon." She flipped up the passenger side vanity mirror and contemplated her reflection. "A trim would only cost me thirty dollars."

I dropped Jolene off at her house and drove Stevie back to the Osprey. My parents texted me that Huey and his wife invited them over for a haddock fish and chips supper, which meant I was on my own that evening. Which is why, despite my screaming muscles, when Stevie's mother invited me to stay for my favorite Maritimes meal, pan-fried Digby scallops and hodge podge with Moon Mist ice cream for dessert, I accepted without hesitation.

Hours later, after I was stuffed with good food and ready for a warm bath like Fiona recommended, I drove home. There was no sound of barking as I walked up the front steps, meaning my parents must have taken Shelly with them. I slipped my key into the lock but paused.

There was a folded piece of paper jammed between the door and the frame. I pulled it free and opened it, expecting to find a note from my mother. My stomach clenched as I read.

The clever fox knows to stay in her own den. Mind your own business, Bishop, OR ELSE.

Chapter Ten

Normally, my reluctance to face the day was because I stayed up too late the previous night, binge-watching baking shows and trying to convince myself I, too, could bake that five-tier wedding cake covered in buttercream roses.

But when I woke up the next morning, the hollow feeling in my chest wasn't due to my lack of icing skills. In accordance with rule number three, I texted a picture of the note to Stevie after finding the paper left in my door. She was immediately concerned, but I assured her I was fine.

But that didn't stop me from obsessing over the note all night. Neither of my parents mentioned it when they came home last night, so it was safe to assume its author hadn't paid me a visit until after they'd left. Honestly, I was more curious about the message than frightened. In my opinion, whoever wrote it wasn't used to threatening people. The wording brought to mind a mustachioed cartoon baddie petting a white cat rather than an actual human.

Unfortunately, this observation didn't do much in the way of providing any clues to the culprit's identity. All I wanted to do was burrow down so deeply under my faded unicorn comforter it would take a team of archeologists years to unearth me. Unfortunately, I still had my interview with Sergeant Finlayson this afternoon.

I also smelled bacon.

I followed the scent through the house, finding my mother standing in front of the old cookstove. A place had already been set for me at the table. My mother did a slight double-take when she saw me, her gaze lingering for a moment on the brown tangled mass sitting atop my head, but she quickly rearranged her expression into what I liked to call her "tourist smile."

She added a few strips of bacon to my plate. "Good morning, my pretty girl. You must be starving. Sit, sit, sit," she fussed, gesturing toward the table with the spatula.

A few drops of bacon grease landed on the floor. Shelly immediately sprung into action, lapping it up. I gingerly took my seat at the table. My mother placed the plate in front of me with a flourish. Two eggs sunny side up, bacon, and toast. Shelly scurried over to the table and planted her round rump at my feet, her sharp little eyes never leaving the food.

My mother cooked me breakfast. My father was still in his favorite recliner chair reading his newspaper, instead of out in his workshop. As much as I was enjoying the aroma of bacon wafting through the air, I smelled something else. An ambush.

I narrowed my eyes in suspicion. "Mum, what are you up to?"

Her eyes widened, adopting the same innocent expression as Shelly whenever someone asked who got into the garbage can. "Can't a mother cook breakfast for her daughter?"

"You hate cooking," I reminded her. "You always say history's greatest invention was the takeout menu, not the wheel. It's also why you insisted the cottages each have a kitchenette."

"I wanted to do something nice for you," she said. "You'll need all your mental strength for your interview with Sergeant Finlayson today."

As if to prove her point, she poured me a cup of coffee and placed it next to my eggs. We stared each other down, each waiting for the other to make the first move. Finally, my rumbling stomach won out against my stubbornness.

Which was exactly what she was waiting for.

As soon as I reached for the plate, my mother swooped in with her true intention. "But, before you leave for your interview, I'd appreciate it if you could explain this."

I looked up from buttering my toast to see her holding the note, now encased in one of the plastic baggies Jolene had provided.

"And this?" She held up my black binder in her other hand.

I tried to grab them from her, but my mother stepped back out of reach. "Aren't I a little too old for you to be snooping through my things?" I asked. "Those were in my purse."

"How could you not tell us about this?" my mother demanded.

I sighed. "It's nothing."

"Really," she said, sounding unconvinced. She cleared her throat dramatically and read the note aloud. "The clever fox knows to stay in her own den. Mind your own business, Bishop, or else."

"That note could be intended for any of us," I said. "Minding our own business isn't exactly a Bishop family trait."

"This is no time for jokes," my mother snapped. "Your father and I deserve to know you've gotten yourself involved in a murder investigation."

"I'm not involved in anything, Mum," I said. "We were just asking a few people some questions about Andy's death."

"Is that the only reason you and Stevie went to visit Jolene on Saturday?" she asked. "What about rekindling old friendships? What about offering someone support in their time of crisis?"

"I can multitask."

"So, you are involved," she crowed.

I looked to my father for help, but he shook his head at me. "Sorry, kiddo," he said, "but you walked right into that one."

"Don't get me wrong," said my mother. "You've always had a knack for this kind of thing, Belinda. If you hadn't gone into journalism, I think you would've followed in your father's footsteps and joined the RCMP."

I let my attention drift back to my breakfast. "Nah, the hats don't suit me."

My mother paced behind me, not listening. "I'm happy that you and Jolene are trying to patch things up. Frankly, I've never understood what went wrong between you two in the first place. "

I took a deep swig of coffee. If my mother was going to drag me down memory lane, I definitely needed more caffeine. "Jolene and I aren't patching anything up, I'm only doing this as a favor to Stevie." And hopefully land a story big enough to catapult me back to Ontario, but my parents didn't need to know that.

She frowned. "But you two were so sweet together as kids. Practically inseparable."

I closed my eyes briefly as I worked up the energy to continue the conversation. "Mum, I love you, but is there a point hidden somewhere in all of this?"

"My point is that when my only daughter starts receiving death threats, I have a right to know about it."

I rolled my eyes. "It's not a death threat."

"'Or else' is written in all caps!" she cried, flapping the note at me.

"Someone is just trying to scare me," I argued. "If they were serious, they'd be more direct. Stop or I'll kill you, that kind of thing."

"That might not be the case," my father said from his recliner.

"See, your father agrees with me," my mother interrupted. "Belinda, while you are living under our roof, we expect you to follow our rules."

I rounded on my father. "Dad, please remind Mum what the age of majority is for this province."

"Kenneth, please remind your daughter how dangerous a murder investigation can be," she countered.

My father looked at the dog, who only had eyes for my bacon. "Shelly, please remind my wife and daughter that I'm retired."

"Are you really not going to back me up on this?" my mother asked him, exasperated.

By way of a response, my father disappeared behind his newspaper again. The silence stretched on as the grandfather clock ticked. "Is your mother still staring at me?" he asked me eventually.

"Yes," she and I answered in unison.

He lowered the newspaper with a sigh. "Ellie, Belinda is a grown woman. She's got a good head on her shoulders, and she knows her limitations. She would never do anything to intentionally impede justice. I trust that she will behave responsibly and not take any unnecessary risks."

"Thank you, Dad," I said proudly.

"Just like I trust her to swallow her pride for the sake of those who care about her and share the note with the sergeant during her interview this afternoon. Along with any other substantial information she may have learned," he added firmly.

Stevie and I had already decided last night that we would both tell Sergeant Finlayson about the note, along with Barry's false alibi and Holly's habit of borrowing the blue scarf, but I figured it would work more in my favor if I let my father believe it was his idea. "Okay, fine. I promise."

He gave me a satisfied nod and returned his attention to the *Foghorn*.

My mother shook her head. "This is going to be the Suede Damon debacle all over again."

I directed my groan toward the ceiling. "No, it isn't. Please give me a little more credit than that."

My father lowered one corner of the sports section. "Four words: elementary school talent show."

I winced. *Of course, he would bring that up again.*

When I was eleven, my school held a talent competition, wherein Ian Huskilson performed a magic act. His first few tricks were relatively simple: disconnecting silver hoops, cutting a rope and then reattaching the two ends, stuff everyone knows. Then, for his big finale, he rolled out a serving cart with a large silver platter and dome sitting on top. He placed his pet rabbit, Buttons, under the dome, spun the cart three times, and lifted the lid to reveal his little sister, Chloe, curled up underneath. The audience went crazy with applause, and he won first prize.

I hounded Ian every day for the next week, demanding to know how he performed the switch, but he wouldn't crack. I read every book on magic at the Little Blue Harbour public library (which, granted, wasn't many). I even snuck into the school cafeteria during recess to inspect the carts for clues. Finally, under threat of losing internet privileges from my parents, I agreed to drop it.

Only to leap to my feet three months later during Jason Zhang's oral report on the emperor penguin and scream, "A false bottom with mirrors!"

So, yes, maybe I did have a history of becoming a little fixated when trying to solve a puzzle.

"Most parents would be proud of their child for figuring out such a cool trick on her own," I muttered sullenly.

"Mrs. Shand had to ban you from the cafeteria kitchen," my father reminded me.

"I won't get carried away this time," I assured them. "Once Sergeant Finlayson hears what I have to tell him, he'll realize Jolene is innocent and turn his attention to other, more viable suspects."

My parents exchanged a cautious glance. "You're saying once Jolene's name is cleared, you'll stop investigating?" asked my mother.

I nodded.

She sized me up for a moment. Finally, she relinquished my murder binder and the note. "I'm going to hold you to that," she warned.

* * *

I spent the rest of the morning covering the reception desk until my mother relieved me at noon for my police interview. Stevie and I had already planned to drive over to the RCMP station together, so I borrowed the Civic and stopped at the Osprey first, where I grabbed a quick lunch with Stevie. Over an order of her mother's lobster roll and sweet potato fries, I showed her the note. While she still wasn't happy that I'd received it, she agreed that it didn't appear to be a serious threat.

"Who do you think wrote it?" Stevie asked as we drove to the RCMP station.

I shrugged one shoulder, my eyes still on the road. "Who knows? It was typed out, so it's not like we can compare handwriting."

"At least Finlayson will be able to check it for fingerprints," she said. "Although I doubt he'll find any on it. If they knew enough to use a computer, they probably also knew to wear gloves."

"Thanks to true crime documentaries and podcasts, that's practically everyone nowadays."

"I don't think it was Fiona," said Stevie. "She didn't take us seriously enough to feel threatened. And it's too abstract to be Holly. If she wanted to threaten us, she'd do it to our faces."

"That leaves Barry," I said, "but this doesn't feel like his style either."

She peered at the note. "What are these?"

"What are what?" I chanced a quick glance from the road to the note, but I didn't see anything that caught my attention.

She tapped a line of tiny black spots at the bottom right corner with her finger. "It looks like they used an old printer with dirty rollers."

I snorted. "So, pretty much every public building in the town."

We pulled into the parking lot in front of the RCMP station and got out of the car. Inside, we checked in with the same officer as before sitting behind the glass and informed her that Sergeant Finlayson was expecting us. Once again, we were instructed to wait in the lobby. Not surprisingly, at exactly one o'clock,

Sergeant Finlayson appeared to collect us. He led us both through the bullpen to an interview room. He motioned for Stevie to wait outside as he opened the door, inviting me to follow him.

Inside was a nondescript room with gray walls, linoleum floor, white ceiling tiles, and a plain metal table with four chairs. To my slight disappointment, there was no large two-way mirror like in the movies. He took a seat and gestured for me to do the same across from him. He took a small recorder from his coat pocket and placed it on the table between us. He turned it on and clearly stated the date and time, as well his name and mine.

"Good afternoon, Miss Bishop," he said politely. "Thank you for coming in today."

Like I had a choice. "Don't mention it," I said. "Where's Randy?"

He took out his pen and notepad, flipping to a blank page. "Given your personal relationship with Corporal Perry, I thought it would be best if I spoke with you alone."

"Are you worried he'll go easier on me because he worked with my father?" I asked, only half joking. "I thought I was just a witness."

"You are," he said, "but I get the sense you don't plan on being a very cooperative one."

I gave him my sweetest, most insincere smile. "I guess you're as good at reading witnesses as you are at determining suspects."

His grip on his pen was so rigid, it looked as though it would snap it into two pieces. "Let's proceed, shall we?"

"Fire away," I said, relishing my small victory.

Sergeant Finlayson asked me to walk him through the night of the reunion; what time I arrived, Andy's demeanor when we spoke, the confrontation on the dance floor between Andy, Trawler, and Jolene. I answered his questions to the best of my recollection, making sure to mention Madeline Barclay's surprise appearance.

Finlayson seemed unconcerned. "We've already spoken to Mrs. Barclay," he said shortly, scribbling his notes. "Can you think of anyone besides Mrs. Dexter who may have held a grudge against the victim?"

"Jo didn't have a grudge against Andy," I reminded him. "They were friends. But to answer your question, yes, I can. Barry and Holly Townsend. Holly and Andy were having an affair. He ended things between them a few months ago, and she didn't handle the breakup well. In fact, Andy had to block her number. Barry knew about them too. Holly came clean after Andy dumped her."

Finlayson's eyebrows twitched upward. "We've been going through Mr. Perch's cell phone. There were quite a few blocked numbers, most of them belonging to women. One was traced back to a prepaid cell phone."

"Ten bucks says it belongs to Holly," I said. "Everyone knows if you're going to send spicy texts to someone other than your spouse, you don't use your regular phone."

He frowned. "Neither Townsend mentioned any of this in their interviews."

"Yeah, because it makes them look guilty." I wasn't too surprised to hear Barry hadn't told the police about the affair. Holly was still the mother of his children, after all. Maybe that afforded her some loyalty on his part. "Barry was in the process of moving out of their house when we showed up yesterday to question them," I said. "They're getting divorced."

His pen froze and he looked up from his notepad, confused. "What do you mean, question them?"

I continued as though he hadn't spoken. "Barry also told us he took a taxi home on Friday night, but we called the cab company. Lottie didn't remember getting the call."

Finlayson dropped his pen and slumped back in his chair, his face incredulous. "You called to check his alibi?"

I shrugged. "Sure, why not? Oh, and I almost forgot." I reached into my purse and took out my cell phone. "Holly loved that blue scarf, she borrowed it from Jo all the time." I found the screenshot of the salon's post and showed it to him. "She freaked out when we asked her about it too."

Finlayson leaned forward, fury radiating from him. "Miss Bishop, just because your father is a former member of the Royal Canadian Mounted Police, it does not mean you have any legal authority whatsoever in this matter."

I looked up from my phone in surprise. "I know that."

"Then why do you seem to be conducting your own investigation into Mr. Perch's death?"

I let out a frustrated sigh. "Because you're focusing your investigation on an innocent woman."

"I have to go where the evidence takes me, Miss Bishop. Right now, it's pointing me toward Mrs. Dexter as the most likely suspect."

"Okay, but you can't deny that confirmation bias isn't an issue with other police investigations," I retorted.

"You can't deny you have a history of showing up where you don't belong." The corner of his mouth twitched, fighting a smile. "Backstage at a charity concert, for example."

A rush of embarrassment warmed my cheeks. My trespassing arrest. In retrospect, it made sense that he'd do a background check on me. I'd been the one to find Andy's body, after all.

Him knowing about it shifted the balance of power between us, though, and I didn't like it.

"Totally different circumstances," I said. "I was in pursuit of a news story." Which was also the case here, but I decided to add his name to the list of people who didn't need to know that. "Besides, everyone knows Suede Damon is a drama llama. Have you ever seen his socials?"

I could tell Finlayson was struggling to maintain his patience. "Miss Bishop."

"Will you please just call me Belinda?" I interrupted. "I'm not the neighborhood spinster in a Jane Austen novel."

He sighed. "Despite what you may think, I'm not trying to railroad anyone here. The fact is, your friend had a personal relationship with the victim that resulted in a physical altercation in front of multiple witnesses. Her personal belongings were found with the victim, and her fingerprints are on the murder weapon."

"Hers and probably half of our graduating class," I reminded him.

"However," he continued, speaking over my objection, "I would not be doing my duty as a police officer if I didn't consider other possibilities, so I will look into the Townsends."

I exhaled a short puff of breath. "Thank you."

His eyebrows flattened into a stern glare. "Is there anyone else you've questioned that I should know about?"

You're lucky I never break a promise to my father. "Yes, we spoke to Andy's ex-wife, Fiona Mahoney," I said. "She and Andy also got into it on the dance floor. It sounded like he was threatening to expose some secret of hers."

"Her settlement agreement," he said, nodding. "Yes, we already know about that. We've also confirmed Ms. Mahoney's alibi with the bartender." He glanced down at his notes. "A Mr. Ethan Suth—"

I considered letting Sergeant Finlayson say Jinx's entire name, but at the last second, I took pity on him. "Just call him Jinx. Everyone else does."

He seemed to struggle with himself for a moment. I suspected this was a man who thrived on proper decorum. "Jinx stated that Ms. Mahoney did not leave the bar until after the police arrived. I assure you, Miss Bishop, that I am capable of conducting a murder investigation without your assistance."

Okay, now he's doing it to annoy me. I crossed my arms defiantly. "You didn't know about Andy and Holly."

He smirked. "Even rookies get lucky."

"If I'm so far off-base, explain this," I said hotly, reaching into my bag again. I pulled out the note, still inside its baggie, and slid it across the table to him.

He read it, frowning. "Where did you get this?"

"I found it stuck in my front door last night, after we questioned Barry and Holly."

Something shifted in his expression. "Did you go straight home after speaking with the Townsends?" he asked eagerly.

"No," I said. "First, I dropped off Jolene at her house, and then I ended up having supper with Stevie and her mother, Diane."

"How long would you say it was between the time you dropped off Mrs. Dexter and the time you returned home?"

"I don't know. After supper, I stayed to visit. Maybe three hours or so?"

He tapped the note with his pen. "Did it ever occur to you that Mrs. Dexter could have left the note?"

I blinked, admittedly caught off guard by his suggestion. "That's ridiculous."

"You said it yourself; you dropped Mrs. Dexter off at least three hours before you found it. She would have had more than enough time to type up the note and leave it on your door."

"Jolene knows we're trying to clear her name. She's helping us."

"In other words, Mrs. Dexter has found a way to insert herself into the investigation," he said.

Immediately, I wanted to kick myself for not realizing how that would sound to a cop. I'd listened to enough *Dateline* podcasts to know what he was thinking. "Yes, but not like a guilty person would," I said in exasperation. "Like a wrongly accused person would."

He gave me a deeply patronizing look. "Which of those two scenarios do you think is more common?"

I closed my eyes and silently counted to ten in an effort to remain calm. This interview was not going at all the way I expected. The note was supposed to prove someone else killed Andy, not further convince him of Jolene's guilt.

"You're wrong about her," I said finally.

"We'll see." He held up the note. "I'm keeping this. If you receive a second note, or if you think of anything else that might be useful, please contact us. But, in the absence of both those occurrences, I strongly urge you to leave the investigating to the professionals, Miss Bishop."

Yep, definitely intentional.

I considered mentioning our concerns about Trawler and his possible involvement with Andy's death, but I doubted Finlayson would take them seriously. Also, I didn't want to give him any more reason to focus on Jolene.

He walked over to the door and opened it, dismissing me. I grabbed my purse and stomped out of the room. Stevie leapt to her feet when she saw me, but Finlayson ordered her inside before she could say anything.

I tried to give her a reassuring smile. "I'll wait for you in the car."

She nodded and stepped inside the interview room. Finlayson gave me one last annoyed glance before he closed the door. I suspected Stevie was about to be subjected to the same lecture as I just was.

Outside in the parking lot, I unlocked the Civic and got inside. I took out my binder and flipped to the back where I'd placed a copy of the note, having xeroxed it at the Osprey before we left. The longer I stared at it, the more I had to admit Finlayson was right. There had been more than enough time for someone to travel from the Dexter's house to Topsail Cottages and back.

But I didn't believe for a second that person was Jolene.

Chapter Eleven

After her interview was concluded, Stevie and I drove back to the boardwalk. Unfortunately, she agreed that, thanks to our interference, Finlayson now seemed more convinced than ever that Jolene was his killer.

"What about Trawler?" I asked her. "Did you mention him to Finlayson?"

She shifted uncomfortably in the passenger seat. "No, did you?"

I shook my head. "He didn't seem that impressed by what I told him about Holly or Barry, so I didn't think he would take it seriously. Besides, we agreed we shouldn't say anything unless all of our other suspects were cleared."

"That's true," she said, still looking unsure. "We still don't know for certain that Trawler is involved. A muddy shovel is hardly a smoking gun."

I dropped Stevie off at the entrance to the boardwalk and began driving back to Topsail Cottages, but I couldn't stop thinking about Finlayson's theory on the note and my nagging suspicions about Trawler. I knew I wasn't going to be able to focus on anything else until I got to the bottom of it. I changed course and headed up Seafarer Road toward the high school. If my parents asked, I would just tell them my interview ran longer than expected. I drove past the front entrance to the school and turned right onto Harbourview Drive, pulling into the school's parking lot.

I glanced across the street at Gull's Quick Stop. Finlayson may not consider Madeline Barclay a suspect, but I still thought she could be involved. I didn't think it was a good idea to approach her on my own, though. I wanted to have Stevie with me, since the two appeared to be on good terms.

There was no police tape marking the west end of the school as closed, so I assumed the police were finished processing the crime scene. I still wasn't in a hurry to see where Andy had died.

Suddenly, the doors swung open, jarring me out of my thoughts. A pair of teenage girls walked past me. I hurried inside before the doors closed, and before I lost my nerve. Next to the staircase, I discovered a small memorial table dedicated to Andy. His framed staff portrait stood in the middle, surrounded by dozens of handwritten sympathy cards and stuffed animals from the students and faculty. On the wall, someone had hung a collage of *Foghorn* articles featuring Andy and the football team.

Coach Perch Leads Muskrats to Victory, one proclaimed. The accompanying picture showed a cheering Andy standing on the sidelines of the football field while the team celebrated.

I continued up the stairs to the administration office. I was just about to enter when I noticed a man wearing a three-piece charcoal suit walking toward me. He was carrying a cardboard box filled with office supplies.

"Vice-Principal Blenkhorn," I said with surprise.

He stopped dead in his tracks, his gray hair shimmering like molten silver under the fluorescent overhead lights. "Ah, Belinda Bishop." He tilted his chin down to peer at me over the top of his glasses. "Yes, I heard you were back in town." With his circular black glasses, round face, unruly eyebrows, and sharp nose, Mr. Blenkhorn still reminded me of a disapproving owl.

I glanced at the box in his arms and the significance of it hit me. "Are those Andy's things?"

He nodded gravely. "His poor sister, Nancy, has enough to worry about, between making the funeral arrangements and everything else. I decided cleaning out his desk for her was the least I could do."

Andy's work desk. He was killed at the school, so odds were good there could be a major clue among his personal effects. "Do you need someone to drive the box out to her?" I asked, probably a little too eagerly. "She still lives in their parents' old place outside of town, doesn't she? The big blue house?"

Nancy graduated a few years before me. I didn't know her well enough to warrant an unannounced pop-in, but dropping off Andy's things to her would be the perfect opportunity to express my condolences, and hopefully ask some questions.

He shook his head. "That's very considerate of you, but Nancy said she would come by herself. In fact, she should be here any moment. I told her I would leave it for her in the administration office."

Okay, not ideal, but I can still work with that. "At least let me carry that heavy box into the office for you," I said, holding out my arms.

"It's not that heavy." He backed up a few paces.

"I'm on my way in to see Jolene anyway." Then, in a last-ditch attempt, I decided I wasn't above stroking his ego. "I'm sure you're a very busy man, especially with the end of the school year."

He hesitated, but eventually relented. "That is true." Finally, he handed over the box. "Thank you, Belinda. It was nice to see you again."

I turned back to the office door and pretended to fumble with the knob. Once Mr. Blenkhorn was out of sight, I set the box on the floor and knelt in front of it. I glanced up and down the corridor to confirm I was completely alone before peering inside.

At first glance, it looked to be mostly office supplies. I picked up a spiral notebook and flipped through it. In the top left-hand corner of one page, Andy had scribbled, *Midterm Exam @ 10:30am, Grade Ten History,* followed by a page of handwritten notes and doodles. I immediately pictured Andy mindlessly scribbling his random thoughts while he supervised a class exam. One drawing near the bottom of the page caught my attention. It was a square with a teardrop in the middle, the words, "always the bad guy" written underneath.

What could that mean? I wondered.

I snapped a picture of the drawing with my cell phone and put the notebook back before continuing to sift through the box's contents. Pens, stacks of blank sticky notes, a stapler in the shape of a dinosaur. The kind of random stuff normally found in a junk drawer.

I was just about to stand up when I noticed a distinctive black sunglasses case at the bottom of the box. As I reached for it to confirm my suspicions, there was a light tapping behind me. I spun around, then breathed a sigh of relief. Jolene stood in the window of the office door, mouthing something at me furiously. I beckoned for her to join me in the hallway. She opened the door a crack and slipped through.

"What are you doing here?" she hissed. "If Donna catches sight of you, it's my butt. She's operating at an impressive level of pettiness today."

I waved aside her objections. "I ran into Mr. Blenkhorn. He said Nancy Perch is coming in today to pick up Andy's belongings from his desk."

She bent down and shooed me aside as she picked up the box, clutching it to her chest protectively. "You can't just go rifling through his things."

I ignored her and grabbed the sunglasses case. "Do you have any idea how expensive this brand of sunglasses is? A grand, easy. I know because my ex, Craig, bragged about buying a pair while I was eating ramen noodles for the third time that week."

Jolene frowned. "Your ex sounds like a jerk."

"He was," I said. "My point is, these sunglasses aren't exactly a brand you see a lot of teachers wearing."

The door to the administration office opened suddenly and I quickly dropped the sunglasses back into the box. Donna emerged, wearing a black-and-white polka dot pencil skirt and ivory ruffled blouse. "Jolene, if you're quite done chatting." Donna's beady eyes zeroed in on the box in her arms. "Are those Andy's personal items? What are you doing with those?"

"Relax, Dickie," I interjected. "I ran into Blenkhorn on my way into the office and offered to carry the box inside for him."

"And you're still in the hallway why?" she asked sarcastically.

"Because you've once again crashed a conversation that doesn't concern you," I replied.

Donna glared at me but pushed the door open wider, allowing room for Jolene to walk past her with the box. Without waiting for an invitation, I followed them both inside.

The school administration office looked almost exactly the same as the last time I had been there. A long, laminate counter with a swinging gate at the end separated the waiting area from the work area and, beyond that, the principal's office. The same generic motivational posters hung on the walls, their corners curled from age. The mustard-yellow wool carpet still smelled vaguely of coffee and mildew. The only thing new was the tiny kitchenette in the corner with a sink, microwave, and coffee machine.

"You guys must be counting the days until you're off for the summer," I said, taking in the shabby surroundings.

Jolene set the box down on the counter next to an outdated desktop computer that I assumed was her workspace. "You're not wrong," she said.

I winced at my inadvertent insensitivity. Of course, I doubted anyone at the school was eager to stick around the scene of Andy's death. "Right, sorry."

"Principal Acker held an assembly for Andy this morning," said Jolene softly.

She reached under the counter and produced a black-and-white memorial service leaflet. Not quite sure what else to do with it, I folded it gingerly and slid it into my purse. "I saw the table by the stairs," I said awkwardly. "Andy must have been a very popular teacher."

Jolene nodded. "They're even talking about renaming the football field after him."

Donna, it seemed, had decided to ignore us and sat down at her desk. Unlike Jolene, she had a separate workspace, complete with an adjustable computer stand, ergonomic office chair, and LED light therapy lamp. The bookcase behind her desk was filled with books, bound procedure manuals, and a couple of spider plants. On the second highest shelf, right at eye level, sat her coveted Teacher's Pet award.

Internally, I rolled my eyes. *Of course, she would have that on display.*

Jolene pulled herself up onto a padded stool in front of her computer. "I'm actually glad you're here, Belinda." She held up a thin USB drive. "The photographer dropped by with the pictures from the reunion," she said in a murmur.

I glanced over at Donna, but she didn't appear to have heard us. "Let's have a look." I took the drive from her and inserted it into the desktop.

Jolene opened the photos and began clicking through them. I leaned against the dividing counter and watched. Most of the images were standard party shots, mostly groups of friends toasting the camera or cutting loose on the dance floor. There were a few pictures of the award ceremony, capturing winners as they accepted their trophies. Nina Gould flashing a peace sign to the photographer as she danced. Barry with the rest of the old defensive line, their arms linked across each other's shoulders.

Jolene and I both froze as the next photo appeared on screen. It was the group photo taken at our table that night. Jolene and Trawler sat next to each other, both of their smiles tight with suppressed emotion. Stevie and I hovered at the edge of the photo, barely wedged into frame. And there in the middle of the shot was Andy, beaming at the camera.

He looked so relaxed and happy, completely unaware of what was coming.

Jolene sniffed softly. I hesitated. *What would Stevie do in this situation?* I gave her arm a gentle squeeze. To my surprise, instead of swatting my hand away, she reached up and squeezed back reassuringly. "I'm okay," she whispered.

Jolene continued to click through the photographs, and I noticed the mood captured in the images seemed to shift from cheerful to somber: Jason Zhang and his husband, Miguel, both looking at something off-camera, their expressions troubled. Amanda, Julie, and Holly embracing in a hug, their heads lowered. Donna wiping her eyes with a mascara-streaked hand as a uniformed RCMP officer stood behind her.

"Did the photographer keep taking pictures after Andy was found dead?" I whispered to Jolene, disturbed.

She sighed. "It would appear so."

I shook my head. "Unbelievable." A thought occurred to me as she reached the end of the photos. "You should save extra copies of these for us," I said, careful to keep my voice low so Donna wouldn't hear.

"Good idea," she murmured back. "I think I have an extra drive somewhere." Jolene opened a drawer and let out an angry squawk. "It's gone!"

Donna groaned and stood up. "Not again," she said, coming over to us.

"What's gone?" I asked, confused.

"Someone has been sneaking into the office and taking stuff," explained Donna. "Probably a student prank, you know teenagers. What did they get this time?" she asked Jolene.

Jolene slammed the drawer shut with a snap. "The little walnut squirrel Sadie made when she was four," she wailed. "I knew I should have taken it home."

"What else has gone missing?" I asked.

Jolene began to list items. "The pen my aunt gave me for my twentieth birthday, my sticky notes dispenser shaped like a handbag, and a little plastic toy alien Andy confiscated from a student."

"Don't forget my snow globe. The one I bought in Whitehorse last year." Donna sighed. "I'll let Principal Acker know it's happened again." She crossed the room and opened his door without knocking, closing it behind her.

I heard a soft ping from the depths of my purse. I took out my cell phone and checked my notifications. It was a text from my mother. I sent her a quick response and dropped my phone back into my bag. "I should go relieve Mum. She's covering my shift."

Jolene glanced up at me, her lips a thin, worried line. "How was your interview with the sergeant?"

I fiddled with my purse strap, stalling. I didn't really want to admit to Jolene that by convincing her to help us find the real killer, I'd only managed to convince Sergeant Finlayson further of her guilt. "It went fine."

Something in my eyes must have given me away. Jolene squinted at me. "Really? You stopped in to see me in the middle of the day because everything is fine?"

I shrugged. "He just wanted to go over my previous statement." She still didn't look convinced. "How are things with Trawler?" I asked, seizing the first topic I could think of to distract her. "He hasn't disappeared on you again, has he?"

She brightened. "No, actually. He was home when I got back last night. He even helped me make supper and stayed in to watch a movie with Sadie and me."

"You guys spent the whole evening together?" I asked, just to confirm.

She nodded. "Yup."

Huh, I guess that means Trawler couldn't have been the one who left the note.

"Except for when he ran out to pick us up some ice cream from Salty Saul's," she added.

Fortunately, Jolene misinterpreted my shocked expression for excitement. "I couldn't believe it either. He said he wants to start spending more time together as a family, and he finally has his priorities in order."

"That's great," I said weakly, doing my best to hide the hollow sensation in the pit of my stomach.

The boardwalk was only a ten-minute drive from my house, fifteen minutes if you hit traffic, and there was no traffic in Little Blue Harbour. That meant Trawler had plenty of time to drive to Topsail Cottages, leave the note, and return home with ice cream without arousing suspicion.

But the same could be said for anyone, whispered the sensible voice in my brain. *It only takes ten minutes to drive anywhere in town.*

Jolene seemed to notice my distracted thoughts. "Why don't we meet up at Right Foot for a quick drink after you get off work?" she suggested. "You and Stevie can tell me more about your interviews."

"Good idea." Like I would ever turn down the opportunity to see my favorite pair of dimples.

I said goodbye to Jolene and left the office. It wasn't until I was walking down the stairs toward the exit that I realized I hadn't had a chance to tell her about the doodle in Andy's notebook. This whole proper communication rule was really starting to bite me in the butt.

Maybe we need to start holding morning briefings or something, like the real cops do. Jolene's little Type-A heart would probably explode with excitement at the idea.

When I reached the west exit, I noticed a dark-haired woman standing in front of Andy's memorial. I recognized her immediately.

Nancy Perch, Andy's older sister.

Chapter Twelve

Nancy had the same black hair and button nose as Andy, as well as his tall stature. She was very thin and gave off the aura of a woman constantly on the move. I didn't remember much about her, only that she'd been a quiet, solemn girl who showed little interest in anything except her family's horses. Thanks to the ever-revolving gossip mill in Little Blue Harbour, I knew Nancy obtained her veterinary license after high school and ran a large animal clinic in Alberta for a while. After her and Andy's parents both passed away, she moved back and took over the animal clinic in the neighboring town of Maryport.

"Nancy," I blurted out without thinking. Quickly, I tried to look more sympathetic. "How are you holding up?"

She gazed at me blankly, followed by a brief spark of recognition. "You're Elizabeth Bishop's daughter. Belinda, right?"

I nodded. "I'm so sorry about your brother."

She surveyed me with the stoic resolve of someone who'd already fought this war twice and survived. "Thank you. The last couple of days have been difficult."

Now that I had the opportunity to speak to her, I found myself at a loss for words. The last thing I wanted to do was come off as invasive or gossipy. “Did you know they were arranging this for him?” I asked, pointing to the pictures on the wall.

She shook her head. “No, but it’s wonderful. Andrew loved this school. So many of his favorite memories were made here.”

“It must have been difficult for him after his injury,” I said.

Her wary expression softened slightly. “He always knew a serious injury could end his football career, but I don’t think Andrew expected it to be over so quickly,” she said. “It would have been easy for him to become bitter over it, but he didn’t. He always said, you’re no use to your team if you cry over every dropped pass; you have to just keep playing the game.”

I smiled. “I like that.”

“Feel free to use it.”

I took a deep breath. “Nancy, I’m not trying to make things worse for you, but I was one of the people who found your brother.” I hesitated, wondering how candid I should be with her.

“After he was murdered?” she asked pointedly.

Okay, that answers that. “Do you have any idea who would want to hurt Andy?”

She stared at the memorial in silence for so long, I worried that I’d overstepped, pushed too hard and too fast. When Nancy finally did speak, her voice was husky. “I know my brother wasn’t perfect. He made a lot of mistakes and hurt a lot of people. Growing up, Andrew and I didn’t always get along. He was loud and extraverted. I preferred the solitude of the fields and my horses. Our parents were so proud to have a gifted athlete in the family. It wasn't hard to tell who their favorite was. He could do no wrong in their eyes. He could be quite cruel at times, especially when he had his friends for an audience."

I nodded. For the most part, Andy had been friendly and upbeat in high school, but there had also been times where I thought I'd glimpsed a darker side, pranks that bordered on cruel, like when Colin Matheson failed the trigonometry final. Andy and his friends started calling him Can't Do Matheson.

"After our parents passed, he was the only family I had left. Whatever his flaws were," Nancy continued, "my brother didn't deserve to have his life stolen like this. Not in the one place he still felt safe." She turned to look at me, her gaze now simmering with fury. "I don't know who killed him. But if I did, there would be no need for the police to punish them. I'd make sure to do to them exactly what they did to my brother."

I swallowed nervously. I thought about Jolene upstairs, waiting to hand over Andy's personal items. Did Nancy believe what people were saying about her? Was she planning to confront Jolene?

"Nancy, I'm not sure what you've heard, but you have to know that Jolene would never do anything to hurt Andy," I said.

Nancy held up a palm, cutting off my next words. "I'm going to stop you right there, Belinda."

I drew myself up to my full height, bracing for trouble.

"I don't believe for a moment Jolene Dexter had anything to do with Andrew's death," she said firmly. "He would be furious if he knew people were saying she did. Andrew adored Jolene."

My shoulders relaxed, but something about her words made them tense up again. “Adored her?”

She nodded. “Yes, he was always talking about her. How much he admired her volunteer work, her work ethic, jokes they shared. Truth be told, I thought he had a little crush on her.”

That's interesting. Jo swore she and Andy were strictly platonic. Perhaps Andy didn't feel the same way.

“That couldn't have been too much of a surprise for you,” I said, “given his past taste in women.”

She sighed. “Yes, I suppose you're right. Personally, I think it was Andrew's way of proving he could still win at something. Unfortunately, he was the only one who thought it was a game.”

“I doubt any of the husbands appreciated it.”

“No, they didn't.” She frowned thoughtfully. “But with Jolene, he was different. It wasn't about winning with her. He wanted her approval, her respect. He became more mindful of others. He found a therapist he really liked and started working through some of his issues surrounding his injury and our parents' deaths.” Her eyes grew moist. “He even began volunteering at my animal clinic in Maryport. He was helping out with our fundraising drive.”

I've seen the flyers posted around town, I realized. The shelter was trying to raise money for a new roof and other renovations. “Did Andy donate money?” I asked.

She nodded. “Yes, quite generously. I tried to tell him it was too much, but he insisted. And it wasn't just the clinic.”

“What do you mean?”

“He surprised me with an all-inclusive ski package to Banff for my birthday in January,” she said.

I whistled softly, impressed. *That couldn't have been cheap.* "Did he usually spend that much on gifts?"

"No, I just assumed he wanted to do something special."

Something definitely wasn't adding up with Andy's finances. How was it he could afford to send his sister to Banff but not pay back Madeline Barclay? "There's a rumor around town that Andy owed money at Gull's," I said. "Can you think of any reason why he wouldn't be able to pay it?"

"No, none," she said, looking slightly bewildered. "Other than their pizza, Andrew hardly shopped there."

I glanced down at my phone and realized the time. "I'm sorry, Nancy, but I have to go."

"Yes, I should be going too."

I dug through my purse and pulled out my binder. I ripped off the corner of a blank page of looseleaf and scribbled my cell phone number on it. "I know we don't know each other that well," I said, handing it to her, "but if you ever need to talk to someone, or even just feel like grabbing a cup of coffee, you can give me a call if you'd like."

She took the sheet of paper from me and stared at it. "I don't come to Little Blue Harbour that often," she said awkwardly.

"Oh," I said, starting to feel foolish. "Well, that's okay. I just thought maybe you could use a friend."

"I really appreciate it," she said, pocketing my number. "I don't have many friends."

I smiled, relieved. "Me either."

I gave her a friendly wave goodbye and left. On the way home, I texted Stevie and let her know Jolene and I were meeting at the Right Foot after work to discuss the case. A few seconds later, she responded with a thumb's up emoji, which I interpreted as confirmation she would be joining us.

We certainly had a lot to discuss.

* * *

When I arrived at the Right Foot later that evening, I managed to snag a table in a secluded corner, away from both the kitchen and the bathrooms. To my slight disappointment, Jinx did not appear to be working tonight. Although, maybe that was for the best. The last thing I wanted was to get distracted, or worse, embarrass him again. I waited impatiently for Stevie and Jolene to arrive, my stomach a ball of knots as I thought about everything I'd learned today.

Starting with the office thefts. The more I thought about it, the more a disturbing possibility circled my brain. I would be the first to admit teenagers can derive a special kind of pleasure from messing with adults, so the idea of an ongoing student prank wasn't far-fetched. But why were students targeting office assistants instead of Principal Acker, the authority figure?

And then there was my conversation with Nancy. From the sounds of it, Andy more than just admired Jolene. He was infatuated with her. Was his confrontation with Trawler on the dance floor driven by jealousy?

Stevie and Jolene arrived within a few minutes of each other. As soon as they were both seated, the server, Hannah, appeared to take our drink orders. Since Jolene and I were driving, she ordered non-alcoholic red wine while I selected a mocktail called the Bluenose Lagoon. Stevie opted for the drink special, a McGrey's Island Iced Tea.

Once we had our drinks, I decided to get down to business. "We need to search Andy's house," I told them bluntly.

Stevie, who was in the process of taking her first sip, choked. Wordlessly, Jolene handed her a napkin to wipe the liquid that dribbled down her chin. "Excuse me?" sputtered Stevie.

Jolene sighed, shaking her head. "Of course, you would want to break into his house," she scolded. "You already went through his work stuff."

I chose to ignore her disparaging tone. "There's something shady about Andy's finances." I relayed what I'd learned from Nancy Perch about Andy's extravagant spending habits of late, as well as her surprise at him owing the Barclays money. "You don't drop money on ski trips and fancy sunglasses if you're in debt."

"Actually, lots of people do that," pointed out Stevie. "It's why the country is in a credit crisis."

"The sunglasses could have been a gift from someone," Jolene added.

"What about this?" I showed them the picture I'd taken of the drawing. "The same sketch, over and over again. A square with a teardrop in the middle."

Stevie took my phone with a sigh. "It's a doodle, Belinda. Almost everyone does it when they're bored. Most of the time they don't mean anything."

"Look what he wrote underneath," I said, pointing. "*Always the bad guy.* I think this drawing has to do with a disagreement Andy had with someone."

"If that's true, he never mentioned it to me," said Jolene, taking my phone from Stevie to study the drawing.

"There's something else," I said.

They shared an exasperated glance. "Of course there is," said Jolene.

I took a deep breath and looked her squarely in the eye. "I think Andy was attracted to you. Maybe even in love with you."

She stared at me for a moment before bursting into laughter. "No, he wasn't."

"What if Andy was the office thief? That could be how he ended up with your blue scarf," I said. "He was a teacher. No one would think twice if he was seen going into or coming out of the admin office."

Jolene sighed and leaned back in her chair, crossing her arms over her chest. "For the sake of conversation, let's pretend there's a tiny chance you're right. And I mean, miniscule. I'm talking, this much chance." She held up her thumb and forefinger, barely a millimeter apart. "Why would Andy steal my things?"

"It could have been a way for him to feel closer to you," I said. "Maybe it was a scheme to throw you into a heightened emotional state he could then use to establish a stronger bond between the two of you."

"I forgot how much *Dateline* you used to watch," said Stevie as she took a sip of her iced tea.

"Hey, listening to Keith Morrison is how I survived my twenties," I said, only half kidding, "but that's beside the point."

"You have a point?" asked Jolene sarcastically.

I leaned forward, placing both palms flat on the table. It was time to break out the big guns. "All of your missing items could be at Andy's house, Jolene. You don't think Finlayson would see that as a possible motive? Or proof of an affair?"

A heavy silence fell over the table as the three of us contemplated that possibility.

"The police would have searched Andy's house by now," said Stevie reasonably. "If they'd found Jolene's things there, we'd know about it."

"Not necessarily," I argued. "Unless her name is engraved on that pen, it would look like any old pen to them."

Stevie rolled her eyes. "So, what's the problem?"

I treated her to an eye roll of my own. "The problem is that if Jolene's things are in Andy's house and Finlayson finds out, it looks like she purposely withheld information. If we're the ones who find them, we can control the narrative."

"Who are you, Olivia Pope?" asked Stevie.

Jolene raised her hand, as if in class. "Are you really suggesting that we break into a murder victim's house and tamper with potential evidence?"

"It wouldn't be tampering," I said, a little insulted. "We'd turn over anything we find to the police. It would show Finlayson you're cooperating."

"Or that I'm the dumbest criminal ever," Jolene countered.

Stevie shook her head. "I'm sorry, Bel, but no," she said. "Rule number two, no breaking the law."

"WWKMD," I said stubbornly. My argument was met with blank looks. "What would Keith Morrison do?"

Stevie rolled her eyes again. "I doubt it would involve breaking and entering."

I knew Stevie was right, but that didn't stop me from feeling incredibly annoyed with her. I sighed. "Fine, we won't search Andy's house." Stevie narrowed her eyes suspiciously, so I held up three fingers. "Girl Guide's promise."

"Thank you," said Stevie. "I don't love that I had to make you promise something like that, but thank you."

"You're welcome, but now what's our next move going to be?" I asked.

"I called the Siren's Sound this afternoon and booked an appointment with Julie to get my hair trimmed tomorrow," said

Stevie. "You can both come with me, and we can ask the Pageant Minions about Holly and Andy's affair."

"They're not going to tell us anything with Holly there," I said.

"We don't have to worry about that," said Stevie. "Holly posted on Instagram that she's going to Prince Edward Island for two weeks."

That certainly got my attention. "Holly's leaving town?"

Stevie nodded. "She's taking an extended mental health excursion."

I snorted. "She's going to eat steamed mussels for two weeks and go on an Anne of Green Gables tour."

Stevie nodded. "It's what we all do in times of stress. But it's very convenient timing, don't you think?"

"Oh, she is so guilty," I breathed. "We're going to have this wrapped up by the end of the week."

Stevie and I shared a high-five over top of our glasses.

Unfortunately, Jolene didn't share our optimism. "I don't know if it's such a good idea for me to come to the Siren's Sound," she said. "What if it just makes things worse with Sergeant Finlayson?"

"Being a suspect doesn't mean you have to stay locked up in your house," I pointed out. "You're still allowed to live your life."

"Maybe you could have something else done while I'm getting my hair cut," suggested Stevie.

"You could get a manicure," I said. "You can question Amanda while Stevie talks to Julie."

"I guess I could do that," said Jolene, still sounding unsure.

With that settled, the three of us quickly finished our drinks. Outside of the pub, I bid them both goodnight with the promise to meet them at the salon tomorrow afternoon. I walked back to my car, making sure to keep my stride as casual as possible, lest I give away the next part of my plan.

I meant what I'd promised Stevie and Jolene. We were not going to search Andy's house.

But I sure as hell was.

Chapter Thirteen

Just after one in the morning, I parked the Civic across from the Little Blue Harbour public library. I slipped out of the car and backtracked two blocks to Elmwood Lane, keeping to the shadows as much as possible. My choice of black clothes for this mission was limited since most of my furniture and personal effects from Ottawa were still in storage, but I managed to find something suitable (albeit unorthodox) in my parents' attic.

It took a little more prodding than usual to get Andy's home address from my mother during supper. She was understandably suspicious, especially after our conversation this morning. In the end, she couldn't resist talking about real estate, especially one of her own sales. Finally, I got her to admit that Andy purchased Edgar Davenport's single-story rancher after the old man moved to Lunenburg to live with his daughter.

Old Man Davenport was a retired English Lit professor and the epitome of a neighborhood crank. At eighty-five years old, his only passions in life were Shakespeare, ceramic lawn ornaments, and home security. It was a Little Blue Harbour High tradition every year on Halloween for students to attempt to steal his prized possession, Winklevine the Garden Gnome.

After the trick-or-treaters returned home and all the porch lights went dark, students prowled through the shadows in pursuit of Winklevine. But each and every year, Mr. Davenport surprised them, ready with the garden hose, or as Stevie and I discovered one year, water balloons filled with ranch dressing.

The hedge border that surrounded the front of Andy's property was easily eight feet tall, providing me with enough cover to creep up the paved driveway without being seen from the road. To my amusement, Winklevine still stood, leaning against his ceramic pitchfork, at the top of the concrete front steps. Once I reached the attached garage, I crouched down in the darkness and contemplated my next move.

Obviously, breaking a window was not an ideal plan. It was too much to hope the front door was unlocked. I considered sneaking around to the back of the house to see if any windows were unlatched, but the hedges didn't extend into the backyard. I would be completely exposed. There was also an annoying lack of trees in this neighborhood.

"No wonder Davenport always saw us coming," I muttered under my breath.

My best bet was to look for Andy's spare door key. I glanced at the neighboring houses across the street. All the windows were dark. Everyone in the neighborhood appeared to be asleep.

I turned my attention back to the front door. In addition to his arsenal of garden hoses and condiment-filled balloons, Old Man Davenport had also installed flood lights with motion sensors above his garage door. Since Winklevine was still prominently displayed, the odds were good the front lawn would be flooded with light at the first sign of movement.

In a flash of inspiration, I remembered an article in the *Bytown Freebie* about an Ottawa man who lost a toe when he accidentally stepped on his neighbor's pet snapping turtle. The animal had moved so slowly, it failed to trigger the man's security lights. Emboldened, I got down on the ground. Very slowly, I began spider-crawling my way across the pavement. With one eye on the front door and the other on the security lights mounted above me, I inched forward.

Easy does it, Bishop. Slow and steady.

When I was halfway to my goal, a shadowy figure sprang up from the hydrangea bushes next to the front steps. "Busted."

My heart shot into my throat as I pressed myself as low to the ground as possible. It took me a moment to recognize the voice. "Stevie? Is that you?" I whispered.

"Yes, it's me," she hissed. "What are you doing?"

"I'm trying to get to the door without activating the flood lights," I hissed back.

A second dark figure emerged from the flower bed. It was Jolene, dressed in a pair of black cargo capris and long-sleeved dark gray T-shirt. Her blond hair was shoved under a black ball-cap. She stepped over the hosta plants bordering the flower bed and hurried toward me. "Andy got rid of the motion sensors years ago," she whispered, pulling me to my feet.

"What about Winklevine?" I asked as Jolene pulled me toward the front door.

She shoved me into the flowers before following suit. "Kids don't try to steal him anymore."

Stevie crouched among the white petals, her bright hair covered by a black knit beanie. She wore black yoga leggings and a black racer-back tank top. "Have you lost your mind?" she whispered. "You're going to get us all thrown in jail."

"Well, popping up in the dark isn't exactly helping me keep a low profile," I snapped back at her. "You almost gave me a heart attack."

"Serves you right for lying to us," she fired back.

"I didn't lie," I said. "I only promised that *we* wouldn't search the house. You're actually the ones breaking my promise."

Stevie rolled her eyes, but I caught a glimpse of a smile. "That's it, I'm installing a tracking app on your phone," she warned me.

"How did you even know I would be here?" I whispered.

"Please," scoffed Jolene. "You hated being a Girl Guide. You quit as soon as they said you'd have to go camping."

Argh, I can't believe I was outsmarted by the Harbour Queen. "Humans weren't meant to sleep on the ground, Jolene," I whispered, my cheeks warm. "It's why we invented houses."

"Not to mention we all know what happened after the elementary school talent show," added Stevie. "Face it, Bel, when it comes to solving a puzzle, you can get a little obsessed."

Honestly, you break into one school cafeteria, and no one ever lets you forget it.

Stevie looked at me and frowned. "What on earth are you wearing? Is that an old Halloween costume?" Her eyes widened in recognition. "Isn't that your costume from the year you went as Catwoman?"

I ran my hands over my black spandex bodysuit self-consciously. "I needed an all-black outfit, and this was the only thing I could find."

Jolene pointed to the black velvet headband on my head. "Doesn't explain the kitty ears."

"They keep the hair out of my face," I said impatiently. "Look, you two don't need to be here. I can do this on my own."

"No one is doing anything," said Jolene. "It's too risky. Finlayson would flip out if he knew we were here."

"He's not going to find out," I assured her.

"How do you know?" asked Jolene. "What if someone saw you on your way here?"

"What if they did?" I argued. "There's nothing suspicious about taking a midnight stroll."

"You're literally dressed as a cat burglar."

Stevie shushed us both. "Look, we're already here." She stood up and climbed out of the flowers. "Let's just see what we can find out."

Grateful, I followed her. Jolene sighed but joined us on the front porch. Stevie pulled vinyl gloves from her pocket, handing one pair to Jolene before putting on her own. Fortunately, I had paired my Catwoman costume with my mother's black gardening gloves.

Stevie felt around the top edge of the door frame. "Do you have any idea where Andy kept his spare key?" she asked Jolene.

"Ooh, I bet I know where it is." I grabbed Winklevine and pulled, but he didn't move. I tried rocking him back and forth, but the gnome refused to budge. I bent down for a closer look at the base.

Davenport, you evil old fossil. I rounded on Jolene and Stevie, furious. "Winklevine is bolted to the porch!"

The two of them broke into suppressed giggles.

"That's why no one tries to steal it anymore," said Jolene. "Andy broke the news to everyone after he moved in. He thought it was hilarious."

After a few more minutes of searching, we finally located the spare key hanging from a magnetic key ring stuck to the back of the metal letterbox. Stevie unlocked the door and slipped inside, beckoning us to follow. As the last one in, I closed the door and locked it again. We each took a moment to survey the dark living room. Stevie walked over to the picture window and drew the curtains as tightly as possible.

"That should keep anyone from seeing inside," she said, walking back over to us. "I don't think we should turn on any lights."

Jolene got out her cell phone and turned on the flashlight app, keeping the beam of light trained on the floor.

I picked up a small pile of mail from the end table by the couch and began to flip through it. "Let's start looking for anything that belongs to Jolene," I whispered. "Also, keep an eye out for bank statements and credit card bills. Anything that would give us a better idea of Andy's financial situation."

Jolene walked around the living room, shining the light on the walls and furniture. A fifty-inch smart TV hung on the wall. Underneath it, the media stand held more electronics, most of which looked current but not new, and nothing that looked overly expensive. There was a Blu-ray player, two video game consoles, and a wireless sound bar. More wireless speakers were mounted on the walls in each corner of the living room for surround sound. The black leather sectional couch looked like four recliners shoved together, complete with individual headrests and cupholders. A sleek-looking black and red ergonomic gaming chair sat in the corner.

"This is all looking pretty basic for a single man in his thirties with no kids," said Stevie as she trailed after Jolene.

The two of them stopped in front of a glass trophy cabinet next to the couch. Having found nothing of interest in the mail, I joined them. Jolene shone the light inside for a better look.

The cabinet was filled with the various sporting awards Andy had won over the years. I recognized some of the framed newspaper articles as the same ones included on his memorial table at the school. On the top shelf, I noticed a signed hockey card of an Edmonton Oilers player.

Jolene noticed it too and gasped softly. "Do you know whose autograph that is?" she asked, sounding awed.

"No, whose?" I asked.

"Wayne Gretzky, the Great One," she squealed. She stood up on her tiptoes to better see it. "Signed in 1989."

"How much would something like that be worth?" asked Stevie.

Jolene shrugged. "Quite a bit, I'd imagine."

Yet another pricey item that a schoolteacher in debt shouldn't be able to afford. "It's strange Andy didn't mention owning something like this to anyone," I said thoughtfully.

Jolene nodded. "Tell me about it. If Trawler ever got his hands on one, he'd never stop talking about it."

We left the living room and continued down the hallway into the back of the house. We checked a few drawers and cupboards in the kitchen but found nothing of interest. The bathroom was even less helpful.

It was somewhat awkward when we got to Andy's bedroom. It felt a little creepy going through his dresser drawers and closet, but it was the most likely place for him to stash anything belonging to Jolene. Both searches turned up nothing, as did the two end tables on either side of his bed. We even looked under his mattress. No luck.

"That's a relief," sighed Jolene. "I really don't know what I would have done if I'd found Sadie's walnut squirrel shoved under his bed." She shuddered.

We left the bedroom and tried the last door at the end of the hallway, expecting to find a guest room. Instead, it was a modest home office consisting of a desk and chair, a stack of unopened moving boxes, and a two-drawer filing cabinet.

Bingo!

Jolene held the light for me as I opened the filing cabinet and began searching through the folders inside. Andy had been surprisingly organized when it came to his home finances. Within minutes, we had his bank statements and credit card bills spread out on the carpet as we knelt over them. To my slight disappointment, nothing suspicious jumped out at me. The ski trip and sunglasses had both been purchased on his Mastercard, with regular payments being made.

"Look at this," said Jolene, picking up a statement. "Andy had a life insurance policy."

"Does it say how much?" I asked eagerly. "Or who the beneficiary is?"

She scanned the page. "No, it just shows the monthly premium payments. I recognize the insurance company, though. I don't think they're known for large payouts. Fifty grand at the most. Hardly life changing."

"Fifty grand would certainly change my life." *And people have killed for less.* I sat back on my heels and sighed. "I guess you two were right. Andy's finances appear to be pretty normal."

"What do you two make of this?" asked Stevie, scooting closer to us with a bank statement in her hand. "Andy made cash deposits almost every Monday. Sometimes as much as five hundred dollars."

I took the statement from her and scanned the list of transactions. "That's a little weird. Did Andy have a weekend job or side hustle?" I asked Jolene.

She shook her head. "He never mentioned one."

My mind flashed back to the night of the reunion and my conversation with Andy by the welcome table. "Poker."

"I don't even know her," joked Stevie.

"No, Andy said he had a weekly poker game with his friends. Remember? He asked if my father would be interested in joining them."

Stevie snapped her fingers. "Maybe he owed money to one of the other players."

"Or someone owed him money and they didn't want to pay," I countered.

Jolene took a couple pictures of the bank statements on her phone before we returned everything to the filing cabinet. Just as I slid the drawer shut, I heard a crash from the side of the house. The three of us froze.

"Did you hear that?" I whispered, my heart pounding in my chest.

"It sounded like a window breaking," breathed Stevie.

We waited in absolute silence, listening closely. A few seconds later, there was the distinct sound of a door opening and footsteps.

"I think someone just came in through the garage," whispered Jolene.

"You've got to be kidding me," I hissed. "There's an actual burglar in the house?"

Frantically, I looked around the office until my gaze fell on a golf bag in the closet. As quietly as possible, I stepped forward and slipped one of the irons from the bag.

"What are you doing?" asked Stevie, panic in her voice.

I shushed her and crept toward the door. I felt Stevie grab for my sleeve, but since I was wearing all spandex, her fingers grasped at nothing. Jolene shook her head emphatically at me and motioned for me to stop. I continued to slink across the office, easing open the door. After a moment of hesitation, they both followed me, taking care to stay behind me. As we crept down the hallway, I raised the golf club, ready to swing at the first sign of movement.

When I reached the living room, a figure stood in front of the trophy case. Whoever it was, they were dressed completely in black like us, their face covered by a balaclava. To my slight relief, they didn't appear to be armed. The burglar opened the trophy case and reached inside.

They're stealing the hockey card, I realized. "Don't even think about it, you vulture!" I yelled.

The burglar jumped back from the case and spun around, eyes wide with shock. Without stopping to let my fear catch up with my senses, I rushed toward the figure and swung the club. Only wanting to scare them away from the display cabinet, I made sure I was far enough away to avoid making contact. The last thing I wanted was another dead body to report to the police.

The burglar ducked on instinct, but then charged forward, shoving me aside. I lost my balance and fell onto the couch. I heard Jolene scream and quickly scrambled back to my feet, my trusty club raised once more.

Fortunately, the burglar paid no attention to Stevie and Jolene standing in the hallway, and instead made a run for the front door. They fumbled with the lock for a moment before throwing open the door and racing out into the night. Despite Stevie's protests, I followed, tossing aside the golf club. But whoever it was, they were much faster than I was and clearly not sore from Barbie's fitness class. I sprinted down the street but lost sight of the burglar after they turned the corner. Hunched over and wheezing from exertion, I came to a stop.

A car engine revved in the distance. I looked up just in time to witness a white sedan with a rusty back bumper speed through the intersection, driving toward the town's center, but it was too far away for me to make out the license plate.

I heard footsteps approaching behind me. I turned and saw Stevie and Jolene hurrying down the sidewalk toward me. For a moment, I was tempted to continue my pursuit, but I knew it was pointless. Whoever it was, they were long gone.

Stevie looked almost beside herself. "What on earth were you thinking, Belinda? You could have gotten yourself killed." She glared at me for a moment before throwing her arms around me. "Never do anything that reckless again."

I extracted myself from her grasp, still trying to catch my breath. "I know, I'm sorry. I wasn't thinking." I shook my head. "I can't believe someone could be so heartless. Andy isn't even buried yet, and someone is trying to steal from him."

"I guess this means he told someone about the hockey card," said Jolene grimly.

"Did either of you recognize the car?" I asked.

They both shook their heads. "I didn't even see it," admitted Stevie.

In the distance, a police siren wailed faintly.

"One of the neighbors must have heard the window breaking," said Jolene nervously. "We need to go."

"Yeah, we definitely don't want to still be here when the cops arrive," agreed Stevie.

As the sirens grew louder, lights started turning on in the houses around us. I slipped off the kitty ears headband in case any of the neighbors looked out their windows. The three of us hurried up the street in the opposite direction, trying to look as inconspicuous as possible.

My head was spinning with questions. Who had just broken into Andy's house? Why were they after the autographed hockey card? Was it just some greedy burglar looking to profit from Andy's death, or was it the reason he'd been killed? Had I just come face-to-face with his killer?

Chapter Fourteen

The next morning, I drove to Siren's Sound on Fishers Avenue where Stevie and Jolene were already waiting. The salon's storefront was more contemporary than most businesses in town, especially for one this close to the boardwalk. I imagined it worked in their favor, having a more modern, edgy look. The salon also had a miniature lighthouse outside of the salon, painted black with hot pink accents and rhinestones. Someone, probably Holly, had added plastic mermaids in a variety of sexy poses sitting on the top of the lighthouse and around the base.

An electronic bell chimed as we entered. Amanda Fleming, the least offensive Pageant Minion, stood behind the reception desk. Her eyes were glued to the laptop screen as she scrolled down with her mouse. Her hair was an ocean of chestnut brown beach waves, and her makeup was subtle but flawless. Her Bohemian-style crop top and denim hip-huggers showed off her hourglass figure. *Flaunt it while you have it, folks.*

"Good morning," trilled Amanda, "and welcome to the Siren's Sound." She looked up from her computer and immediately dropped the professional act. "Oh, my word, Jolene. It's you."

Amanda scooted out from behind the desk and hurried across the lobby toward Jolene, arms outstretched. She engulfed Jolene in what looked like a bone-crushing hug.

Amanda released Jolene before launching into a tirade. "You would not believe the drama going on around here. Four days before the senior prom, Holly just up and completely abandons us. All because Barry finally grew a pair and left her, which we all saw coming. Now Holly has decided to eat-pray-love her way across Prince Edward Island. I've got to call all of her clients, those poor kids less than a week away from what's supposed to be the most romantic night of their young lives, and tell them they no longer have a hair stylist. I haven't been cursed out this much since I worked retail."

Jolene opened her mouth to respond, but Amanda steamrolled over whatever sympathies she'd been about to express.

"I swear, if Holly wasn't my friend, I'd be out of here." Amanda closed her eyes and inhaled sharply. "No, wait; forget I said that." She looked at me. "But you know how it is, right, Belinda? Never work for friends or family."

"If you can help it, I guess," I said. "But I think there's a big difference between working for my parents and working for Holly Townsend."

Stevie quickly covered her laughter with a cough. "Um, I have an appointment with Julie?" she managed to get out.

Amanda cocked her head to the side, drumming her nails against her chin. "Oh, right. Stevie at ten. I'll let Julie know you're here." She walked over to the hair stations, her platform clogs clacking on the tiled floor.

Amanda returned with Julie in tow. Slightly more aloof than the others, Julie always struck me as someone who needed only one glance to pinpoint your every flaw. Her wide-set, heavily mascaraed eyes always seemed to be searching for the slightest imperfection. Every stray hair, smudged eyeliner, or spot of lint, her sharp little eyes saw it and quietly judged.

Sure enough, she did a quick scan of Stevie from head to toe before zeroing in on her hair. “Root touch-up?”

Stevie’s mouth pursed slightly. “Just a trim for today, thanks.”

Julie tilted her head to the side, her amber-blond bangs sweeping across her forehead, and clucked her tongue. “Blue is a tricky color,” she said coolly. “It fades even worse than red. You need to stay on top of it.”

Stevie smiled. “That’s okay, I still have the home dye kit if I need it.”

Julie’s gaze tightened, and Amanda let out an almost inaudible gasp. I turned my head to hide my smirk.

Julie led Stevie back to her station and got her settled. Amanda stood next to me and Jolene expectantly. “Can I get either of you a coffee while you wait?” she asked brightly.

“Actually, Jolene was hoping you had an opening for a manicure,” I said, just as eagerly. Out of the three of them, not only was Amanda the most pleasant, but she also seemed to be the most likely to inadvertently let something slip. A Chatty Cathy, as my mother would say.

Amanda’s eyes lit up. “You’re in luck. My next appointment canceled because she’s prepping for her colonoscopy.” She slapped a hand over her mouth. “Oops. I wasn’t supposed to say anything. Forget I said that.” She paused and, after a few awkward seconds, whispered, “It’s Mrs. Hyatt.”

We followed Amanda over to the manicure table. “This is almost going to be too easy,” I murmured to Jolene.

"Poor Mrs. Hyatt," whispered Jolene.

"At least there's one person having a worse week than you."

Amanda got Jolene settled in her chair and took Jolene's hands in hers, inspecting her nails with professional interest. "Not too bad," she said critically. She picked up a bottle of clear liquid and squirted it into two plastic tubs shaped like scallop shells. She took Jolene's hands and placed her fingers in the tubs to soak. "Did you have a color in mind?" she asked, leaning to the side so we had a better view of the rows of nail polish behind her.

I stood up and walked around the table. Amanda seemed to have every shade I could name. I picked up a light orange pastel color. "How about this one?"

Amanda surveyed my selection. "Passion Peach. Excellent choice."

Jolene frowned pensively. "I think I want something more dramatic."

Amanda and I stopped and looked at her in surprise. Dramatic wasn't exactly Jolene's style, but her face was determined. I turned back to the bottles, intrigued by this new attitude. My gaze landed on a dark purple shade, and I smiled. "This one?" I asked, showing it to Amanda.

"Ooh, no one has ever asked for that color before," she said, clapping her hands in excitement.

Jolene's eyes lit up. "What is it called?"

I found the label and read it aloud. "Goth to a Flame."

Jolene nodded. "Perfect."

Amanda shook her head, looking impressed. "Chickie, I don't know what brought this on, but I am loving it." She took Jolene's hands out of the soaking tubs and wiped her fingers dry with a towel. She picked up a pair of nail clippers and started grooming Jolene's cuticles. "The girls and I haven't heard much from you lately. What have you been up to, Jo?"

Amanda's gaze flickered in my direction, as if to silently ask, *Why are you still hanging out with these goobs from high school?*

"I've been feeling a little overwhelmed lately," said Jolene casually. Then she squared her shoulders as if steeling herself for something. "And I didn't appreciate how Holly spoke to me and my friends in the Right Foot pub."

To my surprise, a flash of remorse crossed Amanda's face. "No, you're right. Holly was out of line." She raised her gaze to meet mine. "Sorry about that."

"Sorry for what?" I asked snidely. "Just sitting there and not saying anything?"

She looked a little less contrite now. "What was I supposed to do, stick my head in the fox's den for someone I haven't seen in over a decade? What would be the point? Holly would have just been after me next."

"The only thing necessary for the triumph of evil is for good men to do nothing," I said.

"That's a bit much, don't you think?" Amanda returned to Jolene's nails. "Besides, Holly is going through a lot right now. What with the divorce, Andy's death, not to mention the whole thing with her daughter, Rena." She squished her eyes closed again and groaned. "Shoot, I wasn't supposed to say anything." She pointed her nail clippers at us. "Forget I said that."

"Of course," said Jolene.

"Rena who?" I joked.

Amanda looked at me, frowning. "I just told you. Her daughter."

Hoo boy. Fortunately, this seemed like the perfect segue for the real reason we were there. "Holly seems pretty broken up about Andy."

"You mean, their epic romance?" asked Amanda sarcastically. She picked up the nail file and began shaping Jolene's fingernails. "Like it was ever going to last. Big Andy was not a one-woman kind of guy. I don't know why Holly thought it would be any different with her."

"Holly doesn't handle disappointment very well, does she?" I asked.

"You are not wrong, chickie," said Amanda. "One time, we were doing inventory, and I made one little mistake. She lost it on me. Threw a box of hair clips at my head."

Jolene and I exchanged a significant glance. "Does Holly normally get violent when she's angry?" I asked.

Amanda shrugged as she started on the first coat of polish. "I mean, it was only a small box. She gave me a day off with pay as an apology." Her lips bunched together in a pout. "Never actually said she was sorry."

There was not a single cell in my body surprised to hear that. "Did Holly ever lose her temper with Andy, like she did with you?"

She shook her head. "Holly wouldn't hurt Andy. She was still holding out hope he'd come back."

"I thought she wanted to work things out with Barry," said Jolene.

Amanda made a sympathetic noise. "Barry is a total sweetheart, but he's a silver medal as far as Holly is concerned."

I glanced across the salon to see how Stevie was getting on with Julie. From the looks of it, not good. Stevie's mouth was stretched in a pained smile as Julie cut her hair, a steady stream of conversation pouring from Julie's mouth almost as fast as her scissors were moving. It didn't look as though Stevie was going to be able to get a single word in edgewise. When I turned my attention back to the manicure station, Amanda and Jolene were discussing the photographer from the reunion, and Jolene's plans for the photos.

"I think I might post some on the reunion committee's website," said Jolene. "Like a memorial collage in honor of Andy."

"Let me know if you need more pictures," said Amanda, applying the final coat of polish to Jolene's nails. "I was snapping pictures the whole night. You're free to look through them for any with Andy that you'd like to use."

"That would be great," said Jolene.

"Do you have them here with you?" I asked.

"Sure do," said Amanda. She set down the nail polish and got up from the table. She walked over to a row of coat hooks on the wall and took down a pink corduroy purse. She took out her cell phone, handing it to me. "Here you go."

The photos were mostly shots of Amanda posing with either her date or Holly and the other Pageant Minions. By the time I reached the end of the gallery, I hadn't found a single picture of Andy.

Then I came across an image that made me pause. At first glance, it was just yet another selfie of Amanda, Holly, Rebecca, and Julie, but what caught my eye was the time on the scoreboard behind them.

"Whoa," I said before I could stop myself.

Jolene looked at me, concerned. "What's wrong?"

I turned the phone around to show them. "This picture of you four was taken at 10:45 PM. That was only minutes before Stevie and I found Andy dead."

"Are you serious?" Amanda took her phone back from me and stared at the screen, horrified. "I can't have this kind of bad mojo on my phone. All of my dating apps are on here!"

She moved to delete the selfie and I almost tackled her. "What are you doing?" I asked, trying to grab the phone.

"You can't delete that picture!" cried Jolene, leaping to her feet.

Amanda held her phone against her chest, safe from our collective reach. "Um, okay, and why's that?" she asked, staring at us like we were completely unhinged.

"I want to use it for the memorial post," Jolene managed to eventually sputter.

Amanda looked even more alarmed. "Why?"

Jolene hesitated.

"In celebration of those of us who are still here," I blurted out in a flash of inspiration, "and the miracle that is life."

Amanda's eyes teared up. "That is such a beautiful idea." She dabbed gingerly at the corners of her eyelids, careful not to smudge her makeup as she wiped away the tears clinging to her lashes. "Okay, I'll text it to you, Jo. But then I'm deleting it."

Amanda's fingers tapped at her screen and a few seconds later, I heard Jolene's cell phone chime in her purse. To spare Jolene's freshly painted nails, I reached into her purse and retrieved the phone for her. I reconsidered our suspect list in my head.

The time on the scoreboard proved that Holly was in the gym as Barry claimed around the time of Andy's murder. She may have had enough time to kill him and make it back to pose with her friends, but not enough time to clean up and bury the evidence in the football field behind the school. With her baby pink dress, it would have been impossible to hide any blood stains.

I guess Barry was right. There's no way Holly could've killed Andy. But that just meant we were one step closer to finding the real murderer.

Stevie joined us at the manicure station. She gave her newly styled hair a shake and struck a supermodel pose. "What do you think?"

Her blue hair was even shorter now, with the sides and back shaved, and the longer hair on top styled into a pompadour.

I laughed, surprised by the sudden change. "I thought you were just getting a trim."

"I decided I wanted to try something a little different," she said.

"Me too," said Jolene proudly, wiggling her dark fingertips.

"Just remember what I warned you about," Julie called over as she swept up the blue hair scattered around her station. "Your face is a little round for such a short cut."

Stevie grimaced. "I hate these people," she muttered to me under her breath.

"You look fabulous," I reassured her. I backed up a few paces and motioned for her to follow me. "Did you learn anything from Julie?"

"You mean, besides that my face is too round and I have uneven eyebrows?"

I shook my head in disbelief. "How does this place stay in business?" Stevie shifted her gaze away from mine sheepishly. "You're going to book an appointment to get your eyebrows fixed, aren't you?"

"I already did. I tipped her too. But this is the best haircut I've ever had," she insisted, pointing to her head. "It's like they practice some kind of hair magic, like they're hair witches."

I snorted. "Only one letter off. So, you didn't get anything out of Julie?"

She sighed. "It was a little difficult to interrupt the constant flow of criticisms."

"And yet you still tipped."

Stevie craned her neck toward Amanda who was still chatting with Jolene, blissfully unaware of our conversation. "How did you guys do?"

As quietly as possible, I told Stevie about the photo of Holly. "We can cross Holly off the suspect list," I concluded.

Stevie sighed. "Yeah, she might be a horrible person, but she's not a killer. Not yet anyway. Who knows what the future holds?"

The front door chimed. "Delivery!" someone called from the lobby.

"Oh, I should get that," said Amanda. "No rush, chickies. Feel free to relax until your nails are dry, and then you can just meet me up front to process your payments." She fluttered her fingers at us in a goodbye wave and tottered back over to the reception desk.

When we went to the front to pay, Madeline Barclay from Gull's Quick Stop was standing in front of the desk, holding a pizza box. As soon as the smell of tomato sauce and cheese hit me, my mouth started to water.

"Ooh, pizza," said Jolene.

"Oh, yeah," said Amanda, wiggling with excitement as she counted the bills in her hand. "You know what they say, when the cat's away—"

"The mice get to eat carbs?" I joked.

Stevie greeted Madeline with a wave. "I didn't know Gull's offered delivery."

Madeline slipped the cash into her pocket. "It's just a trial run for the summer."

"You watch, honey," Amanda told her. "You and Kevin are going to make more money than you know what to do with." After Jolene and Stevie both finished their payments, she picked up the box and carried it back to Becca and Julie. "Drop what you're doing, girls. Pizza's here."

Her statement was followed by a series of appreciative cheers.

"Maddie, this is Belinda Bishop," said Stevie, introducing me. "She recently moved back to Little Blue Harbour."

Madeline turned to look at me properly, and her eyes widened slightly as though in recognition. For a split second, I thought I saw her swallow nervously. But when she spoke, her voice was even. "Hello," she said politely, extending her hand.

Her palm was moist as I shook it. "I went to school with Kevin," I said. "I've been meaning to stop in and say hi to him, but I haven't had a chance."

"Oh, that's a shame," she said flatly. "I'm sure he would love to see you."

I was careful to keep my smile in place, but something felt off about her demeanor. I didn't like the way she was staring at me, sizing me up. "I was surprised to hear Kevin was still living in Little Blue Harbour," I said. "The last I'd heard, he was on the west coast."

"Plans change," she said shortly.

"Yes, I suppose you're right," I said, taken aback by her chilly tone.

An awkward silence settled between us. Why was she acting so defensive toward me? It's not like anything romantic ever happened between me and Kevin, just one awkward slow dance at the junior Winter Wonderland dance when I kept stepping on his toes while he sweated through his suit jacket.

I was just about to make another attempt at conversation when I glanced out the window at the street outside. My heart almost stopped. Parked at the curb in front of the salon was a white sedan with a rusted back bumper.

It was the same car I saw speeding away from Andy's house.

"Is that your car outside?" I asked Madeline, fighting to keep my voice calm.

"Yes, why?" asked Madeline, sounding suspicious.

"I think I've seen that car before," I said with a meaningful glare at Stevie and Jolene.

Madeline gave me an odd look and headed for the door. "I imagine you have. We offer delivery, remember?"

I followed her outside onto the sidewalk, Jolene and Stevie hot on my heels. Madeline opened the driver's side door, but before she could get inside, I slipped in between her and the car.

"Actually, I think I saw you at the reunion," I said, trying to keep my tone as light and breezy as possible. "Too bad we didn't get to hang out. Like I said, I really wanted to catch up with Kevin. You were there that night, weren't you?"

"No," she said quickly. Her cheeks darkened. "I mean, yes, I was there, but Kevin wasn't."

"Oh?" I asked innocently. "Why not?"

"He had a business to run."

Try as I might, I couldn't keep the sarcasm from my voice. "And you, what? Decided to attend in his place?"

Madeline drew herself up to her full height. "That's really none of your business, is it?" She elbowed me out of the way and sat down behind the wheel. She pulled the door shut with a snap. "Nice meeting you," she said curtly.

The three of us watched as Madeline started the engine and drove away. "Oh, yeah. There's no way she could ever be a suspect," I said sarcastically, echoing Stevie's earlier words.

She sighed. "Okay, new rule; no gloating when you turn out to be right."

"What do we do now?" asked Jolene. "Should we contact Sergeant Finlayson? Tell him what we know about the break-in?"

"I don't know about you," I said darkly, "but I could go for some pizza."

Chapter Fifteen

"You do realize you're risking our access to the only decent pizza in town, right?" asked Stevie as we trudged up Harbourview Road after leaving the salon. "Also, don't you need to get to work?"

I powered forward up the hill, not breaking my stride. "I don't need to be there until one o'clock," I said. "Besides, the pursuit of justice far outweighs a good pizza."

"You say that now," said Stevie, "but just wait until it's ten o'clock at night and you have the pizza munchies."

"Madeline recognized me, Stevie," I insisted. "She was the burglar we chased out of Andy's house last night."

"You don't know that," argued Stevie. "She could have recognized you from the reunion."

I spun around to face her. "How do you explain her driving the same car I saw?"

Stevie rolled her eyes. "You didn't actually see the thief get into a car. None of us did. You only saw a white car driving down the street."

"Speeding down the street. As if fleeing the scene."

She ignored me. "Do you have any idea how many people own white cars in this town?"

I folded my arms across my chest. "White cars that also have a rusty back bumper?"

"This is the Maritimes, Bel. We're right on the ocean." Stevie pointed to a blue sedan parked ahead of us. "See? Rusty bumper. That brown hatchback across the street? Rusty bumper." She gestured toward a passing pickup truck. "More rust."

I started walking again. "People in this town really need to start taking better care of their vehicles."

Stevie hurried after me. "All I'm saying is we should discuss this before we get ourselves banned from the best pizza in town. None of us got a license plate number, remember."

"No one is going to be banned," said Jolene sensibly. "Obviously, we're not going to just burst in with accusations." She tapped her pink binder. "Rule number one, no accusations without evidence."

I threw up my hands in frustration. "We have evidence. Eyewitness testimony is a form of evidence."

Stevie gave me a highly skeptical glare. "You once thought you saw Prince Harry on the same flight as you."

"The royal family travels too, Stevie."

"Not in economy seats."

I came to a stop again, planting my fists firmly on my hips. "It was Madeline's car that I saw last night. She's the same height and build as the thief. Plus, she lied about why she was looking for Andy at the reunion. One plus one plus one equals guilty."

"Less than twenty-four hours ago, you were saying the same thing about Holly," snapped Stevie. "Madeline is my friend, Belinda."

Jolene stepped between us, her hands outstretched beseechingly. "I know she's your friend, Stevie," she said kindly, "but Maddie is on our suspect list for a reason. We need to talk to her." She glanced at me. "Respectfully."

"Until she lies to us again," I said.

Stevie sighed, puffing out her cheeks. "I hate this," she said eventually. "I hate to think someone I trusted could be capable of something so horrible."

She looked so sad and defeated, my irritation with her instantly dried up, leaving only remorse. I was so focused on getting to the bottom of Andy's murder, I was treating this as just another story. But for Jolene and Stevie, these people were their friends and neighbors.

"I'm sorry, Stevie," I said softly. "It's only natural you would want to think the best of her."

She sighed, nodding. "Madeline is acting very suspiciously. I just hope there's an explanation for it all." She paused. "Something other than she's guilty."

As we approached Gull's Quick Stop, I noticed the sign had been updated with a new logo, a cartoon seagull wearing a sailor's cap and holding a fresh pizza. New wooden picnic tables had also been added, each with a white and red striped patio umbrella for shade. Inside, the layout was exactly the same. The convenience store, which was currently empty, was up front and the pizza counter, pool tables and arcade games at the back.

We approached the pizza counter where a young man in his late teens stood texting on his phone. I didn't recognize the kid, but he bore a strong resemblance to Kevin.

"S'up?" He greeted us without looking up from his screen. "You here for pizza?"

No, we're here to buy a used car, I almost retorted.

Jolene, on the other hand, greeted him with familiarity. "Hello, Gavin. I'm surprised to see you working today. Have you finished writing your final exams already?"

Her question earned her a brief glance up from his phone. "Oh, hey, Mrs. Dee. Yeah, I wrote my last one on Friday."

"Are you excited for prom?" she asked teasingly.

Gavin's blond hair was twisted back into a bun and his sharp jawline was covered in patches of pale facial hair. His faded green Star Wars T-shirt had grease stains on it, and he had yet to make direct eye contact with any of us. Yet there was no doubt in my mind this kid had no shortage of prom dates. This particular brand of laid-back confidence and "too cool to care about being cool" attitude was like catnip to teenagers. It certainly was in my day.

He shrugged, still texting. "Not really my thing, but Mum's freaking out. Keeps crying about the passage of time and humming some old song about cats and a cradle." He finally raised his head, looking baffled. "I mean, it's just a dance, right?"

"Gavin's mother is Carla Doane," explained Jolene.

Ah, Kevin's older cousin. That explains how the kid has a job. But I wasn't interested in comparing family trees. I did a quick scan of the menu on the wall behind him. "A large pizza with the works?" I asked Jolene and Stevie.

They both nodded. I waited for Gavin to put down his cell phone before repeating our order. As he started assembling the ingredients, I looked around the store. "Is your boss here?" I asked him. "Kevin Barclay?"

Gavin nodded as he spread tomato sauce liberally over the uncooked dough. "Yeah, but he must have gone out back or something."

"Do you like working here?" I figured I might as well take the opportunity to do a little questioning while I waited for

Kevin to come back. Gavin didn't strike me as the most observant, but it was still possible he'd seen or heard something that might explain Madeline's sudden interest in home invasions. My father always said the smallest detail could lead to the biggest break.

He hitched one shoulder higher in a half-hearted shrug as he added mushrooms to the pizza. "Sure."

I waited for him to elaborate, but he didn't. Clearly, Gavin wasn't going to be as forthcoming as Amanda. "How do you like working for Kevin and Madeline?" I tried again.

"They're alright," he said vaguely, his eyes drifting back to his phone.

For a moment, I considered just texting him my questions, since the kid was obviously incapable of any other form of communication.

Stevie, sensing my frustration, stepped in to help. "Business must be booming with the new delivery service."

Another shrug. "About the same, I guess."

What does that mean? I wanted to scream at him. *Are Kevin and Madeline flat broke, or are they diving into a swimming pool filled with gold coins every night like Scrooge McDuck?*

The back door opened just as Gavin slid our pizza into the oven. "Yo, boss! Customers here to see you!" the kid bellowed without turning around.

A tall, gangly man with thinning blond hair and glasses appeared from a back room. "You don't have to yell, Gavin. I'm right behind you. It's not a large space," he said with a soft-spoken voice. His light blue eyes lit up in surprise when he saw me. "Hello, Belinda. I heard you were back in town."

In high school, Kevin made the basketball team simply by showing up for tryouts. He towered over the rest of the students, and most of the teachers. In fact, he'd always reminded me of Stephen Merchant. He was a little heavier now and had replaced his thick frames with more modern ones, but he'd retained his mild good looks and kind smile.

He pushed his rimless frames back into position. "What brings you three by?" he asked fondly.

We were just in the neighborhood and thought we'd pop in to question your wife about a B&E last night. Oh, and do you think it's possible she killed Big Andy?

But that hardly felt like the best way to start a conversation. I gestured vaguely toward the pizza counter. "Who can resist the call of Gull's pizza?"

The four of us chatted while we waited for our order, with Kevin and I each sharing an abridged version of life events. He was detailing his plans to sponsor the upcoming Miss Harbour Queen pageant at the end of the summer when Madeline entered the store through the rear entrance, having obviously just arrived back from her deliveries.

Kevin waved her over to us. "Hey, Mads. I want you to meet my old friend, Belinda Bishop. We went to high school together."

Her expression soured slightly when she spotted us, but she joined us at the pizza counter. "We've already met," she said somewhat reluctantly. "Today at the Siren's Sound."

"Actually, I'm pretty sure we met last night," I said sweetly.

I felt Jolene go still beside me, and Stevie sucked in a sudden breath. Madeline's face became as smooth and emotionless as beach glass.

Kevin glanced between the two of us, looking politely confused. "Last night? Where?"

"Order up," said Gavin, returning with our pizza. He held out the flat, square box.

Before I could take it from him, Madeline stepped in front of me and seized the pizza box. "I can ring in you ladies up front,"she said tightly.

We followed Madeline and Kevin to the cash registers while Gavin went back to his phone. Madeline stabbed at the register buttons, punching in the amount owed. She looked me squarely in the eye, and I realized this woman would never willingly admit to anything.

Forget Rule number one; I wasn't going to get anything out of her without backing her into a corner.

Kevin joined Madeline behind the register. "I don't understand," he said. "Where would you two have met last night? Maddie and I closed together."

Madeline remained as defiant as ever. "I don't know what she's talking about, Kevin. I met her for the first time this morning at the salon." She gave me a flat smile. "You must be mistaken."

I opened my mouth, ready to tell her just how unmistaken I was, when Stevie suddenly elbowed me in the ribs. She pointed to the wall behind Kevin and Madeline. Tacked up between the enclosed cigarette shelves and an advertisement for Pepsi, there was an Edmonton Oilers poster circa 1984 of the team posing with the Stanley Cup. Below that, there was a picture of a young Kevin with an older man, both wearing Oilers jerseys and holding hockey sticks.

The truth hit me like a lightning bolt. "The doodle!" I exclaimed.

Kevin frowned. "The what?"

The Oilers team logo. Andy was doodling the hockey card. Quickly, I swerved tactics. I pointed to the poster. "I didn't know you were an Oilers fan, Kevin."

He glanced over his shoulder at it. "Dad got me hooked as a kid," he said proudly. "You should see his study. If it has an Oilers logo on it, my father owns it."

So, Kevin's father is ill and a huge Oilers fan. I imagined Andy's hockey card would be quite valuable to someone like that. Or his devoted son, maybe? Anyone prepared to give up their dreams of being the next tech mogul to care for their ailing father might also be willing to kill for him.

"That will be $25.28," said Madeline sharply. She turned to her husband. "Kevin, you need to stop talking to these people."

"Why?" asked Stevie. Her mouth was set in a firm grimace as she stared at her friend. "What don't you want us to know, Maddie?"

Madeline mirrored her hard expression. "No offense, Stevie, but it's none of your business."

"Does it have anything to do with the fact you crashed our high school reunion looking for Andy right before he died?" I asked.

She glared at me, and I could almost see her back go up like an angry alley cat. "Still none of your business."

"I beg to differ," snapped Jolene, "seeing as how I'm the one everyone thinks killed him."

"Maybe you shouldn't have had an affair with him," Madeline fired back.

Apparently, Madeline wasn't above playing a little hardball herself. *Two can play that game.* I turned to Kevin. "We know Andy owned a hockey card that was autographed by Wayne Gretzky. Your wife tried to steal it last night."

Kevin took a step back, looking baffled. "Maddie tried to do what?" He shook his head as though trying to jostle his thoughts back on track. "Why would you say such a thing?"

"Yeah, where's your proof?" asked Madeline.

I pursed my lips to keep myself from blurting out the truth. *Maybe Stevie was right. Maybe I should have waited to confront Madeline.* No wonder she looked so smug. The only way to explain how we knew it was Madeline who broke into Andy's house was if we admitted that we'd broken in first.

Then again, maybe not. "The three of us happened to be walking by and saw the whole thing."

Madeline's eyes became two slits. "Oh, really?"

I returned her narrowed glare. "Really."

Her nostrils flared and I relished the thrill of victory. I was lying, we both knew it, but she couldn't call me out on it without giving herself away. Mutually assured destruction.

I took out my cell phone and pulled up the snapshot of the doodle. "Andy drew this before he died," I said, showing them. "It's the Oilers team logo." I slipped my phone back into my pocket. "What happened? Did you two approach him about selling the card and Andy turned you down? Is that why you tried to corner him at the reunion?"

Madeline shook her head. "This is ridiculous."

"When he refused again, you lost your temper and killed him," I continued. "Then, after the police had already searched Andy's house, you went there to steal the card."

"I wasn't going to steal anything," said Madeline.

"The burglar drove off in a white car that looked exactly like Gull's delivery vehicle. I recognized it at the hair salon this morning." I pointed a finger at Madeline. "You were determined to get your hands on that hockey card."

Madeline lurched forward suddenly, and I pulled back on instinct, half expecting her to claw her way over the counter. "Of course, I wanted that card!" she cried.

Jolene gasped next to me as Stevie clamped onto my forearm in a death grip. The three of us stared back at Madeline, dumbfounded. *Did we just goad her into a murder confession?*

Kevin shook his head. "Maddie, you promised you would drop it," he groaned. "I remember waking up as you were getting out of bed last night, but I thought you were just getting up to use the bathroom or something." He sighed heavily. "This is all my fault."

Madeline took his hand, clasping it tightly. "No, Kevin. I'm the one who screwed up."

She dropped down onto a wooden stool wedged behind the counter. We watched as the fight seemed to drain out of her. While Madeline had no problem lying to the three of us, lying to her husband seemed to be a bridge she couldn't bring herself to cross.

"I did break into Andy's house to steal the card. But not for the reasons you think," she said, calmer now. "Andy stole the Gretzky card from Kevin."

Kevin slid one arm across his wife's shoulders before responding. "In 1989, my father went to an Oilers game in Edmonton. Gretzky signed it for him after the game. He gave it to me when I was eighteen as a graduation present."

I pressed my fingertips against my forehead, still reeling. "Wait, are you saying you killed Andy because he stole the card from you two first?"

Madeline scoffed. "We didn't kill Andy. I never even saw him at the reunion. When I couldn't find him in the gym, I went to check the rest of the school for him. When Kevin realized where I was, he called my cell phone and talked some sense into me, so I went back to the store."

"Just like that?" I asked, raising my eyebrows.

"Kevin asked me to drop it, so I did," said Madeline. "But after Andy died, I decided the card was fair game. He certainly had no use for it anymore. As far as I knew, Andy hadn't told anyone else about it." She shrugged. "Can you blame me for trying to get it back?"

Stevie shook her head, looking just as confused as I was. "Okay, but again: how did Andy end up with it in the first place?"

"I lost it to him," said Kevin softly.

"Lost it?" I asked. "How?"

Kevin looked at his wife, and the two seemed to reach an unspoken agreement before he continued. "I used to attend Andy's weekly poker games. He invited me to join last fall. I'm a gambling addict," he said sadly. "It's the reason I dropped out of university. Most people assumed it was because of my father's health issues, and I never corrected them. Only my parents and Maddie know the truth."

I guess Andy was right, I thought. *No one comes back to Little Blue Harbour for good reasons.* "You bet your father's card?" I asked Kevin, aghast. "If you have an issue with gambling, why would you even join the game?"

"I don't know," he said helplessly. "Money has been tight the last couple of years. The store has been barely scraping by. I thought I could make a few extra bucks. It'd been so long, I thought I could keep it under control this time."

"I'm not sure that's how addictions work," Jolene said gently.

Kevin nodded. "I know, it was foolish of me to think that. I kept losing money and convincing myself that I could win it back. Finally, I owed Andy more money than I could pay him. So, I challenged him to one last game. If I won, he'd forgive the debt. If I lost, I'd give him the Gretzky card." He covered his face in shame. "I can't even bring myself to tell my father. The fact that I was willing to risk something so important to me. That's when I knew I needed help."

"Did Andy know you're a recovering gambling addict?" asked Stevie.

"No," he said. "Not until Madeline told him."

Madeline snorted angrily. "I thought once he knew the truth, Andy would do the decent thing and return the hockey card. Instead, he said it was Kevin's responsibility to manage his issues."

"That's why you crashed the reunion," said Stevie. "You went to confront Andy."

"I went to expose him," she said angrily. "Everyone in this town treated him like he was some kind of god. Every football season, he'd be in the local newspaper talking about teamwork and good sportsmanship. What a crock." She pressed her fingers to her forehead. "I was just trying to protect my husband."

That much was obvious. Exactly how far had she been willing to go to do that?

I surveyed Madeline closely, looking for any sign of deception. Her body language was still defiant, but there was no fear in her eyes. Not exactly what I'd expect from someone about to be exposed as a murderer. Which meant there were two possible explanations for her angry yet steady demeanor; either Madeline Barclay felt zero remorse for killing the man who (in her mind) ruined her husband's life or she was telling the truth.

The bell over the door chimed. I glanced over my shoulder and saw Barry Townsend standing in the doorway. Just as he was about to enter, he stepped back and held the door for someone. Donna Dickie, dressed in a multicolored shift dress with a black belt and matching gloves, strode into the store without even a thank-you for Barry.

"Hi, Maddie. Hi, Kevin," said Donna as she walked over to the magazine rack. "Just grabbing my usual."

Madeline greeted her in an overly cheerful tone. "Hello, Donna."

Donna slipped a copy of *Hello! Canada* magazine under her arm. She grabbed a bag of chocolate-covered pretzels and joined us at the cash register. "Oh, hello, Jolene." Her gaze fell to Jolene's fresh manicure. "Nice color. That will certainly get you noticed."

The three of us didn't even bother to acknowledge her. "Which exit did you take when you left the school?" Stevie asked Madeline.

"The west one," she answered irritably. "Why?"

"And you didn't see any sign of Andy or anyone else?" I asked.

"No." Madeline paused. "But I did hear voices."

I perked up in interest. "Voices? Coming from where?"

I glanced at Donna and caught her quickly looking away. Behind her, Barry got in line, carrying two jugs of milk, looking entirely too nonchalant. *Great.* I doubted Keith Morrison ever had to question a suspect in full view of the peanut gallery.

"I don't know," she said, "the voices were too muffled. I can't even say for sure one of them was Andy."

"Who else could it have been?" I asked irritably.

She shrugged. "I thought maybe a couple sneaked away from the reunion for a little private time together in one of the classrooms. I told Sergeant Finlayson about it."

"You mean after you lied about Andy running up a tab at your store?"

Madeline raised her eyebrows, her expression cool. "I never said anything about a tab. All I said was that Andy and I needed to discuss a debt."

"Yes, I'm sure Finlayson will make that distinction," I said sarcastically.

"Maddie, why didn't you just speak to his sister, Nancy Perch, about the card?" asked Stevie.

Madeline curled her lip in disgust. "For all I know, his sister is just as bad as Andy was, a heartless jerk who didn't care about anyone but himself."

"Excuse me," interrupted Donna, "but Andrew Perch devoted his life to the students of this town. He was an amazing teacher and a wonderful man."

"Only when it suited him," said Madeline.

"Truth," Barry muttered.

Donna tossed her intended purchases onto the counter. "I think from now on I'll buy my snacks from the gas station down the street. At least they know how to show a little respect for the dead."

Madeline gaped after Donna's retreating back as she left the store. She turned her outraged expression in my direction. "Now you're costing us customers."

She started to gather up Donna's abandoned purchases. Barry cleared his throat and reached for them. "You don't have to put those back," he said. "My mother reads *Hello! Canada*, and the kids love chocolate."

Madeline sighed gratefully. "Thanks, Barry."

Kevin rubbed the back of his neck. "Look, I know what Maddie did was wrong, but she was just trying to help. She wouldn't do anything to harm Andy. I think maybe you three should leave now," he said awkwardly.

I opened my mouth to protest, but Jolene gave me a warning look. For once, I acquiesced. If we refused, there was nothing to stop Madeline and Kevin from calling the police. I already knew how well that would work out for us. "We'll just pay for our pizza," I mumbled.

Madeline shoved the pizza box across the counter toward me. "It's on the house, Belinda."

"Really?" I exchanged a surprised glance with Stevie. "Thanks."

"Provided you never step foot in this store again," she added.

Yeah, that tracks.

I grabbed the pizza box and the three of us hurried out of the store. Unfortunately, it looked as though unless we could prove Madeline Barclay was our cold-blooded killer, this slice of Gull's pizza, deliciously brimming with melted cheese, pepperoni, and vegetables, was going to be my last.

Chapter Sixteen

I didn't need to be back at Topsail for another thirty minutes, so we decided to take our (now banned) pizza down to the boardwalk and have lunch in the picnic area while we discussed everything we'd learned that morning.

I flipped open the pizza box lid and selected the most cheese-laden piece. "Let's go over our suspect list again."

Jolene handed around the napkins before getting out her pink binder. "Holly's out." She made a note on Holly's profile before flipping to another page. "So that's at least one down. Barry is still a possibility. Have you heard anything from Sergeant Finlayson or Randy about his fake alibi?" she asked me.

"Finlayson doesn't want Randy anywhere near me. He thinks I might use my personal relationship with Randy to manipulate him into sharing information about the case."

"Which is a fair assessment," said Stevie, smirking.

I nodded. "Oh, yeah, I'd totally do that."

Jolene made another note on the page. "Either way, we need to tell the police about this new development with Madeline and Kevin," she said.

"I'm sure Finlayson will be so appreciative," muttered Stevie.

"Even more so if he finds out exactly how we learned about it," I added.

"Maybe we don't have to tell him about breaking into Andy's house," said Jolene. "It's not like Maddie will be eager to admit that herself."

"I almost don't want her to get in trouble for it," I said. "I think she has a point about Andy."

Jolene frowned, her expression outraged. "What, like, he got what he deserved?"

"Of course not," I said, "but it was a jerk move to keep the hockey card after he knew the truth about Kevin. I can't blame her for feeling like Andy took advantage of her husband."

"It's Kevin's responsibility to manage his addictions," argued Jolene.

I raised my palms in mild defense. "I'm just saying, we've seen Andy's finances. He may have been owed the money, but he didn't actually need it. He could have forgiven the debt and returned the card if he'd wanted to."

Stevie took a thoughtful bite of her pizza. "I wonder if that's what Andy intended to do."

"What do you mean?" asked Jolene, still looking discomforted.

Stevie wiped the grease from her fingers with a napkin. "Doesn't it strike you as odd that he was found in the west end of the school?" she asked.

I thought about it for a moment. "The school parking lot is at the west exit. I assumed Andy was headed to his car when he was attacked."

Jolene shook her head. "Andy was extremely cautious when it came to drinking and driving. There's no way he was planning to drive home that night."

"And Gull's Quick Stop is across the street from the parking lot," added Stevie, raising her eyebrows significantly.

"I invited Andy to join us for pizza," I reminded them. "He acted like he didn't want to be anywhere near Gull's."

"Well, it was hardly a conversation he'd want to have with Kevin in front of us," said Stevie.

"Doesn't that increase the likelihood that Madeline is our killer?" I asked.

"Not necessarily. If Andy was going to return the hockey card, she'd have no motive to kill him," said Stevie.

"Unless she killed him before he had a chance to tell her that," I suggested.

"That still wouldn't explain how my blue scarf ended up with Andy's body," said Jolene.

"Ugh, that stupid scarf." I dropped my half-eaten slice in frustration. "It's the one clue that keeps gumming up all of our theories."

"Unless Andy was the office thief," said Stevie.

"We didn't find any of my stuff at his house," said Jolene.

"We were also interrupted," I said. "Maybe he had a secret altar set up somewhere we didn't find, with all your stuff surrounded by a bunch of lit candles and pictures of you."

Jolene shuddered. "Okay, you need to cut back on the true crime podcasts."

I brushed off her concern. "Think about it." I raised one hand, palm facing up. "Andy was the office thief." I held up the other hand in the same fashion. "Madeline blamed him for her husband's relapse." I brought my two palms together in a loud clap. "Boom! Jolene ends up implicated in a murder."

Stevie opened her blue binder and slid the Right Foot pub coaster from an inside pocket, considering the suspect list scribbled on it. "Belinda might be on to something."

"Andy did not have a secret altar for me," sighed Jolene.

"No, I mean Madeline as our strongest suspect," she said, rolling her eyes. "She had the means, motive, and opportunity to do it."

"The only problem is, how do we bring what we know to the cops without ending up in jail ourselves?" I wondered aloud.

Suddenly, Stevie straightened, her eyes wide. She pointed behind us toward the boardwalk. "Speak of the surprisingly handsome devil."

Jolene and I both turned to look over our respective shoulders. Striding across the grass with Randy trailing behind him, Sergeant Finlayson looked like a school principal about to hand out detentions. My defenses went up, fearing the worst. What was he doing here? Had the killer planted another piece of evidence against Jolene?

But for once, Finlayson didn't seem concerned with her. His furious gaze locked on to me as he approached our picnic table, a now-familiar scowl etched on his handsome face. Quick as a flash, Jolene grabbed the coaster from the table while Stevie hid the binders under the pizza box.

I gave Finlayson my brightest smile. "Good afternoon, Sergeant. Would you like some pizza?"

"The Little Blue Harbour RCMP detachment received a very interesting phone call last night," he said, ignoring my offer. "Apparently, someone broke into Mr. Perch's house."

I pointed to the box. "Is that a no to the pizza?"

A muscle in his clenched jaw popped. "A witness reported seeing three women flee the scene before officers arrived."

Jolene and Stevie both froze in their seats. My chest suddenly felt hollow. "A witness?" I asked. "Who?"

Sergeant Finlayson opened his mouth, presumably to tell me it was none of my business, but Randy spoke first. "Estelle Demings," he said. "She lives across the street."

My entire body sagged with relief. "Mrs. Demings is in her nineties and likes to call the detachment whenever animals knock over her compost bins. Are you sure she didn't just see three stray cats?"

Randy chuckled. "No, but oddly enough, she swears one of the burglars was dressed as one."

I forced a strained laugh. "Obviously, she's a little confused."

Stevie made a noise as if suppressing a snort of laughter. "Her eyesight is going, the poor thing," she said, her own eyes shining. "When she comes into the Osprey, my mother and I always have to read the menu specials for her."

Finlayson crossed his arms and fixed me with a firm stare. "Miss Bishop, please tell me that you and your friends were not foolish enough to break into Mr. Perch's house to search for clues. Especially after I very specifically warned you about further involving yourself in my investigation."

"Of course not, Sergeant," I said innocently.

Randy burst out laughing. "Come on, Finlayson. Belinda's father was a cop. Even if she was dumb enough to break into a house, she'd know better to wear something as conspicuous as a Halloween costume."

I couldn't help but shoot him an offended frown. Jolene and Stevie suddenly became very interested in their pizza slices, but I still caught the shared smirk between them.

Finlayson sighed irritably and withdrew his notebook and pen from his pocket. "In that case, Miss Bishop, I'm sure you won't mind telling me, just for the record, where you three ladies were last night between one and two o'clock in the morning."

I maintained a neutral expression, but inside I was screaming. We were so focused on talking to Amanda and Madeline this morning, we didn't even think to agree on a cover story for last night. "We were watching a movie together."

"Yes, the new superhero movie that just started streaming," lied Stevie quickly.

Finlayson wrote down our responses. "And you were at Topsail Cottages?"

I hesitated. As understanding as my folks were, it was too much to hope they would back up a false alibi. And given the current tensions in his and Jolene's relationship, the same could probably be said for Trawler.

"No, the Osprey," Stevie answered. "I live on the second floor."

He switched his gaze to her. "Can anyone else verify your alibi?"

"Probably not," she said, biting her lip nervously. "My mother lives on the other side of town."

He raised one eyebrow. "I see," he said, writing. "Who is the star of this new superhero movie you were supposedly watching?"

Argh, why don't I follow celebrity news more closely? "It stars Ryan Reynolds." Even to my own ears, it sounded like a guess.

Finlayson flipped his notepad closed and clasped his hands in front of him expectantly. "Tell me about the plot."

"He gets superpowers."

"And?"

"And he uses them," I finished weakly.

Stevie snapped her fingers a few times. "He uses them to track down the man who killed his father," she said triumphantly.

Jolene jumped in. "Yes, and the actress from that Scottish historical drama plays the scientist he falls in love with."

"How did the movie end?" asked Finlayson, still glaring at us.

Bless movie executives and their strict adherence to genre formulas. "He learns to use his powers for good and not revenge," I said confidently.

The sudden flare of his nostrils and tightening of his lips told me I guessed correctly. "What was your favorite part of the movie?" he asked, his words barely discernible through his clenched jaw.

"The explosions," I said.

"The witty banter," added Stevie.

"I liked the surprise celebrity cameo at the end," said Jolene.

Randy frowned, looking disappointed. "This new movie isn't very original. It sounds like the plot to every other superhero film."

Finlayson closed his eyes as though praying for strength. He inhaled deeply and let out a calming breath before opening them again. "You ladies realize, of course, that it is a crime to lie to the police. And that online streaming activities can be traced."

There was a short pause as the three of us processed that tidbit of new information.

"Of course, we do," I managed to say eventually. Unfortunately, knowing and remembering were two different things. "Even if you did trace it, it would still only be considered circumstantial evidence and not enough for an arrest warrant, I'd imagine."

To my surprise, he laughed and shook his head, albeit wearily. "You know, Miss Bishop, your kind has always fascinated me," he said, each word dripping with contempt.

I felt my shoulders tense and tried to relax them before he noticed. "What kind would that be?"

He smirked. "My father liked to call them Small Town Fish. Kids who thrive in the fishbowl, but flounder when tossed into the ocean." He rocked back and forth on his heels, as if preparing to dive off a cliff. "Let me guess: you were kind of plain growing up, but just smart enough that adults started using words like *gifted* and *brilliant*, even though they never bothered to formally test you. But then you got out into the real world and realized you're just as mediocre as everyone else. Now you've forced your way into my murder investigation in a pathetic attempt to prove to yourself and everyone else you're as smart as you've always claimed to be."

My cheeks burned, but my hands felt strangely cold. I recalled Randy's warning on the boardwalk about Finlayson being determined to use this case to make a name for himself. *Okay, buddy, two can play the revealing deep-seated insecurities game.* "Let me guess, Sergeant Finlayson: your father is in law enforcement too. Judging by your apparent need for validation from superiors, he's most likely high ranking. You've probably spent your entire career desperately trying to prove you're just as good, if not better, than him in a hollow attempt to win Daddy's love and approval."

Finlayson's eyes widened and his nostrils flared again. *Direct hit.*

He took a step forward, but Randy quickly slipped in between us. "Whoa, okay, everyone back to your corners. Things are starting to turn a little personal here."

Finlayson ignored him. "Did you break into Mr. Perch's house?" he demanded.

"Absolutely not," I said, equally defiant. *We used the key,* I added silently.

"I'm very glad to hear that," he said, "because if I find even *one* speck of evidence that places any of you in that house, I will be back. And all three of you will be charged with breaking and entering. Have I made myself clear?"

The intoxicating scent of his woodsy aftershave made the back of my neck tingle, and I chastised myself for even noticing. "Yes."

"Crystal clear," said Stevie.

"Absolutely," said Jolene meekly.

"I sincerely hope so." Finlayson turned to Jolene, and she shrank back a little, as if expecting him to yell at her next. But he just cleared his throat awkwardly. "Mrs. Dexter, we received the lab results back from the clothing you were wearing the night of the murder. No traces of any blood or DNA from the victim were found on them."

"No traces." She blinked at him. "Does that mean I'm cleared? As a suspect?"

The muscle in his jaw jumped again. "While you are still considered to be a person of interest in this matter, we are considering other suspects."

Which was basically cop-speak for her being cleared.

But the happy dance would have to wait. "What about Barry Townsend?" I asked.

When it became obvious Finlayson had no intention of answering my question, Randy did. "We spoke to Iggy Saxton. Barry's alibi checked out."

"But Lottie said he never called for a cab," countered Stevie.

"That's because he didn't," said Randy. "Iggy was driving past the high school and saw Barry passed out on the front steps. He took pity on him and drove him home for free. He didn't mention it to Lottie because he didn't want to embarrass Barry any more than he already was."

I guess this means Barry's alibi checks out. Or did it? "What time did Iggy find him on the front steps?" I asked.

Finlayson, however, seemed to be at his wits' end with me. "Do not answer that, Corporal Perry," he barked. "That is a direct order."

Randy, who'd obviously been about to answer my question, dutifully closed his mouth.

Finlayson pointed a finger at me. "Consider this your last warning, Miss Bishop. Stop interfering in my investigation." Without waiting for a reply, he spun on the heels of his very shiny black shoes and walked away.

Randy shook his head as we watched Finlayson storm off down the boardwalk. "The drive back to the station with him should be fun."

"Maybe you should buy him a snow cone from Salty Saul's," I suggested.

He chuckled at my joke before turning serious. "He's right, you know. There isn't any reason for you to get involved now. Your friend is in the clear."

That may be true, but I still don't know who was responsible. And that was like an itch under my skin, too deep to fully scratch.

Randy didn't care for my silence. "Belinda," he said, a warning in his voice. "Ellie said you were only doing this to clear Jo's name."

"Finlayson said she's still a person of interest," I reminded him.

"He has to say that in order to save face. As stubborn as he is, even the sergeant knows how much head wounds can bleed. Whoever whacked Andy over the head would have gotten *some* of his blood on their hands or their clothes."

"Especially if the victim had been drinking alcohol," I realized. I turned to Stevie. "Remember when Trudy Spencer walked into that tree at her house party? Her forehead bled like crazy."

"Exactly," said Randy. "Since the lab didn't find any blood on Jolene's dress, it's unlikely she's the killer." He looked at Jolene, his eyes kind. "You're good, sweetie."

She exhaled deeply, relieved. "Thank you, Randy."

Randy noticed my pensive expression and frowned. "Something else bothering you, Belinda?"

I hesitated. Iggy Saxton vouching for Barry's alibi should have been enough to cross him off the suspect list, but I kept picturing the dark brown suit he wore to the reunion. Holly's pink dress may have been too light to hide blood stains, but that suit wasn't. Without knowing what time Iggy saw him on the front steps, Barry could still have had enough time to kill Andy and bury the trophy in the football field before passing out on the front steps.

There was also the matter of Madeline Barclay. "Have you spoken to Andy's poker buddies yet?" I asked Randy.

He nodded. "Yeah, they all have solid alibis. Why?"

"What about Kevin Barclay?"

Randy nodded. "Same. He and his wife were at his store when Andy died."

"You might want to double-check that," I advised. "We found out the truth behind the debt Andy owed them." As briefly as possible, I explained about the hockey card, trusting that Randy would be discreet. "Madeline blamed Andy for her husband losing it."

"Okay," he said, looking intrigued. "I'll mention it to Finlayson."

"But don't tell him you heard it from me."

He winked at me. "I always protect my informants," he assured me, touching two fingers to the brim of his hat before departing.

Stevie began to gather up the napkins strewn across the picnic table. "Finally, some good news! Randy is going to look into Madeline. Jo is basically cleared as a murder suspect, and Barry has an alibi."

"Right," I said, distracted by the questions still swirling in my brain.

"What's wrong?" she asked me.

"Nothing." I paused. "Except for one thing."

Stevie sighed. "And there it is."

"Barry might have still had enough time to kill Andy and bury his trophy in the football field before Iggy found him passed out on the steps. His brown suit might have been dark enough to hide blood stains, especially outside or in a car at that time of night."

"You're using the word *might* too much for my liking," said Stevie.

I shrugged. "I'm just saying, I don't think we're done yet."

"No," said Jolene, her voice strangely tense. "There's definitely at least one more thing we still need to discuss."

She held up the Right Foot pub drink coaster.

Oh, no.

"Would either of you care to explain what my husband's name is doing on our suspect list?" she demanded.

Chapter Seventeen

By five o'clock the next evening, I still hadn't heard from Jolene, despite my numerous apology texts and phone calls.

For the next twenty minutes, I alternated between performing my closing duties and checking my phone for any notifications from Jolene. I finished balancing the cash float and returned it to the small safe under the desk. I entered the code into the reception phone to ensure any calls would be forwarded to my parent's cell phone before signing out our booking system and shutting down my computer. The DeLuca family wasn't expected to arrive until late that evening, so I grabbed the keys to the Zwicker cottage they'd booked and deposited them into the dropbox outside before locking the door.

I considered returning to the main house, but decided I wasn't in the mood to be interrogated by my mother about our stalled investigation, so I sent her a short text telling her I was going to grab a drink at the Right Foot pub. As I started down the trail to the boardwalk, my phone chimed, but it was just a text from Stevie letting me know she was having just as much trouble as I was getting a hold of Jolene. Foot traffic on the boardwalk was light, and the pub almost empty. An elderly couple sat by the windows overlooking the harbor, while a dark-haired woman sat by herself in the corner with her back to me.

The only other customer was a solitary man seated at the end of the bar, drinking a bottle of beer as he watched the baseball game on the television. I took a seat at the opposite end from him and looked around hopefully. Hannah was on serving duty tonight, chatting with the couple by the windows. A second server, a young man I didn't recognize, wiped down the tables next to the empty stage. So my odds of seeing my favorite bartender were good.

Sure enough, the doors to the kitchen swung open and Jinx appeared, carrying a tray of freshly washed glasses. He was wearing dark blue jeans and a green plaid button-down shirt with the sleeves rolled up, looking like he'd just stepped off the pages of a Mark's Work Warehouse ad. (Even as a teen, I was never really into boy bands. Give me a handcrafted hutch over a love ballad any day.)

"Hey, stranger," he said, flashing those killer dimples at me. He returned the glasses to their shelf before facing me. "What can I get you?"

I sighed. "Anything with bourbon in it."

He winced. "That can't be good. Rough week?"

I braced my elbows on the bar and tented my fingers. "Let's see, I exposed someone's very personal secret, got myself banned from Gull's Quick Stop, managed to get on the wrong side of a cop, and helped further erode Jolene's marriage."

His brows rose. "You've been busy." He was about to add a shot of brown liquor to my glass when he paused. "Wait, were you seriously banned from Gull's?"

I nodded.

He whistled softly. "Kevin and Maddie never ban people. Not even that kid who kept shaking up all the pop bottles."

"What can I say? I'm gifted," I said bitterly, remembering Finlayson's words.

Jinx finished making my drink and slid it across the bar to me. "There you go. Wild rhubarb gin, ginger beer, and a sprig of mint. I call it a Pucker Up."

I wish. My cheeks warmed, and I dropped my gaze as I took an experimental sip. The spice of the ginger beer combined with the tang of the rhubarb was so delicious, I almost wanted to down it all in one gulp. "This is amazing," I said, taking a second, deeper, swallow.

He chuckled, looking pleased with himself. "It's my go-to drink whenever I need a little pick-me-up."

"I definitely needed one of those, so thank you." I took another sip, savoring the sweet and bitter taste.

Hannah approached the bar with a drink order, and Jinx moved down a few paces to speak to her. After he handed her the two drinks, he checked in with the guy at the other end of the bar. Jinx laughed at something the man said, opening another bottle for him. When the two began discussing the game, I knew it would be a while before those dimples returned.

To pass the time, I took another sip of my drink and looked around the pub. The brunette woman seated in the back corner got up from her table and approached with her wallet in hand.

As she got closer, I realized that I recognized her. "Nancy."

She jumped and spun around to face me. Her anxious expression eased into one of polite surprise. "Belinda, I didn't see you there." She smiled ruefully. "I'm sorry, I'm a little jumpy tonight."

"I didn't mean to frighten you," I said. "I was just surprised to see you. You said you don't come into town very often."

"I had an appointment with Charles Bennett this evening."

Of course, Andy's funeral. Charles Bennett and his wife, Yvonna, owned and operated the town's only funeral home and crematorium. "Is there anything I can help with?" I had no idea how exactly I could be of any assistance, but it felt like the right thing to say.

"Thank you, but it's all arranged. The service is next week. I wanted to hold it sooner, but the police only just released Andrew's body. Not to mention everything else I've had to deal with in settling his estate." She gave me an incredulous look. "Can you believe someone actually broke into his house a couple of days ago?"

I paused longer than I should have before reacting. "What? No! You're kidding!" I yelped. *Ugh, nice cover, Bishop.* I may as well have held up a sign that said, *It was me.*

"Yes, but luckily, Mrs. Demings from next door heard the window break and phoned the police. They arrived before the thief had a chance to steal anything, but whoever it was got away."

"That's too bad." Then, just to be sure I really sold the performance, I snarled, "People like that deserve to be locked away for life."

Nancy gave me an odd look, but fortunately chose to ignore my strange behavior. "I think I know what they were after. Andrew owned a valuable hockey card signed by a very famous player."

"You knew about that?" I asked without thinking. Instantly, I wanted to snatch the question back from the air, mainly because there was no reason I should know about it.

She nodded. "Yes, he showed it to me after he bought it. For quite a steal, apparently."

Interesting choice of words. Evidently, Andy felt some guilt in acquiring the hockey card; otherwise, why would he lead Nancy to think he purchased it?

She sighed and shook her head. "Frankly, I'll be happy when this whole mess is over, and I can go back to focusing on what's important in my life: my clinic and my horses. Fortunately, there is one bright side to everything that's happened. Apparently, Andrew changed his will before he died. He wanted part of his estate to be used to set up a bursary award through the high school, and the rest to go to my animal clinic." She gave me a sad smile. "Andrew promised he would help me raise the money for a new roof. I just wish he could have kept his word another way."

I invited Nancy to join me for a drink, but she declined. Hannah came over to help settle her bill, and we said our goodbyes. After she was gone, Jinx returned to my end of the bar and offered to make me another drink, which I accepted. I sipped my fresh drink in silence, pondering everything that had happened over the past couple of days, while Jinx busied himself tidying behind the bar.

"You know, normally I hate the sympathetic bartender stereotype," he said, resuming his casual lean across from me. "Mainly because most people use it as an excuse to trauma dump on a stranger just doing their job." He shot me a wink. "I'll make an exception in your case."

I hesitated. As much as I enjoyed the wink, I wasn't sure how much I could share with him. While I didn't think he would repeat it, discussing Kevin's gambling problems with Jinx wasn't the same as telling Randy.

He raised his hands placatingly. "Only if you want to talk, of course."

"Honestly, I wouldn't even know where to start," I admitted.

"How about with whatever is bothering you the most?"

I mulled this over for a few seconds. "Actually, I think it all happened for the same reason."

He made a little whirling motion with his hand, urging me to elaborate. "Which is?"

I inhaled deeply before taking the plunge. "Do you think I'm a know-it-all? Do I think I'm smarter than everyone else?"

He hesitated just long enough to confirm my fears.

"You do, don't you?" I wailed.

"We haven't seen each other in over ten years, Belinda," he said reasonably. "Give me a chance to remember."

Okay, that's fair but also a bit of a kick to the ego.

He drummed his fingers against the bar top. "I remember you had a lot of opinions and observations," he said eventually, "and you weren't shy about sharing them."

I groaned and rested my forehead on the bar. "That's the definition of a know-it-all." I raised my head. "The thing is, I'm not. I know I'm not smarter than other people. I make dumb mistakes all the time."

He shook his head, his chocolate brown locks gleaming under the soft light from the chandelier. "Being a know-it-all isn't about intelligence. It's having an unwavering conviction that you're always right or know what's best for other people."

"You're not helping."

He chuckled. "But that's not how I see you. I thought you were an incredibly perceptive person who also sucked at reading the room."

I sat up straight. "What's that supposed to mean?"

He gave me a knowing look. "Mr. Donnelly? You announced his divorce to the entire homeroom class."

I rolled my eyes. "Well, it was pretty obvious. He went from wearing ironed shirts and eating homemade lunches to crew neck sweaters and bologna sandwiches over the course of one summer." I shifted in my seat, embarrassed. "And I didn't announce it. I just offered to give him my mother's card. He was the one who asked why he would need it."

"My point is, you are smart. You're observant. You notice things that others miss. Which means you sometimes see things that people don't want to be seen." He looked at me, his gaze oddly intense. "And you don't always pick up on social cues."

Suddenly, my chest felt light and fluttery. I took another sip of my drink in an effort to cover my nerves.

"Where's this coming from, anyway?" he asked. "It's not like you to care if someone thinks you're a know-it-all."

"I thought you said I wasn't a know-it-all."

"Answer the question."

"I don't know." I sighed. "It just got me thinking. What if that's why everything fell apart in Ottawa? Because I keep butting into situations that don't concern me and blurting out every revelation as soon as it hits me. Maybe Donna Dickie is right: you get farther along in life sucking up to people instead of calling them out."

Jinx snorted. "Depends on what kind of life you want to live. You know who you are, and you're not afraid to show it. In fact, that's something I always admired about you. Your confidence."

I caught a whiff of Old Spice cologne, the same scent he wore in high school. It was subtle, just enough to make my forearms break out in goosebumps.

Confidence. Jinx was right; it didn't matter if Finlayson thought I was only meddling because of my own insecurities. I was smart. I could see what others missed. I also knew to always trust my gut, and right now it was telling me that Trawler was hiding something. Something big.

I jumped to my feet and grabbed my purse. "Thanks for the sympathetic ear," I told Jinx, coughing a little as I swallowed the last of my drink. I slapped enough cash down on the bar to cover my bill, plus a tip. "You really helped put things in perspective for me. You should have been a therapist."

"Thanks," he said, his expression muddled by my sudden departure. "I prefer the pub life. Better hours, cash tips. And I get to flirt with the customers," he finished with a grin.

I gripped the bar in an effort to stop my knees from buckling. But the playful banter would have to wait for another day. There was still one more suspect on our list to deal with.

* * *

Fifteen minutes later, I was standing outside of Jolene's house, knocking on her door. I heard the sound of approaching footsteps and braced myself. But when the door swung open, it was only Sadie, her dark hair twisted on top of her head in a bun and held in place with a yellow pencil. Once again, I was struck by her resemblance to Trawler.

"Hi," I said after an awkward pause. "Is your mother home?"

"Who wants to know?" the girl asked bluntly.

I frowned down at her, a little offended. "You don't remember me? I brought your mother a box of pastries."

"Those scones tasted weird," she said. "I like the Sand Dollar's apple fritters."

What a weird, serious kid. "I'll keep that in mind next time."

She cocked her head to the side and pushed her dark bangs out of her eyes. "Your name's Belinda, right?" I nodded. She surveyed me, her eyes squinting as she determined my fate. "Okay, you can come in," she said eventually, stepping aside so I could enter.

The scent of onions and spices emanated from the direction of the kitchen. Sadie closed the door behind me. In the living room, hidden from view by a glass partition wall, I heard Trawler speaking softly. Instinctively, I leaned against the wall under the guise of struggling to undo a stubborn shoelace to hear better. After a few moments, I realized he was on the telephone.

"No, not yet," I heard him murmur. "Soon, I promise. I just need a little more time." He paused and I strained to hear more. *More time for what?* "No, Jo doesn't suspect a thing."

Sadie chose that moment to announce my arrival in typical kid fashion, which was bellowing for the entire neighborhood to hear. "Mum! Dad! Someone is at the door!"

"I have to go," I heard Trawler whisper hastily. "I love you too."

I scrambled away from the wall as Trawler appeared around the corner, kicking off my other shoe and arranging my face to look as nonchalant as possible.

"Who is it, Sadie?" He stopped short when he saw me. "Oh, Belinda, it's you."

Call me paranoid, but he looked less than pleased to see me. In fact, he looked downright perturbed. His posture was stiff, and he held his arms awkwardly by his sides. I remembered what Jinx said about my ability to see the things other people didn't want to be seen, and I wondered if Trawler's uneasiness had anything to do with that.

Having properly alerted her parents of their visitor, Sadie now seemed bored with my company. She spun on her heels and bounded back up the stairs "I'm going to read my book in my bedroom," she told her father.

"I think supper is almost ready," he said.

"One more chapter," she yelled back, followed by the sound of a door closing.

I pointed to the cell phone in his hand. "Am I interrupting?"

My question seemed to snap Trawler out of some kind of daze. He shoved his phone into his pocket and gave me a smile eerily similar to his wife's pageant grin. "Uh, no, not at all. I assume you're here to see Jo. She's in the kitchen, cooking."

He motioned for me to follow him, so I did, keeping a close eye on his demeanor. "Great news about Jo, isn't it?" I asked. "Being cleared as a suspect so quickly. Now the police can focus on finding the real killer."

His chuckle sounded too forced to be genuine. "It's been a huge load off us all."

"It's a good thing she offered her dress for analysis," I continued. "Did the sergeant ask for your clothes too?"

He stopped and stared at me. "No, why would they? I wasn't even in the school when Andy was killed."

I snapped my fingers as though I'd just remembered something. "Oh, that's right. Jolene said you told the police that you went for a walk to cool down."

Was it my imagination, or did Trawler shift his gaze away from mine? "That's right."

"And that worked?"

His brow creased, and I thought I saw his Adam's apple jump. "What?"

"The walk helped calm you down," I clarified.

He hesitated. "Sure did."

When we reached the kitchen, we found Jolene in the middle of preparing a spaghetti supper. With the timed precision of a Royal Nova Scotia Tattoo performance, she scooped up a handful of chopped mushrooms and bell peppers from the wooden cutting board on the counter, dropped them into the tomato sauce bubbling on the stove, adjusted the heat under the pot of noodles boiling next to it, before adding the now empty wooden board to the sink filled with soapy water. She then scooted back over to the stove to taste the sauce.

Without turning around, she said, "Trawler, can you please pop the garlic bread into the oven while I get some of these dishes done? The oven is already preheated, and the timer is set."

"I can do that, if you'd like," I offered.

She looked up, her expression immediately clouding over. "What are you doing here?" she demanded.

"We need to talk," I said. I glanced at Trawler. "In private."

He hesitated and looked at Jolene for direction. She nodded, albeit reluctantly, and he left the kitchen, but not before sliding the garlic bread into the oven as requested.

Jolene picked up a tea towel and tossed it to me. "If you want to talk, you have to dry."

"Understood." I walked over to the dish rack and got to work. "I know you're mad at us for not telling you about Trawler."

She snorted as she began scrubbing the cutting board. "And here comes the rationalization."

I lowered my voice. "I know you don't want to hear this, but the fact is we can't account for his whereabouts at the time of Andy's death, he won't explain where he's been disappearing to, and he had a muddy shovel in the back of his truck, which you two drove to the reunion. Admit it, if he was anyone besides your husband, you would have added him to the suspects list too."

She let the cutting board she was scrubbing slide back into the soapy water, spinning around to face me. "You think that's why I'm angry?" she asked. "Of course, I would have added him."

I was so shocked, I almost dropped the plate I was holding. "You would?"

She glanced toward the living room before continuing. "He's been acting strangely ever since this whole thing started. I'm not upset that you and Stevie think he may have done it. I'm upset you didn't warn me. I thought we were friends again."

To my dismay, I realized she was right.

Jolene plunged her hands back into the soapy water and resumed scrubbing. "I'm not completely naive, Belinda. I know how his recent behavior looks. But I told myself if Belinda Bishop, the most cynical and suspicious person I know, doesn't suspect him, I must be overreacting. But now, I find out that you do suspect him," she said, her voice raising slightly with emotion.

Quickly, I shushed her. "We weren't sure how you would take it. Most people wouldn't be thrilled to hear that about their spouse. We were going to tell you, just not until we'd eliminated all of our other suspects."

She glared at me. "I have a daughter with this man."

"We didn't think you or Sadie were in any real danger," I tried again to explain. "Everyone knows you don't kill the patsy."

"What are you talking about?" she hissed. "It's much easier to frame someone if they're not around to defend themselves."

The timer on the oven beeped, signaling the garlic bread was ready. Without prompting, I pulled on one of the oven mitts on the kitchen island and took it out, setting the bread on a cooling rack. Despite the tension in the room, my mouth still watered at the sight of it.

I allowed myself one deep inhale, savoring the scent of buttery garlic and melted cheese, before turning back to Jolene. "We messed up, okay? I'm sorry," I said sincerely.

She surveyed me for a moment and then let out a gusty sigh. "You're forgiven. What do we do now?" she asked, crossing her arms.

"I think you already know."

She looked down at the floor and nodded. "We have to investigate my husband."

Chapter Eighteen

The next afternoon, Stevie and I parked our car across the street from Jolene's house and waited. Since there was a good chance Trawler would recognize the Civic (I really needed to get my own vehicle soon), Stevie borrowed Diane's battered green Volkswagen Golf.

"What time did Jo say Trawler would be leaving the house?" she asked, turning off the engine.

"She didn't," I said, watching the front door. "Just that he said he had some errands to run this afternoon."

"Is he back to not telling her what those errands are?"

"All he would say was that it was a surprise," I said. "Which is already annoying when guys do that, but when there's the possibility they're a murderer . . ." I trailed off meaningfully.

Stevie craned her neck to check her appearance in the rear-view mirror, adjusting her curly auburn wig. "I'm still not convinced we need disguises."

I pulled at my own brunette pageboy wig. "How else are we supposed to follow Trawler without him knowing it's us?"

Fortunately, my parents regularly attended the Haunted Harbour Masquerade Ball every year on McGrey's Island. Since my mother refused to throw away anything even remotely arts-and-crafts related, Stevie and I had access to a literal treasure chest (from the year my father went as Jack Sparrow) of old costumes and wigs.

"I still can't believe you and Jo cooked up this plan without me," she said. "Rule number three, remember? Our first real stakeout, the coolest part of any investigation, and I didn't even get to help plan it."

I squirmed in my seat, trying to alleviate the guilt roiling in my stomach. "I know, I'm sorry."

"We wouldn't even be doing this investigation if it wasn't for me," she said for the umpteenth time.

"Technically speaking, you only wanted to bring Jo the pastries," I pointed out. "I was the one who said we should try to clear her name."

"I'm the only reason you went to her house in the first place," she argued.

I sighed. "Stevie, I've already apologized a million times. What more do you want from me?"

"I know, and I forgive you." She skimmed her fingers down the sides of the steering wheel, avoiding my gaze. "I don't like being left out of things," she said softly. "My cousins did that to me all the time when I was a kid."

The wriggling guilt monster in my stomach kicked again. Stevie didn't usually talk about her family in Alberta. From what she did share, her wealthy paternal grandparents didn't approve of their son's marriage to Diane, whose parents were grocery store clerks. On the rare occasions she and Diane were invited to family events, Stevie was often ignored and excluded. After the divorce, her father moved overseas for work, and his parents cut contact with both Diane and Stevie.

I groaned and closed my eyes, letting my head flop back against the headrest. "You're right. That was really insensitive on my part. I should have waited until the three of us could have talked." I opened my eyes and looked at her. "It won't happen again."

She gave me a reluctant side glance. "Even if there's a really big break in the case and I'm not around?"

I placed one hand over my heart. "I promise, next time Jo and I will wait for you or at least send a text."

Stevie didn't respond, but she looked slightly mollified.

The front door opened, and Trawler stepped outside. As if on cue, Stevie and I both slid down in our seats to avoid being seen by him. The only problem was that now we couldn't see him either.

"We need to see which direction he's headed," I whispered.

"I'm on it," murmured Stevie, groping in the back seat while trying to stay hidden. Finally, she found her purse and pulled out her compact mirror. Opening it, she tilted it until the house came into view. "He's getting into his truck."

A few seconds later, we heard the engine start, followed by the sound of tires crunching on the gravel driveway as he reversed into the street. We both sat up cautiously as the truck drove past us. The front door flew open again and Jolene hurried down her walkway, making a beeline for the Golf. She was wearing a baby pink sweatshirt and matching yoga pants, with a large cooler bag slung over her shoulder. Her blond ponytail was covered with a Little Blue Harbour High ballcap, and she wore a pair of dark, oversized sunglasses.

"She looks like Reese Witherspoon trying to avoid the paparazzi," I muttered.

Jolene opened the passenger side door and dove into the back seat. "Go, go, go," she ordered, pulling the door shut behind her. "Before we lose him."

I twisted in my seat to face her. "What's with the cooler?"

"Trawler said he wouldn't be home until five thirty. Since we're probably going to be following him all afternoon, I brought stakeout snacks," she said, patting it. "Anyone want a sandwich?"

"Um, yes, please," I said, holding out my hand.

"You ate at the Osprey before we left," said Stevie, laughing as she followed Trawler down the street. "You had two helpings of blueberry grunt."

"Snacking is an essential part of the stakeout experience."

Jolene unzipped the cooler and handed me a sandwich wrapped in parchment paper. "Stevie, would you like one too?" she asked.

She shook her head. "I'm good, thanks."

I unwrapped the sandwich and took a bite. I almost swooned from the taste. "This is incredible," I said, fighting the urge to go limp with pleasure. "What's in it?"

Jolene unwrapped a sandwich for herself. "Chicken salad with chopped crabapple and brie cheese on ciabatta bread."

"What?" squawked Stevie, tapping the brakes abruptly. "When you said snacks, I thought you meant stuff like beef jerky or processed cheese sandwiches."

I laughed, trying not to spray the dashboard with crumbs. "Like Jolene Dexter, supermom, would ever be caught dead offering someone packaged food."

Jolene pursed her lips, but her eyes danced with amusement. "I'll have you know Trawler and Sadie love beef jerky. We always have some in the house," she said smugly.

"Yeah, but do you buy it or make it yourself?" I asked. "You strike me as a woman who owns her own food dehydrator."

Her sheepish silence told me I was right.

"How has Trawler been acting?" asked Stevie. Any concern in her voice was muffled by the fact she was currently biting into her own sandwich with the same ferocity as a black bear attacking its prey.

"Oddly upbeat," said Jolene, her brow furrowed. "His mother, Kathleen, came by this morning and picked up Sadie for a weekend sleepover. Apparently, Trawler arranged it with her. When I asked why, he just said he wanted it to be just the two of us tonight. Normally, I'd find that sweet."

"But now you're worried his big surprise is just a Jolene-sized hole dug in the woods?" I asked.

Stevie choked on her sandwich. "Sheesh, Belinda. Would you please cut it out with the true crime dramatics?"

I rolled my eyes. "Right, because we're following Trawler out of sheer curiosity," I whispered sarcastically.

"I know, but you're going to freak her out," she whispered back.

"I can still hear you," Jolene stage-whispered from the back seat.

Stevie shot me an exasperated look before continuing at normal volume. "I just think we should keep an open mind with Trawler."

"You do that," I said. "I, on the other hand, am only going to trust him as far as I could throw him, which as you saw at Boot Camp on the Boardwalk, wouldn't be very far."

Stevie turned to me, eyebrows raised. "That's a weird thing to brag about."

We followed Trawler's truck down Schooner Lane and onto Seafarer Road. He continued through the town core, passing the high school and movie theater, before turning onto Roseway Street. His brake lights flashed in front of the Home Hardware Building Centre, and he turned into their small parking lot. Stevie steered the Golf into an empty parking space on the opposite side of the street. The three of us watched as Trawler strolled into the store.

"What do you think he needs to pick up here?" I asked.

"No idea," said Jolene, frowning. "I do the majority of the household shopping, and I can't think of anything we'd need from here."

I reached for the door handle. "Maybe one of us should follow him inside."

Stevie shook her head. "It's too risky. Lurking across the street from him in bad wigs is one thing, but any closer than that, and he's bound to recognize us."

I couldn't help but feel a stab of indignation on behalf of my mother, who prides herself on her costumes.

"Besides, it's just a hardware store," said Jolene, her eyes still glued to the storefront. "What's the worst he could buy in there?"

I started to answer her, but Stevie pushed the last bite of my sandwich into my mouth, effectively cutting off my words. Point taken, I chewed in silence, my eyes also trained on the store.

The minutes seemed to crawl by as we waited for Trawler to reappear. I began to realize why they don't show the entire stakeout in movies or television. Any tension and excitement I'd felt in the beginning soon curdled into impatience. Stevie drummed her fingers on the steering wheel, mimicking my own restlessness. Only Jolene remained completely still, staring at the store entrance.

After thirty minutes passed with no new developments, I flopped back in my seat with a groan. "What is taking so long?"

"Maybe he can't find what he's looking for," said Stevie, her voice flat with boredom. "You know how some guys are—they'd rather die of old age in the aisles than ask for help."

"It's more likely Trawler just ran into someone he knows," said Jolene reasonably.

We lapsed into frustrated silence again.

"Did Finlayson ever give you the impression he suspected Trawler?" Stevie asked Jolene.

"He asked a lot of questions about the fight between him and Andy, but he was more focused on me as a suspect," she said grimly.

"That's probably because there isn't any physical evidence tying Trawler to the scene," I said thoughtfully. "Whereas with you, Finlayson had the blue scarf."

"Still, you'd think Finlayson would have looked into Trawler a little closer," said Stevie, "especially considering his weak alibi. I mean, taking a walk to clear his head? Hardly iron-clad."

"True," I agreed, "but again, no physical evidence at the scene. It's not like we can prove he *wasn't* taking a walk." Suddenly, Trawler reappeared, carrying a large canvas shopping bag with the store's logo. I sat up in my seat. "We have a bag, people."

Stevie squinted in his direction. "Can either of you make out what's inside?"

"It doesn't appear to be anything heavy," said Jolene hopefully. "That's promising, right?"

I decided not to point out that plenty of items commonly used in a murder were lightweight and could be easily purchased at any hardware store.

Trawler unlocked the truck and climbed back inside, casually tossing the bag into the back seat. To be safe, the three of us ducked as his truck drove out of the parking lot. Instead of turning onto Seafarer Road, he continued straight through the intersection. After a few more minutes of driving, he parked on a side street and got out. Stevie guided the car into a space a few spots down from him while Jolene and I watched him cross the street. He approached a bright blue building, taking the concrete stairs at a jog. He pushed against the glass door and disappeared inside.

I read the sign over the entrance. "Sea You Go Travel." I looked at the others. "I didn't know Little Blue Harbour had a travel agent."

They both nodded. "Wendy Snow," said Stevie.

I wracked my brain for a few minutes before finally placing the name. "Wait, wasn't she the little brat you used to babysit? Didn't she once pour an entire carton of apple juice into your backpack because you wouldn't let her stay up to watch *Freddy vs. Jason*?"

"Yes, the little ingrate," said Stevie. "I saved her from watching a truly terrible movie."

"Why would Trawler need a travel agent?" asked Jolene, worried.

"Maybe he's planning a romantic getaway for the two of you," suggested Stevie hopefully.

Jolene snorted derisively. "Trawler? Please. He didn't even take me out to dinner for my last birthday, and all he gave me for a present was a new vacuum cleaner."

"His only gift was chores?" I asked, appalled. "Ugh, that's what we should send him to jail for." The two of them stared at me, and I reconsidered my stance. "No, you're right; murder is worse."

We watched the building for a moment in silence.

"Well, I guess now is our chance," I said.

I threw open the car door and moved to get out, but Stevie reached across the console and grabbed my arm. "Chance for what?"

"We're going to search his truck and see what he bought," I said, like it was obvious.

"What if Trawler comes out and catches us?" she asked. "Or someone drives by and sees us? Remember what Finlayson said, he's looking for any reason to charge us."

"It's not like we have to break into the truck." I turned to Jolene. "You have a set of spare keys in your purse, right?"

Jolene nodded.

"See? Totally legal." I got out before either of them could further object.

They shared a hesitant glance before following me. The three of us walked over to the black truck as casually as possible. Jolene found her set of keys and clicked the remote entry fob twice, unlocking the passenger doors. Stevie kept watch while I opened the door and picked up the shopping bag. I turned it over, dumping out its contents.

My stomach dropped. "Oh, no."

"What is it?" asked Jolene. "What did you find?"

I moved to block her view, but she slipped past me. I winced at the sharp gasp that escaped her. Piled on the back seat of the truck was a large heavy-duty tarp, a bag of nylon zip ties, and a canister of lye.

Chapter Nineteen

The three of us stared down at the items, each silently processing this new discovery.

Jolene was right, I thought, my stomach sinking. *He is going to kill the patsy.*

I may have been the first to say Trawler shouldn't be trusted, but there was still a tiny part of my brain that believed there was another, less nefarious, explanation for his recent strange behavior. Kind of like when you were little and believed a monster lived under your bed. You still made your parents check every night, but deep down you knew they wouldn't find anything.

But the pile of items on the back seat was the equivalent of looking under the bed yourself and being grabbed by a scaly hand.

Stevie was the first to speak. "Okay, let's not jump to conclusions."

I grabbed the sales receipt. "Where else are we supposed to jump?" I asked. "A tarp? Zip ties? Lye? This is practically a serial killer starter kit."

Jolene shook her head. "No, we can't think like that. Like Stevie said, we can't jump to conclusions." But her voice was strained several notes higher than usual.

My mind flew back to Trawler's odd behavior the previous night. I glanced down at the jumble of items. Is this what he needed more time to complete?

Something must have shown on my face because Stevie frowned at me, her eyes now clouded with suspicion. "Belinda, why do you have that look?"

I swallowed thickly. "What look? I don't have a look."

Stevie pointed to my mouth. "Yes, you do. You're squishing your lips to the side. That's your *I've-realized-something-huge* look," she answered.

I sighed. *It's probably a good thing I didn't join Andy's poker game.* "Okay, I'm busted." With a grimace, I shared the clandestine telephone conversation I'd overheard the previous night.

"Belinda," Stevie chided me wearily as Jolene groaned. "Seriously?"

I looked at Jolene. "Are you mad?"

"No. Yes." Jolene slumped against the truck. "I don't know, to be honest. I feel like everything I thought I knew has been turned upside-down. Andy was running around with half of the town. The people I thought were my friends all think I could be capable of murder. And now, we've discovered so-called murder supplies in the back of my husband's vehicle. I don't know who to trust anymore."

My cheeks stung a little at the implication. "You can trust me."

Jolene looked up at me, and I noticed her eyes were glazed, as though she was holding back tears. "Can I? You didn't tell me about this phone call. You didn't tell me about the muddy shovel in Trawler's truck. Do you really care about rebuilding our friendship, or are you still just after an exciting news story you can sell?"

Stevie quickly jumped in to vouch for me. "Of course, you can trust Belinda. The last thing she cares about is a silly news story. Right?" She looked to me for confirmation, but I hesitated. "Right, Belinda?" she repeated, her question now laced with warning.

I sighed. "Look, I won't lie; finding a murder kit in the back seat of your husband's truck is an amazing plot twist. But that's not the only thing I care about," I added hastily. "There's a chance Trawler could present a real threat to you." I hesitated. "I don't want anything bad to happen to you, Jolene. Or Sadie."

Jolene glanced back into the interior of the pickup truck and seemed to steel herself. "You're right. This has gone on long enough. Trawler needs to explain himself."

I glanced at the glass doors and saw Trawler talking to a shorter woman with black hair. She nodded and handed him what looked like a travel brochure.

"Here's your chance," I told her, "because he's coming outside."

Her eyes widened and she grabbed us both by the arm, dragging us with her into the alley. The three of us crouched down behind the dumpster and watched as Trawler approached his truck, whistling softly.

"I thought you wanted to confront him," I hissed in Jolene's ear.

"I know, but I panicked," she whispered back.

Trawler started the truck and pulled away from the curb. Stevie cautiously edged out from behind the dumpster. "How long do you think we should wait before we go after him?"

Jolene shook her head. "Let him go. I want to talk to Wendy instead."

"But we're supposed to be following him," said Stevie. She dropped her voice and muttered to me, "What if he's not done shopping for her surprise?"

"We already found his bag of murder tools," I muttered back.

Jolene sighed irritably. "You two are so bad at whispering." She stood up and marched toward the entrance. "Come on."

* * *

We stepped inside the Sea You Go Travel office and were immediately engulfed by a chorus of tropical birds, accompanied by steel drums. It was smaller than I expected, or maybe it just seemed that way because of the many leafy plants and miniature palm trees filling the lobby. A massive aquarium with brightly colored fish sat in the middle of the waiting area.

"Okay, if this is intended to send people into vacation mode, it's definitely working," I said, gesturing to our surroundings. "I only have approximately eighteen dollars in my savings account, and I still want to book a trip to the Bahamas right now."

The brunette woman suddenly appeared from behind the fish tank. "It's the coconut air freshener," she said. "Folks get a whiff of it and start picturing themselves on a tropical beach."

I sniffed the air and realized she was right.

The last time I saw Wendy Snow, she was a rowdy ten-year-old in corduroy overalls and pigtails, with a penchant for minor property damage whenever she didn't get her way. Now she stood in front of me wearing a fitted burgundy pantsuit and matching slingback heels, her hair styled in an asymmetrical bob.

"We have some very affordable packages, if you ladies are interested," she said.

Jolene took off her sunglasses. "Wendy, it's me."

Wendy did a double take, placing hand on her chest. "I'm sorry, Jolene. I didn't even recognize you." Her gaze shifted to me and Stevie, and her expression changed from surprise, to recognition, and finally confusion. "You're Stevie and Belinda, right? " She pointed to our heads. "What's with the wigs?"

There was a short beat of silence as I scrambled for a plausible cover story. "We're both trying out a new look."

She stared at us for a moment before nodding. "Fair enough." She turned her attention back to Jolene. "What brings you in today?"

"Have you recently booked any travel for Lawrence?" she asked.

Wendy frowned for a moment. "Oh, Trawler. Yes," she said. "I helped him finalize his plans today."

Jolene waited expectantly, but Wendy clearly had no intention of providing any more information unprompted. "Where exactly is he going?" asked Jolene.

Wendy shook her head. "I'm sorry, but I can't divulge any details to a third party. Unless it's the police," she added as an afterthought.

The one time Sergeant Finlayson would have come in handy. "We just saw Trawler leaving your office," I said.

Wendy clucked her tongue and wagged a finger scoldingly. "That may be true, but we at Sea You Go take our confidentiality policy very seriously. I've worked very hard to maintain a stellar reputation. You don't get that by blabbing your clients' business all over town."

"Wendy, he's my husband. You and I are in the same book club," said Jolene, sounding aggravated.

Wendy arched one eyebrow. "And? I didn't even tell my cousin when his wife booked a two-week package on a singles cruise."

"You really should've told him that," said Stevie.

"I'm a travel agent, not a marriage counselor. Besides, the doofus told on herself when she came back without a tan line on her ring finger," she said.

I huffed and crossed my arms over my chest. "What's it going to take for you to tell us what we want to know?"

She cocked her head at me, amused. "Are you trying to bribe me? I just heard you admit to only having eighteen dollars." Wendy turned to Jolene. "Did it ever occur to you to just ask your husband?"

Jolene sighed deeply as she took off her baseball cap, smoothing back her ponytail. "I can't. He hasn't exactly been forthcoming lately, especially when it comes to issues in our marriage."

Wendy waved her off dismissively. "None of this sounds like my problem. Like I said, I'm not a marriage counselor. Take it up with your husband."

Unwilling to yield, I played the last card we held. "You owe Stevie for dumping apple juice in her backpack."

She stared at me, baffled. "I was eight years old. My parents compensated her for that."

"What about her first love note from Holden Darryls that was in the backpack?" I asked. "How do you intend to compensate her for that?"

Wendy sighed. "Now you're just reaching. Wasn't Holden Darryls the drunk teen who tried to climb the water tower on a dare before having to be rescued by the fire department?"

"Yes," said Stevie. "But in my defense, I was only sixteen and he had very soulful eyes."

Wendy directed us toward the exit with a shooing motion. "Jolene, I'm sorry you're having marriage issues," she said, not sounding sorry at all, "but I'm a very busy woman. Can you three please go play *Charlie's Angels* somewhere else?"

"I thought we were supposed to be Nancy Drew," Stevie muttered to me.

"*Charlie's Angels* was just a sexy seventies reboot of Nancy Drew," said Wendy.

I stared at her. "You just blew my mind."

"Glad to have helped," said Wendy flatly. "Now get out of my office."

"Wait, wait!" I cried, skirting past her, much to her obvious exasperation.

Wendy let out a low growl of frustration. "You're wasting your time. I'm not giving you any details."

"Okay, but what if we ask you questions and you only respond with yes or no answers? No one could ever accuse you of giving us any details. After all, you can't be held responsible for what we might infer from a simple, one-word response, right?"

Wendy tapped her manicured nails against her leg as she considered it. Finally, she exhaled sharply through her nose. "I'm listening."

"Domestic flights?" I asked.

Wendy nodded. "Yes."

"Was it just the one seat booked?" asked Stevie.

"No," sighed Wendy.

"Someone else is traveling with him?" asked Jolene furiously. "Who?"

Wendy raised both eyebrows pointedly, and I realized our mistake. "Is the second ticket for a man?" I asked.

She gave me an almost pitying look. "No."

Jolene's face fell. "It's under a woman's name?"

"Yes," said Wendy, her eyes wide as she nodded meaningfully.

In the past week alone, Jolene had been questioned by the police in the death of her friend, shunned by the town she loved, and started to suspect her husband of murder, but Wendy's words made her face crumble in a way I hadn't yet seen. I almost couldn't bring myself to ask my last question.

Unfortunately, I had to know. "Were they round-trip tickets?"

Wendy glanced at Jolene. "No, one-way."

Chapter Twenty

After thanking Wendy for her time, Jolene walked outside without saying a word, Stevie and me following her. The three of us got back into the Golf and sat, each silently staring ahead.

Finally, I couldn't take the tension anymore. "So," I began tentatively.

"So," repeated Jolene, her voice tense enough to snap.

"How are you doing with all this?" Stevie asked her gently.

"Great," she drawled, each syllable dripping with sarcasm. "Just peachy."

I looked at Stevie. "Is it too late to go back to that *let's-not-jump-to-conclusions* suggestion you had earlier?"

She sighed and let her head fall back against the headrest. "Way too late for that."

I fell silent for a moment, quickly running through everything we knew so far about Trawler in my head, before twisting to face Jolene in the back seat. "Are you absolutely sure you didn't find anything that pointed to Trawler being the killer when you searched your house for clues?" I asked her.

She blinked at me. "What are you talking about? I didn't search my house for clues."

"What?" I practically screeched.

"Was I supposed to?" she asked.

I cradled my head in my hands, groaning. "Do you mean to tell me Trawler has been acting strangely for almost an entire week after a close friend was murdered and you didn't go through his stuff?"

"Of course not," she said, her expression scandalized. "He's my husband."

"To be fair, it's kind of our fault, Belinda," said Stevie, "It's not like we told her about our suspicions."

I waved aside her protest. "We need to search your house before he has a chance to destroy any evidence. Assuming he hasn't already," I added.

As Stevie started the engine, Jolene's cell phone rang. She glanced down at the screen and paled. "It's Trawler."

"Don't let him know we're on to him," I told her. "Act normal."

Jolene swiped up to answer the call. "What?" she barked into the phone.

"Normal as in happy," I hissed at her.

A high-pitched voice spoke from the other end. "Hello?"

"Sadie," said Jolene, wincing. "I'm sorry, sweetie. Why are you calling from your father's phone? Aren't you still at your grandparents' house?"

"Yes, but Dad's here too," she said.

Jolene glanced at us, concerned. "What's he doing there?"

"He's outside with Grampy, looking at their shrubs. Are you and Dad fighting again?"

Talk about a loaded question. Like any parent, Jolene dodged it. "Did you forget something at home?"

And like any kid, Sadie refused to drop it. "You sound angry, and the only time you get angry is when you and Dad are fighting. Or when you haven't eaten."

Blunt criticism must just be Sadie's default setting. I had to admit, the kid was growing on me.

"We're not fighting," Jolene snapped. She closed her eyes and exhaled before continuing. "It's been a rough day. Why did you call me, sweetie?"

"I wanted to ask if you'd mind if I went to McGrey's Island tonight with Nanny and Grampy to visit their friends," said Sadie.

"Which friends?" asked Jolene. "I thought you and Nanny were having a sleepover weekend."

"We still are. Tonight, we're going to make popcorn and watch the new shark documentary on Netflix. But Mrs. Stoddard called an hour ago and invited them to supper. They're having creamed lobster. Mrs. Stoddard also promised to show me how she makes her beeswax candles. She said I could help her add the scents. Please, can I go? Dad said I could, but only if you say yes too."

To my surprise, Jolene's eyes teared up. "Of course you can, sweetie. I can't wait to see your candles."

"You can have one for your office, if you want," offered Sadie. "After they set, I mean."

"I'd really like that."

"Do you want to talk to Dad?"

"No," said Jolene quickly. She cleared her throat before continuing. "No, that's okay, sweetie. I've got to go now, but text me a picture of the candles."

"Okay, love you."

"I love you too," said Jolene, smiling. It slipped off her face as soon as she disconnected the call.

"You realize that you're getting candles for your next birthday, right?" I asked her.

"And probably every holiday for the next year," added Stevie.

Jolene didn't even seem to be listening, staring down at her phone with a frown. "It's bad enough Trawler is planning to leave me for another woman, but how can he abandon such a great kid?" She shook her head. "I can't believe he would be so selfish."

"At least now we know where Trawler is," I said. "That means your house is safe to search."

"You're right," she said firmly. She clicked her seat belt in place. "Let's go."

"And if we find something that proves he really did kill Andy?" asked Stevie.

She pursed her lips. "We are going straight to the police and singing like it's halftime at the Grey Cup."

* * *

Even though I'd already been inside Jolene's home, I still needed a moment to stop and appreciate the level of cleanliness and organization on display.

Like the kitchen, her living room was filled with white furnishings, in open defiance of children and gravity. The plush ivory sectional sofa, with not a single stain to be seen, almost gleamed against the matching espresso-stained coffee and end tables. A white faux-fur rug complemented the ebony hardwood flooring, which did not appear to have a single scuff. A white

Provençal grandfather clock stood next to a contemporary gas fireplace with a marbled mantelpiece. Both were flanked by built-in bookcases filled with an assortment of artfully placed books and accent pieces.

I couldn't help but give a low, appreciative whistle. "How is it even after an entire week of being considered a murder suspect, your house still looks ready for a photo shoot?"

"It's not like having a dirty house was going to clear my name." Jolene pointed to my feet. "Shoes off, please."

"Like I would dare keep them on," I said, kicking them off and sweeping them to the side of the entryway. I pointed to the fireplace. "I'll bet if I swiped my finger along the mantle, I wouldn't find a speck of dust." I crossed the room and did just that. As predicted, my finger came up empty. "See?" I wiggled my bare finger at her.

Jolene rolled her eyes. "We're here to find clues, not judge my coping mechanisms."

I shrugged. "Hey, no judgment. It's healthier than my own. Wine, mini cupcakes, and light internet stalking."

"Still, it could come in handy," said Stevie to Jolene, grinning. "Maybe the next time you're accused of murder, you can help me clean out my basement."

"Ha, ha," said Jolene sarcastically. She glanced at the clock. "All this playful ribbing is costing us time." She clapped her hands together, loud enough to make Stevie and me jump. "Divide and conquer. I'll take the upstairs; Stevie, you can search the living room and kitchen; and Belinda, you can check the guest room and Trawler's office," she commanded, pointing us each in the right direction.

I decided to search the guest room first. As expected, it was as tastefully decorated and spotless as the rest of the house. If I hadn't known otherwise, I'd have assumed it was a room in a high-end Airbnb. The walls were painted a pastel green and coordinated perfectly with the white antique dresser. The queen-sized bed, with its beautiful tulip patterned duvet cover, looked soft enough to sink into completely. The room even came with a great view of the bubbling creek and green space that ran behind their house.

For a moment, I was tempted to ask Jolene whether I could move in as a tenant if Trawler went to prison.

I didn't hold much hope of finding anything significant in the guest room. Not only did it appear to be the smallest room in the house, it was also the least furnished. The closet was a good size, but free from the usual clutter, making it an unlikely hiding spot for anything incriminating. I might not have been very impressed with Trawler's behavior lately, but even I had to give him more credit than that. I checked the dresser drawers and found nothing but extra towels and bedsheets. Eventually, when I felt I had exhausted my search of the guest room, I moved on to Trawler's office, located at the back of the house.

It's my personal belief that you can always tell what matters most to a person by what they add to their workspace. Trawler's two passions appeared to be football and his family. I counted no fewer than three Toronto Argonauts jackets in the tiny closet. An oversized leather loveseat sat on one side of the room, with a thirty-six-inch flatscreen television mounted on the opposite wall. There was a console controller on the loveseat, suggesting that Trawler was a gamer, but nothing like what we saw at Andy's house. I took my time looking through the desk, filing cabinet, and closet but didn't find anything of interest. I even checked under the loveseat but found only a disturbing lack of dust bunnies.

The walls of his office were covered with picture frames, a mixture of professional family portraits and candid holiday photos. Trawler and Jolene's wedding portrait was displayed prominently on the filing cabinet, along with a photo of the two of them with a swaddled newborn Sadie. There was a picture of the three of them on Trawler's fishing boat, grinning as the sun set behind them. Another photo, this time of Trawler with toddler-aged Sadie, their faces dusted with flour as they proudly displayed a plate filled with misshapen sugar cookies, hung next to the television, placing it directly in his line of sight when watching football or playing video games.

A tiny seed of doubt took root in my mind. After everything Jolene had shared regarding her marriage, combined with what we'd learned from Wendy Snow, I was expecting a full-blown "man cave" decorated with nothing but beer can pyramids and posters of half-naked models sprawled on top of sports cars. However, this was the office of a devoted family man, or at least a devoted father. And yet, now it looked as though he was planning to flee Little Blue Harbour, and possibly a murder charge, with another woman. After trying to frame his current wife for his crime, no less. What changed? What could possibly make someone go from Danny Tanner to Tywin Lannister?

Stevie walked into the office, one hand on her hip as she ran the other through her hair. "Well, I came up empty." She slumped against the wall. "Did you have any luck?"

"None so far," I said, sitting back on my heels.

She groaned. "I thought for sure we'd find something in his office."

I sighed and stood up. "I'm starting to wonder if we have this all wrong."

Stevie chuckled wearily and shook her head. "Belinda, you're giving me whiplash. First, you say you don't trust Trawler, and now you think we're wrong about him. Which is it?"

"I don't know anymore. This whole case is giving me whiplash. What we've learned about Trawler doesn't line up with what I'm seeing," I said, gesturing toward the walls. "I mean, even if Trawler is planning to run away with another woman, I'd expect him to at least take Sadie with him."

"Maybe that was his original plan, before Jo was cleared as a suspect."

"And who is this other woman?" I asked, beginning to pace. "Why is it that Jo can't even have lunch with a male friend without the entire town believing they're having an affair, but Trawler can run off with some mystery woman without anyone noticing?"

Stevie cocked her head to the side, eyebrows raised. "You mean, besides sexism?"

I shook my head. "The one time this town's gossip mill would've come in handy."

There was a loud thud overhead, followed by the sound of muffled cursing. The two of us tilted our heads to gaze up at the ceiling.

"Do you think Jolene is okay?" asked Stevie, looking concerned.

"Not really," I said honestly.

"Do you think we should go help?"

"Probably." We both winced at the sudden bang of a drawer slammed shut. "Then again, she might prefer some privacy," I amended.

Stevie sighed. "No, we should be up there with her for moral support."

With one last shared look of concern, we made our way to the second floor. We followed the sounds of activity down the hallway and into the master bedroom. The closet door was open, and I could hear Jolene moving around inside.

"Hey, Jo. Stevie and I thought you could use some company." The words died in my throat as I stepped over the threshold. Next to me, Stevie's eyes went as wide as saucers.

"Don't come in here!" cried Jolene, throwing out her arms as if trying to block her surroundings from our view.

It was a walk-in closet but only in the technical sense. The clothing rods were stuffed to capacity, and the wire shelves were crammed to the top with a jumbled assortment of plastic bins, old children's toys, folded blankets, and outdated Christmas decorations. There were enough shoe boxes lined up along the walls to fill a stockroom. I could barely make out the carpet under my feet as I stepped over the various piles of hobby and crafting supplies. I moved carefully, lest I dislodge something and bury us all. Stevie, smartly, chose to remain in the doorway.

Jolene groaned, dropping her arms. "Go ahead, let the mocking begin."

I pointed to a shelf stuffed with packs of tube socks still in the plastic wrappings. "This is actually very comforting. The lack of dust bunnies in this house was starting to freak me out."

"I know it doesn't look like it, but there is actually a system in place," said Jolene nervously.

"Is that system to just cram everything in and hope for the best?" I asked.

"Like one of my exes," joked Stevie.

Jolene sighed. "I know. It's my own Room of Secret Shame."

My chuckle faded as the significance of her words hit me. "That's exactly what it is."

"Thank you, Belinda, very supportive," deadpanned Jolene.

"I don't mean it like that. This is the only spot in your entire house where Trawler could possibly try to hide something from you. It's crowded, it's messy, and you probably go out of your way to avoid staring directly into the face of your failure." I surveyed the chaos around us. "Does anything in here look different or out of place?"

Stevie and I watched closely as Jolene silently considered the surrounding shelves and clothing racks. If something had been moved or added to the closet, I didn't doubt for a moment that she would be able to spot it. Jolene might avoid this room like the plague, but I was willing to bet she knew every single item in here, right down to the number of broken Christmas tree lights.

Finally, her gaze landed on one of the (many) rows of shoeboxes and her brow creased. "That shouldn't be here," she said, pointing to a black and white box with the logo of a popular sneakers brand.

My heart rate picked up in anticipation. "Are you sure?"

She nodded. "Positive. This room haunts my dreams." Squaring her shoulders, she walked forward and picked up the shoebox, flipping back the lid. Her mouth dropped open and her eyebrows shot upward.

"What?" I asked, my stomach squirming with dread. "What is it?"

She looked up at me, her expression still frozen in horror. "These are the shoes Trawler wore to the reunion."

She tilted the box to show Stevie and me its contents. Inside, a pair of men's Oxford shoes lay amidst the crumpled tissue paper.

"The soles," gasped Stevie.

"They're caked with mud and grass," I finished grimly. "Trawler was in the football field that night."

Chapter Twenty-One

After a few awkward moments of silence, I took the box from Jolene, carefully closed the top, and tucked it under my arm. Finally, I settled on the one thought repeating through my brain. "Police station?"

"Yup," agreed Stevie readily.

The most Jolene could manage was a stunned, muted nod. Without a single word, Stevie and I each seized an elbow and led her, as docile as a ragdoll, out of the closet and into the upstairs hallway.

"I can't believe it," said Jolene weakly as we steered her down the stairs. "I know we thought it might be Trawler, but I didn't actually think it would turn out to be him. I just thought I'd find out who his travel partner was, and then you two would help me throw all of his things out onto the lawn just as he pulled into the driveway."

"Jo, honey, you're spiraling," said Stevie gently.

"But you were right, Belinda. He was there," she continued, oblivious. "He was on the football field that night. Trawler buried the award statue. He killed Andy."

When we reached the front door, Stevie and I both slipped on our shoes. However, Jolene, still looking dazed, just sagged against the partition wall.

"What am I going to do?" she asked. "How am I going to tell Sadie? Do I still have to help him find a lawyer?"

As Jolene continued to ramble on about the sanctity of marriage and just what exactly constitutes marital obligations, Stevie bent down to lift one of Jolene's legs. I inserted her foot into the corresponding sneaker, repeating the process with her other shoe. When we finally had her sorted, I reached for the doorknob.

Suddenly, it turned, and the door flew open, almost smacking me in the face. The three of us leapt backward as Trawler came barreling into the house.

He stopped short when he saw us. "Sorry about that." He smiled good-naturedly as he closed the door behind him. "I didn't realize someone was standing on the other side." He raised a hand to give Stevie and me a friendly wave, the hardware store shopping bag swinging from his wrist.

I looked from the bag, over to Stevie and Jolene, and then back at the bag again. "Oh, I don't think so." I spun around and tossed the shoebox to Jolene. "Run! I'll hold him off."

She clutched it to her chest and took off for the back door, with Stevie right behind her.

"Wait," Trawler called. "Jo, what's wrong? Come back!"

He tried to give chase, but I stood my ground, waving both arms in a wild attempt to block his path. Unfortunately for me, Trawler was a former football player. I only managed to delay him for a moment before he slipped past me, feinting left before dodging right.

But unfortunately for him, I was a know-it-all who didn't know when to quit.

As he shot past me, I leapt onto his back, clamping my arms around his shoulders, but my added weight didn't appear to slow him down. Stevie and Jolene seemed to realize they wouldn't reach the back door before Trawler caught up with them, so they switched tactics and ran into the kitchen, putting the marble countertop between them and him.

Trawler rushed into the kitchen, me still swinging from his back like a deranged orangutan. Finally, he managed to shake me off and I fell onto the linoleum floor, landing painfully on my tailbone. I scrambled to my feet and joined Stevie and Jolene, both huddled on the other side of the kitchen island.

Trawler braced himself against the countertop and rubbed his collarbone, wincing. He looked both aggravated and completely baffled. "What is going on?"

As he took a step forward, I reached for the knife block, seizing the first handle I touched. I yanked the blade free like I was King Arthur pulling Excalibur from the rock and brandished it at Trawler. "This is what's going on!" I exclaimed.

He stared at my clenched fist. "That's a butter knife."

I looked down at my hand, momentarily stumped. *What kind of wuss knife company includes a butter knife in the set?* Trawler took another step closer to the edge of the island, and I quickly raised it again. "It's still pretty sharp," I warned him.

"Belinda, have you completely lost your mind?" He looked to Jolene for a response, but Stevie and I quickly each stepped forward protectively, as though shielding her.

"I know what you did, Lawrence," she told Trawler, leaning to the side before quickly retreating.

"You know? I was so careful," he groaned.

The three of us gasped, shocked at such a casual admission.

He leaned against the kitchen island. "I have to say, Jo, I really thought you'd be more appreciative of all the effort I've made in planning this." He sighed, shaking his head. "Who told you? Was it my mother? That woman cannot keep a secret to save her life."

"Kathleen knew about this?" Jolene managed to choke.

He shrugged. "Of course she knew. Someone needs to take care of Sadie after we're both gone."

I curled my lip in disgust. "Oh, you are a sick individual, Trawler."

"Excuse me?" he sputtered.

"Don't play innocent with us. We know what you did, and we know exactly what you're planning to do next." I reached into my back pocket and pulled out the hardware store receipt. "Heavy duty tarp, zip ties, and lye."

"How did you get that?" His eyes widened with outrage. "Did you three follow me?"

"Of course we did," I snapped, "and we're not going to let you get away with this." I pointed to Jolene. "This woman has given you a child. Not to mention, the best years of her life."

"I mean, I'm only thirty-two," she muttered behind me.

I ignored her. "You think you can just do to her what you did to Andy and then skip town with your new squeeze?"

Trawler placed one hand to his temple and closed his eyes. He took a long, steadying breath before opening them again. "The lye was for my father. My parents want to re-landscape their backyard this summer."

"A likely story." I trailed off as I remembered Sadie's telephone conversation with Jolene. She mentioned that Trawler was in the backyard with his father, discussing shrubs. I rallied quickly, though. "What about the tarp and zip ties?"

He made a frustrated noise. "They're for the fishing boat. Swordfish season starts next month." I didn't think Trawler's expression could get any more incredulous, but he managed it. He looked past me at his wife. "Jolene, do you really think I murdered Andy?"

"We have evidence it was you," I said.

"Oh, really?" Trawler crossed his arms, amusement now creeping into his befuddled expression.

I ticked each example off on my fingers as I listed them. "You were jealous of the attention Andy paid to Jolene. You argued with him shortly before his death. You weren't in the gymnasium when he was killed. You've been acting shady ever since he died. Last but not least, when you came to pick Jolene up from the police station, there was a muddy shovel in the back of your pickup truck."

Trawler stared at us, all traces of humor now gone. "Wow," he said after a moment. "You're right, that's a lot of evidence against me. Without the proper context, I mean," he added hastily.

"Well, perhaps you won't mind providing the proper context for these." I took the box from Jolene and dumped the shoes onto the countertop, turning one over to expose the dirty soles. "Your shoes from the reunion, covered in mud and grass. You weren't on any walk that night. You were in the football field, burying Andy's trophy after you killed him with it."

I tossed the shoe back down on the counter. Beside me, Jolene flinched as bits of dried mud and grass scattered across her pristine countertop.

"We also know you've been meeting with Wendy Snow, the travel agent," Stevie added. "She told us you bought two one-way plane tickets, for yourself and an unknown woman."

I nodded to her in appreciation. "That's right. Add it all up and it can only mean one thing."

Trawler flinched too. "Jolene, is that really the kind of person you think I am?"

Jolene sighed. "I'm scared, Trawler. I don't understand what's happening between us anymore. I don't know what you're hiding from me."

His shoulders slumped. "It was never about hiding something. It was about finding something."

He left the kitchen, taking the shoes with him. The three of us cautiously followed and found him in the living room, standing in front of the grandfather clock. To my surprise, he pulled on the front panel, and it swung open, revealing not the clock's internal workings as I expected, but shelves of neatly arranged Blu-ray discs. Trawler slipped his hand behind the movie cases and pulled out a thin, rusted metal cookie tin.

He handed it to Jolene. "I wasn't on the football field that night. The grass on my shoes is from the high school courtyard. I was there, looking for this."

She gasped with recognition. "I don't believe it," she whispered, sinking down onto the sofa. "It's the time capsule we buried together fourteen years ago on prom night."

Trawler smiled. "Under the tree where we had our first kiss."

She opened the lid. Inside, there was a Polaroid picture, a few small trinkets, and two folded pieces of paper. "The letters we wrote to each other that night," she said softly. She picked up the photograph. A younger Jolene and Trawler stood with their arms wrapped around each other, wearing matching burgundy prom outfits, smiling widely at the camera. "Mama took this right before we left for the dance."

He sat down next to her. "Jolene, what you said the night of the reunion was true." He pointed to the papers on her lap. "I realized I haven't kept a single promise I made to you in that letter. I thought if I could find the capsule and give it back to you, you'd realize how much I still love you."

"Why wouldn't you just tell her that?" I asked him, exasperated. "And if you knew it was buried under the tree, why did you keep disappearing on her?"

Trawler shifted awkwardly. "To be honest, I had a little trouble remembering exactly *which* tree it was," he admitted. "It took me a few tries to find it."

Jolene groaned and covered her face with her palm. "Hence the muddy shoes and shovel."

"How does Wendy factor into this?" I asked. "Why do you need a travel agent if you're not planning a dramatic flight from the law?"

"I needed her for the other part of my surprise. I was going to wait until after supper tonight." He reached into his shopping bag and handed Jolene the travel brochure packet Wendy gave him.

Her confused expression turned to one of delight. "Niagara Falls?" she gasped with excitement.

"You always said that was your idea of the perfect honeymoon," he said proudly. "We couldn't afford one when we got married. And since I've spent the last thirteen years taking you for granted, I thought you deserved it. I've already talked to my parents, and they've agreed to take care of Sadie."

"After you're both gone," I finished wearily, echoing his earlier statement. "You know, Trawler, you could have been a little clearer."

He glared at me. "In my defense, I didn't realize you three suspected me of murder."

Stevie raised her hand as if answering a question in class. "If you were planning a romantic trip for the two of you, why is the second ticket under another woman's name?" She groaned. "It's under Jolene's name. Wendy never said it was under another woman's name, just a woman's name."

I sighed. "Wendy is still such a brat." I turned back to Trawler. "Why only book one-way tickets?"

"One-way plane tickets," he explained. "We're taking the VIA Rail train home."

Jolene clapped her hands in excitement. "Like you've wanted to, Trawler."

"Exactly," he said, just as excited.

Unfortunately, I was still coming to terms with the fact our case against our prime suspect had just gone up in a mushroom cloud of romantic gestures. "So you didn't leave a threatening note on my door?" I asked him.

He gave me a confused frown. "What note?"

Jolene pressed the Polaroid picture and letters against her chest. "Oh, Trawler, and here I was thinking the worst of you, literally. You must be so angry with me," she moaned. "I know better than anyone how it feels to be accused of something you didn't do. I am so, so sorry."

He took her hand. "No, I'm sorry. You lost a close friend, and then had to deal with the police and town gossip. I should have been more supportive. I thought surprising you with this trip would help, but I just ended up causing you more stress. No more secrets, I promise."

Jolene threw herself into his arms, the contents of the time capsule spilling onto the rug. "I love you, Lawrence."

"I love you too," he said, hugging her tightly. "Everything is going to be different from now on, Jolene. I promise."

"This is so romantic," breathed Stevie. "You planned your big reveal for the same night as the senior prom, just like when you two first buried your time capsule."

But there was a new suspicion needling me. "You're being awfully forgiving about all of this," I said to Trawler.

Stevie sighed irritably. "You can't turn it off, can you?"

I really can't. "If I found out my spouse thought I killed their friend, I'd be a little upset."

"It's not like Jo didn't have any encouragement." Stevie gave Trawler an apologetic smile. "Sorry about that, by the way. If it makes you feel any better, you weren't our only suspect."

"That's true," said Jolene. "We offended a lot of people this week."

"All water under the bridge," Trawler said kindly. "I think the best thing for us to do is just put this all behind us."

I narrowed my gaze at him as I realized the truth. "You thought Jo killed Andy, didn't you?"

Panic flashed in his eyes. "No." I fixed him with a hard stare, doing my best to imitate Sergeant Finlayson. "Okay, maybe a little," he admitted.

Jolene stared at him, her mouth pursed in a scowl. *Jinx was right; I do not know how to read the room.*

"What?" he asked as our silence stretched on. "Her scarf was found with the body. No one else saw Jolene in the women's bathroom that night. It was only until I realized you and Stevie were helping her clear her name," he insisted. "I knew you would only do that if Jolene were innocent."

Jolene sighed, and all tension drained from her expression. "So, basically, we suspected each other of murder." She gave her husband a weary smile. "I don't think either of us were at our best this week."

Trawler's body sagged with relief. "Should we just call it even?"

Jolene nodded. "Yes, please."

They embraced again while Stevie and I just stood there, unsure of what to do next. As relieved as I was that Trawler was not a killer (or a cheater), I couldn't help but feel disappointed with our failure to crack the case. Not to mention the bone-crushing embarrassment that was coursing through my veins.

Maybe I was as arrogant as Finlayson thought I was. I must have been. I accused a man of murder when he was actually trying desperately to save his marriage. I was no detective; I was just a failed journalist who couldn't write and still lived with her parents.

I cleared my throat awkwardly. "Well," I said, edging toward the door, "we'll just get out of your hair."

"Yeah," said Stevie, following my lead, "we'll let you two get started on your special evening."

Trawler chuckled. "I'm pretty sure that ship has sunk."

My face burned with shame. "Again, very sorry about that."

Jolene stood up and placed her hands on her hips. "I don't know about the rest of you, but I think we should celebrate."

Stevie and I shared a dubious glance. "You do?" she asked.

"Yes," said Jolene. "We accomplished everything we set out to do. I've been cleared as a suspect, as well as Trawler. I'll finally get to see Niagara Falls. And now that everything's out in the open, Trawler and I can reconnect as a couple and work on our communication skills. We should all go to the Right Foot pub for drinks."

Trawler and Stevie voiced their enthusiasm for the idea. They looked at me expectantly. "Sure," I said, still feeling deflated. "That sounds great."

The four of us left the house together and began walking toward the boardwalk. Stevie and I hung back a few paces behind Jolene and Trawler, who seemed to be in full-on lovey-dovey mode, holding hands and giggling like the teenagers they used to be. I watched them with an air of wistfulness.

Stevie nudged me playfully with her shoulder. "You're disappointed, aren't you?"

"That Trawler isn't a murderer? Not at all."

She laughed. "No, that we couldn't solve this puzzle."

I shrugged. "Can't win 'em all, right?" I only lasted a few seconds under her knowing gaze before I cracked. "But I'd be lying if I said I couldn't have used the win."

She pointed to Jolene and Trawler walking in front of us. "I prefer this ending."

"Agreed," I said, linking my arm through hers.

"We may not have solved a murder, but we helped save a marriage."

"Right after we almost destroyed it," I joked.

She laughed. "At least now we can just let the police handle it. We can all go back to normal."

I hesitated before giving her a nod of agreement. *Right, normal.*

Chapter Twenty-Two

The Right Foot pub was surprisingly busy, even for a Friday night. Apparently, the parents in town decided the high school seniors weren't the only ones who deserved a night out. It was standing room only; every table was full, and every barstool was occupied.

We hesitated by the doors, taking in the crowd. "Wow, this place is packed tonight," said Trawler.

Stevie nodded in the direction of a small stage in the back corner, musical instruments already set up and waiting. "That's probably why."

"I forgot the Albatross Boys are playing tonight," said Jolene. "Did you guys want to go somewhere quieter?"

Just then, I saw Jinx carrying a tray of dirty dishes over his head as he made his way through the throng of patrons back to the kitchen, his bicep muscles straining against the sleeves of his flannel shirt. "I'm good here," I assured her, my eyes following him across the pub.

We wove our way through the crowd as politely and unobtrusively as possible until a couple seated near the stage finished eating and stood up. Suddenly, every standing patron descended on the now-empty table like ravenous birds of prey. Stevie motioned for us to follow her before plowing her way through the hoard like Katniss Everdeen, armed with elbow jabs instead of arrows.

"Very impressive," said Trawler, claiming one of the chairs. "You should have played football with us in high school."

"I'm really more of a bowler," said Stevie. She offered the other chair to Jolene, who accepted.

I looked around the pub, ignoring the multiple death stares aimed in our direction. Hannah and the other servers were making their way around the room, taking orders and chatting with customers, while Jinx was back behind the bar.

"With the size of this crowd, it's going to take Hannah ages to make it over here to take our drink orders," I said. "The second we get up from this table, the other tributes are going to make a play for it."

Stevie rolled her eyes. "Let me guess," she said. "You're offering to go order our drinks, but really it's just a flimsy excuse to flirt with Jinx."

I shot off in the direction of the bar. "I'll be right back."

"You don't know what we want to order!" she yelled after me.

While I waited patiently for my turn at the bar, I couldn't help but admire Jinx as he worked. He was right—running a pub suited him. I watched as he chatted with customers, mixed their drinks, and took the money all in a seamless blend of charisma and efficiency. It reminded me of when we were in high school, how he'd always had a joke or greeting for every kid he passed in the hall while never once being late for class. I wondered whether it was a natural affability or a concentrated effort to counteract the supposed curse.

A little ironic when you think about it, I realized. *The guy goes out of his way to acknowledge everyone, but the rest of us are scared to say his real name.*

I pushed that depressing thought aside as he finally reached me. "Good to see you, Belinda," he greeted me with a smile. "I didn't know you were a fan of the Albatross Boys."

"I'm not," I admitted. "What kind of music do they play?"

"Mostly East Coast folk rock."

I grimaced. "Do I need to brace myself for an evening of bagpipes?"

He chuckled. "You're safe. It's the one instrument I've banned from the building."

I laughed. "Four Pucker Ups, please." That would at least give me a few extra minutes with him while he mixed the cocktails.

"Uh-oh," he said, grabbing the glasses. "In need of another pick-me-up?"

I shook my head. "Officially speaking, these are celebratory drinks."

He gave me a wry look, his hazel-and-green-speckled eyes twinkling. "And unofficially?"

I took a moment to consider his question. "Have you ever been so sure you're on to something big, only for it to blow up in your face multiple times?"

He finished mixing the first drink and slid it to me. "I take it your investigation into Andy's death isn't going well."

"How did you know about that?" I sputtered.

"It's not a big town." He winked. "Also, I caught a glimpse of your coaster suspect list that day you ate lunch out on the deck."

"I guess we're not exactly Columbo, are we?" *Or Nancy Drew.* I braced one elbow on the bar. "Is it weird I actually thought I could solve it?"

"I'd expect nothing less from a know–it-all," he teased.

My laugh quickly turned into a groan. "Maybe Finlayson was right; I let myself become obsessed with Andy's death as a way to avoid dealing with my own problems. This is the fifth-grade talent show all over again."

Jinx cocked his head, curious.

"Ian Huskilson's magic act," I explained. "Remember? He turned his pet rabbit into his little sister."

He nodded fondly. "Oh, yeah. That was pretty clever of him, using mirrors and a false bottom on the serving cart."

"You figured out how he did it that night?" I asked, mildly annoyed. "It took me months."

He shrugged. "When he stepped behind the cart, I noticed I couldn't see his legs."

"That would have been useful information before I ran up my parents' internet bill," I said ruefully.

Jinx slid the last three cocktails in front of me. "It's the secret to every great magic trick, what you don't see."

As much as I enjoyed flirty banter, I didn't want to monopolize his time when the pub was so slammed. "How much do I owe you?" I asked, opening my purse.

I dug for my wallet, but instead my fingers kept brushing against the same crumpled piece of paper. It was the program for the memorial assembly Principal Acker held for Andy at the high school. Just as I was about to shove it back down into the depths of my purse, I noticed a line of vertical black dots at the bottom of the page.

Suddenly, the pieces of the puzzle snapped into place, and I could see the image of the killer clearly in my mind.

What you don't see.

I crumpled the program in my fist and leaned across the bar, throwing my arms around Jinx. I pressed my face into those glorious copper whiskers. "Sutherland, you are a brilliant human being."

"Thanks?" When I let go of him, his cheeks were almost as red as his beard. "Hey, what are you doing after the show? I thought we could—"

But I was only half listening. "Keep the change," I told him, slapping down two twenty-dollar bills.

I hurried back into the surrounding crowd, a giddy energy coursing through my body. I made my way across the pub, weaving in between crowded tables and standing patrons with rushed apologies. I reached Jolene and Trawler just as the band took the stage. A loud cheer went up from the crowd as they began to play.

I deposited the drinks on the table, upsetting the liquid in my haste. "It's a magic trick," I said excitedly.

"What is?" asked Jolene as she dabbed at the spill with a napkin, raising her voice over the cheering crowd.

"Andy's death. This whole time we've been focused on what happened, but we should have been paying attention to what didn't happen."

Jolene scrunched her lips in a pink pout. "I can tell from your tone you've realized something important, but I have no clue what you're talking about."

My mind was racing too quickly to fully address her confusion. "The photographs from the reunion," I said instead. "Where are they?"

"They're still on my work computer at the school," she answered.

"You said you were going to make us copies," I said, not even trying to keep the exasperation from my tone.

Jolene shrugged. "I was, but I got distracted when I realized Sadie's walnut squirrel had been stolen."

I opened my mouth to retort but suddenly noticed who was missing from the table. "Where's Stevie?"

"Her mother called while you were at the bar," said Trawler, yelling over the music. "There's a leaky pipe at the Osprey. Diane didn't know how to shut off the water, so Stevie went to help. She said she'd be back."

I urged Jolene out of her seat. "We'll have to text her to meet us there."

Jolene gaped at me as I grabbed her leather tote from the back of her chair and slipped it over her arm. "Meet us where?"

"The high school," I said, pulling her toward the exit.

"Belinda, slow down," she said, dragging her heels. "We can't just leave Trawler here by himself."

"We'll only be gone for a few minutes," I argued. "I just have to verify something."

She let out an aggravated huff and came to a complete stop, yanking her arm free from my grasp. "I am not going anywhere until you tell me what exactly is going on."

"I know who killed Andy."

* * *

As we approached the high school, I felt the throb of the bass music emanating from the building in my chest. Or maybe it was just my heart pounding with nerves. There was a small group of teenagers gathered outside the front entrance, giggling and taking pictures with each other. A couple of the dates stood off to the side, smoking and pulling awkwardly at their formal attire. I couldn't be sure from this distance, but I could have sworn one of the boys was Gavin from Gull's Quick Stop. For a split second, I considered asking him if I was still banned from the store.

One problem at a time, Bishop.

I didn't actually go to my prom. Stevie and her mother were out of town that night, and Jinx already had a date who wasn't me. I suppose I could have accepted Richard Spencer's invitation, but a night spent watching cheesy horror movies and eating my weight in cookie dough was far more appealing than one spent with the guy who wiped his boogers on the curtains in elementary school.

Since we knew the school chaperones probably wouldn't take too kindly to a pair of grown adults, one of whom was in no way affiliated with the school, showing up at the senior prom, we decided to sneak in through the west doors.

"I'm only supposed to use this key for emergencies," muttered Jolene as she unlocked them.

"There's a killer on the loose," I reminded her. "How is that not an emergency?"

We crept up the stairs, each keeping a close eye out for anyone who could bust us. Once we saw the coast was clear, Jolene used her key again to unlock the administration office, and we both slipped inside. We dropped our purses on the lobby chairs and continued through the swinging gate. Rather than risk turning on the main office lights, Jolene flicked on the lamp on Donna's desk.

She sat down in front of her work computer and turned it on. "If you're so sure of your theory, why are we crashing a high school prom instead of going to Sergeant Finlayson with this?"

"We need something concrete; otherwise, he'll never believe us."

She looked at me. "Understandable. I'm not even sure I believe you."

I pulled the crumpled program from my purse and flattened it against the counter. "These black dots," I said, running my finger down the side of the paper. "They're the same ones Stevie noticed on the note that was left on my door. Whoever wrote it used the same printer to make Andy's memorial program. And since I know you didn't leave it, that only leaves one person."

But Jolene failed to seem convinced.

I huffed irritably. "Just pull up the reunion photographs that were taken after Andy's body was found and I'll show you." I waited as she clicked through them, until the image of Donna Dickie filled the screen. "There, that one."

Jolene stared at the photo, unimpressed. "What exactly am I supposed to see?"

"It's what you don't see." I pointed to Donna's mascara-streaked hands. "Her white Chanel gloves. She was wearing them before Andy died, but now they're gone. We haven't seen her wear them since that night, either. Same with her white shawl."

"That doesn't prove anything," argued Jolene.

"You saw how much Donna enjoyed showing off those gloves. The only reason she would take them off is if they pointed to her as the killer."

The first seed of doubt took root on her face. "Randy said the killer would have blood splatter on their clothes."

"Exactly. Her green dress would've been dark enough to hide any stains but definitely not the gloves and shawl." A restless, almost giddy, energy seized me as I began to pace, going back over everything we knew. "We've had multiple run-ins with Donna while we were questioning people about Andy's death, and she hasn't butted into our investigation once. Three small town idiots try to solve a murder themselves, and she doesn't have an opinion about that? Does that sound like the Donna you know? It's the same with the office thefts. Some kid was supposedly stealing right out from under her nose, but she didn't do anything about it. Why not?" I answered before Jolene could. "Because she already knew who the thief was. Her."

"Donna had things taken too," said Jolene. "Her snow globe."

"Did she really? She could have just pretended it was stolen to avoid suspicion."

Jolene seemed to consider this for a moment before shaking her head. "Donna was at the bar with Fiona when Andy died."

Another piece of the puzzle clicked into place. "No, she wasn't." I took control of the mouse and clicked back through the other pictures until I found the one of Fiona downing her glass of red wine. The photographer had been standing far enough away to capture the entire bar. As I suspected, Donna was nowhere to be seen in the photo.

Jolene got to her feet. "This doesn't make any sense," she said. "Why would Donna vouch for Fiona if she wasn't with her?"

I thought back to that afternoon on the boardwalk after our fitness class, how Donna didn't approach us until Fiona was out of earshot. "She did it because confirming Fiona's alibi gave her one too. Think about it: Donna has been Little Blue Harbour's self-appointed hall monitor for as long as we've known her. If she said she was at the bar, why wouldn't we believe her?"

"Why would anyone believe us?" asked Jolene. "Don't get me wrong, you're definitely on to something here; but we don't have any evidence physically linking Donna to the crime."

"We have the note. It was left after Donna overheard us questioning Fiona. The police should be able to recover a copy of it from her work computer."

Jolene stared at the computer screen, her expression troubled. "We still need a motive. Why would Donna kill Andy? They barely spoke outside of work."

I resumed my pacing. "If that's true, why did Donna react so strongly when Madeline spoke badly about him? When did your things start disappearing from the office?" I asked Jolene.

She tapped her fingers against her chin, thinking. "The first time would have been in October, just before the Thanksgiving long weekend."

I nodded grimly. "That was after the dance-a-thon fundraiser, wasn't it? When everyone thought you and Andy sneaked off together."

"It was." Her eyes widened with shock. "You think Donna was the one who was stealing from me? Why would she do that?"

"She's spent most of her life trying to get in with the Pageant Minions and Andy. It's pretty obvious she resents you for being part of the group, like you took her spot." A startling thought occurred to me. "Maybe in more ways than one. She thought you and Andy were an item, remember? Maybe she killed him in a fit of jealous rage."

Jolene looked back at the image on the computer screen. "We need to show these pictures to Sergeant Finlayson."

I started opening random desk drawers. "Where do you keep your thumb drives?"

Jolene hopped down from her stool. "We should have some in the supply closet."

Together, we made a beeline across the office. We opened the door to the supply closet and hurried inside. I scanned the surrounding shelves, unable to make out anything in the dark. "Where's the light switch?"

"On the outside wall," she said. "I'll get it."

But as she turned, the door slammed shut, plunging the closet into darkness. I heard the unmistakable click of the lock sliding into place.

I rushed forward, pounding on the door. "Someone's in here!" I cried, thinking maybe it was the school janitor.

I heard a sugary voice answer from the other side. "Oh, hello, Belinda."

My stomach turned to ice. There was only one person in the world who could sound so sweet and yet so condescending.

Donna Dickie.

Chapter Twenty-Three

I struggled to keep my voice as breezy as possible, like her sudden appearance was a pleasant surprise when in reality it was far from it. "Donna! So crazy running into you like this. What are you doing here?"

"I volunteered as a chaperone for the prom. Of course, a better question would be what exactly are you two doing here?" asked Donna sweetly.

"You know how it is," I said, stalling for time. "Jo forgot something at the office, so we just popped in to grab it. Be a lamb and unlock the door?"

Unfortunately, Donna seemed content to keep us where we were. "It's the strangest thing. I was just checking the halls to make sure none of the students had left the dance when I noticed the office door was ajar and my desk lamp was on. Naturally, I decided to investigate. Quite an interesting theory you have regarding Andy's death."

I couldn't see Jolene's expression in the dark, but I imagined it looked as alarmed as I felt. "There are a few things we haven't figured out yet. Obviously, you had a thing for Andy."

"It was more than a thing," interrupted Donna. "Andrew Perch was the love of my life."

"Really? You and Andy?" I winced. I probably shouldn't have sounded so surprised.

"Not that he'd ever admit it, of course, " she answered bitterly. "I've loved him ever since I was fifteen years old. I went to every single one of his football games, not to mention all of his practices. Not even Fiona did that for him. When she and Andy started having relationship issues before prom, it wasn't Holly or Jolene that he turned to for comfort. It was me. He knew I understood what it felt like to be lonely. Completely unheard and unseen."

"Andy was one of the most popular students in school," I reminded her.

"They didn't know the real Andy. Everyone else just saw what they wanted to see. He told me he felt like he could tell me anything, I was the only one who truly understood him. That's why he asked me to prom."

"I thought he just offered you a seat in their limo," said Jolene.

"I was his date," snarled Donna. "He came by the house one afternoon while my grandmother was out to pick up donations for the prom bottle drive. He and Fiona had another fight and she dumped him, again. I invited him inside and we spent hours talking." Her voice caught. "When he kissed me that afternoon, it was like my prayers had been answered. Finally, someone in this town saw me, accepted me for who I was. For the first time in my life, I felt like someone who mattered."

"Did you know about any of this?" I whispered to Jolene.

"No, Andy never said a word," she whispered back.

Donna's laughter through the door was as bitter as fresh rhubarb. "No sooner had I bought my dress, which cost me over two hundred dollars, Fiona was back in the picture. Suddenly, the best day of my life was a mistake, something that should have never happened. We weren't supposed to talk about it. I was supposed to just move on, get over it."

"I can't believe Andy would use you like that, Donna," said Jolene. "That must have been heartbreaking."

"What would you know about it, Harbour Queen?" spat Donna. "You're just as bad as he was. You knew Andy had feelings for you, but you just kept stringing him along. It wasn't enough that you already had the perfect life: friends, a successful husband, a gifted daughter, and the admiration of the entire town. Playing with him like a toy to be tossed aside once the novelty wore off."

We need to keep her talking until Stevie gets here. "From what I've heard, it was usually the other way around with Andy," I said.

"That's a lie," snarled Donna. "He was too good for them. None of those women deserved him."

"I don't understand, Donna," said Jolene. "If you loved Andy so much, why would you kill him?"

I realized the truth as soon as she asked. Andy intended to leave through the west exit. He would have walked right past the administration office. "Andy caught you taking something from Jolene's work desk as he was leaving the school, didn't he, Donna? He realized you were the office thief."

Donna harrumphed loud enough to penetrate the thick wooden door. "I wasn't even planning to take anything that night. I just wanted to arrange my award on my shelf for Monday morning. But after that embarrassing display of marital drama on the dance floor between Jolene and Lawrence, and Andy coming to her defense. It was practically a public declaration of his feelings for her, feelings that he should have felt for me. So I stole your blue scarf from your desk. Andy always complimented you when you wore it."

"Oh, now I kind of feel bad for suspecting Andy as the thief," I murmured to Jolene.

"I told you it wasn't him," Jolene hissed in the darkness.

"At least I was still right about the thief being fixated on you." It wasn't much help to us at the moment, but I decided to cling to whatever comfort I could find.

"I didn't even hear Andy come into the office," continued Donna, becoming increasingly agitated. "When he saw me with the scarf, he grabbed it out of my hands. I tried to explain. I tried to tell him that I still loved him, even after all this time, but he just kept ranting about how I was nothing but a thief. He threatened to tell Principal Acker everything. I followed him out of the office to the stairs and tried to get the scarf back from him. I was going to put it back inside your desk. I told him I'd return everything, but he wouldn't let go. He stumbled and lost his footing. I wasn't trying to push him down the stairs, I swear."

There was a long pause, and I began to worry if Donna had left. When she finally spoke, it was with such cold, hard fury it sent shivers down my spine. "I ran down after him, but when I tried to help him stand, he wouldn't even let me touch him. He said he was going to call the police, that I was going to jail for theft and assault. I panicked. His award statue was laying at the bottom of the stairs, so I picked it up and . . ." I heard her let out a shaky breath. "I loved Andy. I didn't want to kill him, but I had no choice. I couldn't let him humiliate me like that. Not again."

I closed my eyes, trying to picture the scene in my head: Donna crouched over the body in the darkness, checking for a pulse like I had, her pristine gloves now red with Andy's blood. "That's when you got rid of your gloves."

"I took his award and wrapped it in my shawl along with the gloves before hiding everything in an unassigned locker. I managed to sneak back to the gymnasium before the police arrived. Then I waited until the coast was clear to bury his award in the football field later that night."

The same place where she used to watch Andy play football all those years ago, dreaming of a future with him that would never happen.

What was taking Stevie so long to get here? I wondered frantically. We really could have used her. She was so much better at relating to people. Unfortunately, I didn't have much of a choice. I was going to have to empathize with Donna Dickie of all people.

"It must have been so horrible for you," I said, pouring as much sympathy as I could muster into my words.

"Andy was wrong to treat you like that," added Jolene, catching on.

"You were emotionally distraught," I said. "I'm sure Sergeant Finlayson will understand."

"We'll go with you to the RCMP station and help you explain," offered Jolene.

"I suppose that's one option," said Donna.

I felt Jolene grasp my hand in the dark, and I squeezed back, hope coursing through our skin.

"But then again, I could just walk down the hall to the science lab and grab the leftover jugs of acetone from Mr. Blackburn's disappearing Styrofoam experiment," she finished.

I turned to Jolene. "Acetone? Wasn't that the super-flammable stuff Amy Marsh was using when she accidentally set her braid on fire in chemistry class?"

Jolene's response was lanced with quiet panic. "Yes, it is."

"That's your plan, Donna?" I yelled through the door. "You're going to burn down the school just to keep us quiet?"

"Don't worry, Belinda. Nine times out of ten, the smoke kills you before the flames do."

Gee, that's comforting. "This is an incredibly stupid plan, Donna, and I'm not just saying that because you want to kill us."

"It's a good plan," she said, sounding offended.

"Donna, the vapors from acetone are flammable too," said Jolene. "If you douse the room and then light a match, the whole office will explode."

"Exactly." Donna's voice was softer, more muffled, as though moving away from us. "Problem solved. For me, anyway. Not so much for you two."

"There's a gymnasium full of kids downstairs!" pleaded Jolene.

"Relax, the school does regular fire drills," said Donna, thankfully sounding like she was back outside of the door.

Okay, this definitely isn't going as well as I hoped. "Fine, Jo and I will just call the police," I threatened.

"With what exactly?" asked Donna, her voice dripping with scorn. "You both forgot your purses on the chairs out here."

Frantically, I patted down my jean pockets. "You've to be kidding me," I groaned, scolding myself more than anyone else. "We don't have our phones."

Jolene sighed. "We really are bad at this."

As if on cue, I heard my phone begin to ring. A moment later, Jolene's phone followed suit. Their upbeat tunes were an odd contrast to our dire situation.

Okay, this is bad, but we're still not beat. "It doesn't matter because as soon as you leave, we're just going to yell until someone hears us," I told Donna.

"Scream all you want," she said. "No one will hear you at the other end of the school over the loud music."

My stomach sank as I realized she was right. But I was nothing if not tenacious. "If we figured out that you killed Andy, Sergeant Finlayson will too," I tried again. "What are you going to do, murder an RCMP officer?"

"Don't be silly," said Donna. "He already suspects Jo. Which wasn't intentional on my part, to be honest, but I'm happy with how things worked out. Now I can spin this to suggest you two dummies accidentally blew yourselves up while trying to destroy evidence. People will be so outraged that their beloved Harbour Queen almost killed their children to cover her tracks, Sergeant Finlayson will pin it all on Jolene just to save his reputation. Then I can simply leave town."

I turned to Jolene, exhaling sharply. "I hate to admit it, but this is starting to sound like a good plan."

"What did I tell you?" Jolene wailed. "Patsies do get killed!"

"Donna, listen to me," I said urgently. "I get it. From the outside, Jolene's life looks perfect. Annoyingly perfect. I mean, the hair, the stylish clothes, and the hero-worship."

"Is this really helpful?" whispered Jolene.

"I'm trying to establish a bond with her, like hostage negotiators," I whispered back.

"You can't do that without insulting me?"

I shrugged her off before turning back to the door. "I'm just saying, I know how you feel, Donna. My life hasn't exactly turned out the way I expected either. Sometimes other people's good fortune feels like the universe is twisting the knife. At some point, though, you need to stop blaming others and take responsibility for your life."

There was a beat of silence, and Jolene and I waited hopefully. *Maybe I actually got through to her.*

"Yeah, no," said Donna. "If I wasn't willing to go to jail for the man I loved, why would I do it for you two?" "

Then again, maybe not.

There was a high-pitched squeal I recognized as a chair being jammed under the doorknob. "Okay, you two ladies sit tight." The clacking of her heels faded as she left the office.

A sudden panic seized both of us, and we resumed our frantic banging and shouting. After what felt like a long, unsuccessful stretch of pounding on the wooden door, we fell silent.

"We are totally screwed," groaned Jolene.

"No, we aren't," I argued, pushing down the fear clawing at my chest. "You texted Stevie on our way over here and told her everything. As soon as she gets here and lets us out, we'll call the police."

There was a long pause from Jolene that I really didn't like. "I didn't text Stevie."

"What?" I screeched before I could stop myself. "I said we needed to text her before we left the pub. Stevie is going to think we ditched her again."

"Is that really our biggest concern right now?" snapped Jolene.

Good point. "You're right. Escape now, apologize later." My eyes darted around the closet as I willed them to adjust to the darkness, my mind racing with a hundred desperate ideas. "We can break down the door," I said, choosing the least complicated one.

I heard rather than saw Jolene's frustration. "Is one of us secretly She-Hulk?"

"We have to try. There are some things in life I simply refuse to do—parallel park, try kale, and be murdered by Donna Dickie."

Unfortunately, it only took a few attempts of throwing myself against the steadfast slab of wood for me to abandon my plan. "I don't understand," I said, rubbing my sore shoulder. "How did people escape locked rooms in the olden days?"

"They didn't," said Jolene. "They starved to death and eventually their skeletons were found."

"You know, for an overachiever, I really expected you to perform better under pressure," I said, trying to ignore the terrible thoughts racing through my mind. Like the fact we were moments away from certain death.

"I can't die," moaned Jolene. "Trawler and I just started repairing our marriage. Sadie is entering her teen years. He won't be able to handle that on his own."

I decided not to press the issue. "There must be a way for us to get out of here. This building is almost a century old." There was a strange shuffling noise to my left. "What are you doing?" I asked Jolene.

"Looking for the door hinges," she said. "When Sadie was three, she accidentally locked herself inside the bathroom at her grandparents' house. It was built in the early 1900s and still has all of its original doors. Kathleen and I just removed the hinges to get her out. It was easy; we tapped out the pins, and it came right off." She was quiet for a moment, and I could hear the sound of soft pats against the wooden door. "Aha, I was right," she crowed. "These are the same kind of hinges. We just need something similar to a screwdriver and a hammer."

"Too bad Donna didn't lock us in the janitor's closet." A flash of inspiration hit me. "Wait, letter openers."

"They should be on the shelf with the pens."

I felt her brush past me and followed her over to the shelves as best I could in the dark, groping blindly for anything remotely shaped like a letter opener.

"Found it!" I heard Jolene cry to my left.

My hand landed on an oddly shaped lump. "I think I found something to use as a hammer." I felt around some more, trying to figure out what it was that I was touching. "It feels like some kind of jagged rock."

"My amethyst paperweight. I moved it from my desk to the supply closet when things started to go missing," said Jolene. "I bought it because it's supposed to promote wisdom and calmness."

"Both of which you would definitely need to work with Donna."

We both fumbled our way back over the door and got to work. I listened closely as I held the door steady while Jolene gently tapped at the hinge bolts. On the other side of the door, I heard approaching footsteps. Jolene and I both froze.

Donna was back.

Chapter Twenty-Four

There was an ominous scraping noise beyond the closet door, like furniture being moved. *Donna must be piling the furniture into the center of the room to start a bonfire*, I thought wildly. I sniffed the air, searching for any whiff of an accelerant. For a split second, I could have sworn I heard multiple voices on the other side of the door.

Does Donna have an accomplice? My mind raced at the possibility. I couldn't think of anyone willing to help Donna move a couch, let alone commit another murder.

"Hurry, hurry," I moaned, one hand already on the knob, ready to move as soon as the last hinge was free.

"I just need to do the last one at the top," whispered Jolene. Two more taps, and I felt the door shift. "Last pin is out."

No sooner had she uttered those victorious words, the chair braced against the other side vanished, causing me to lose my grip on the door. It fell forward with a loud thud, followed by a sharp shout of pain. "Ow!" a deep voice protested.

Two figures stuck their heads into the closet on either side of the fallen door, but it was too dark to make out their faces. Thankfully, both of them appeared to be too tall to be Donna.

When the shorter one spoke, I recognized the voice. "Belinda? Jo? Are you two okay?"

"Stevie?"

Someone flipped on the light switch. I blinked a few times, wincing against the sudden blaze of light. Trawler's face came into focus. "Hey, babe," he greeted his wife with a grin. "We were wondering where you two went."

I realized there was a third person in the room, their face still blocked by the door in their hands. They pushed it aside with a loud, wooden clunk. It took me a moment to recognize Sergeant Finlayson, wearing a black cotton polo shirt tucked into beige chinos with a brown belt. It was the first time I had ever seen him without a tie.

He rubbed the top of his head, a pained expression on his face. "Is this how you thank all your rescuers? With head trauma?"

I knew I should be more grateful, but his choice of words irritated me. "Excuse me, but we were just in the middle of rescuing ourselves, thank you very much. How did you know where to find us?" I gasped as a disturbing thought occurred to me. "Is the RCMP tracking us?"

Stevie pulled Jolene and me into a tight hug. "No, I am," she said, squeezing me hard enough to make my breath catch. "Remember? I said I was going to install a tracking app on your phone."

"I didn't think you were being serious. Not that I'm complaining," I added quickly.

"Yes, we are both very glad that you did," said Jolene.

Stevie handed us our purses and phones. "By the time I made it back to the pub, Trawler was alone at the table. Neither of us knew where you'd gone. I tried calling both of your cell phones, but there was no answer. We got worried, so I checked your location and saw you were at the school. We ran into Sergeant Finlayson as we were leaving the pub, and he offered to come with us."

"For the record, we didn't intentionally ditch you," I told her. "There was a slight miscommunication over which one of us was supposed to text you."

"Jolene," said Stevie, without hesitation. "She's the responsible one."

"Unbelievable," Jolene muttered under her breath.

"Why did you run out of the pub like that?" asked Stevie.

Trawler asked the obvious question. "Why were you locked in the supply closet?"

As quickly as possible, I brought them up to speed.

Stevie's eyes looked like they were about to pop out of her head. "Donna killed Andy?"

Trawler whistled quietly under his breath. "When goody-two-shoes go bad."

Finlayson shook his head, looking bewildered. "I suspected she wasn't telling me everything. I'm supposed to speak with her again tomorrow about her alibi. I noticed none of the reunion photographs show her near the bar that night, even though it's where she claimed she was at the time of the victim's death."

"Didn't notice the missing gloves, did you?" I couldn't resist asking.

He gave me an aggravated look. "You do realize the event photographer already provided me with copies of the photographs he took that night, don't you? There was never any need for you to come to the school. Why didn't you just call me with your theory?"

I frowned. "Oh, sure, because you've been so receptive to our help."

"Can you two please do this later?" interjected Stevie. "We need to stop Donna before she hurts anyone else."

Sergeant Finlayson and I grudgingly turned our attention back to the matter at hand. "She said she was going to the science lab," I said, hurrying to the door.

"Or she could still be checking this end of the building to make sure it's empty," said Jolene, right on my heels.

As a group, we ran out of the office into the hallway. Thankfully, it was just as deserted as it was when Jolene and I first arrived. The music in the gymnasium was so loud, I could feel it vibrating in my chest.

"We need to split up and look for Donna," I said.

"No, we need to stay together. There's safety in numbers," said Jolene.

Finlayson took out his phone. "You're civilians, so none of you will be doing any such thing," he told us firmly. He unlocked his screen and dialed. "Corporal Perry, this is Sergeant Finlayson. I've got an attempted 10–80 in progress at the Little Blue Harbour high school. Requesting immediate backup; suspect should be considered dangerous."

Huh. That firm tone is kind of sexy when it's directed at someone else. Of course, it didn't hurt that he'd just *almost* rescued us from a killer. Or that his black polo shirt made his blue eyes look even brighter.

Finlayson paused. "A 10–80, Corporal. It means arson," he said. "Yes, I know we're speaking on a phone and not the radio. Yes, I'm aware this was supposed to be my night off."

I grabbed his phone and jammed it against my ear. "Randy, it's Belinda. Listen, we found the killer. It's Donna Dickie. She's about to barbecue the high school to cover it up. Now get your butt down here and bring every cop in Little Blue Harbour with you."

I ended the call without waiting for Randy's response and handed the phone back to Finlayson.

His irritated sigh sounded mixed with gratitude. "I'm going to search for Miss Dickie in the downstairs hallway. I want you four to head to the gymnasium and inform the chaperones about what is happening. Help them get all the kids out of the building."

I noticed the fire alarm on the wall behind him. "I think I have a better idea." I flipped open the plastic covering and pulled down on the lever.

A shrill ringing blasted throughout the school.

Trawler flinched and covered his ears. "Well, that's certainly faster," he yelled, barely audible over the alarm.

Jolene caught sight of something behind me, her mouth dropping open with surprise. "There she is!" she shouted, pointing.

I spun around in time to see Donna, wearing yet another amazing vintage cocktail dress and Mary Jane heels, racing out of the science lab with two plastic jugs of clear liquid cradled in her arms. Her head swiveled wildly from side to side, looking for the source of the fire alarm. For a split second, she stared at us like a porcupine in the middle of the highway. Before any of us could react, she dropped the plastic jugs and sprinted down the hallway.

I took off after her. "Stop, you're under arrest!"

"I'm supposed to say that," Finlayson yelled behind me.

We gave chase, following her downstairs into the school lobby, but lost her in the crowd of students gathered in front of the doors, waiting to exit the building in a calm and orderly manner.

"Did anyone see where she went?" I yelled as I pushed my way through the throng, taking care not to step on any hemlines.

"No," answered Jolene, her petite stature barely able to see over the heads of the students.

Stevie, who was almost as tall as Finlayson, pointed in the direction of the gymnasium. "I think she ran in there."

"She's heading for the fire exit door next to the assembly stage," I realized, changing course.

Luckily for us, the gym was almost empty, the remaining students filing outside through the fire exit next to the still-creepy inflatable Manny the Muskrat. And there, scurrying to the front of the line, was Donna.

"Oh, no, you don't, Dickie!" I cried, pursuing her.

Just as she reached the exit, I launched myself at her in a flying tackle, knocking her into the mascot balloon with enough force to rip the fan's plug out of the wall. The remaining students cried out in shock as the balloon slowly deflated on top of us. Donna and I hit the floor hard, my knees taking the brunt of the fall. Unfortunately, the pain was enough of a distraction for Donna to get the drop on me. She scrambled on top of me and wrapped her hands around my neck.

"Why couldn't you just let it go?" she panted as she began to squeeze. "Why can't you ever just mind your own business, Bishop?"

"That's rich coming from you," I managed to gasp through the pressure on my throat.

I could hear the sounds of Finlayson and the others trying to fight their way through the layers of nylon to get to us. Rather than wait, I jabbed two fingers upward, poking Donna in both eyes. She howled in pain, and I felt the pressure lift. I gasped for air as I rolled her off me and onto her back. I sat on her chest, pinning her to the floor. I swung my fist, striking her on the jaw.

Finlayson pulled aside the last of the deflated balloon and helped me to my feet. Randy and the other officers had arrived, running up behind him. The fire department must have turned off the alarm because I could hear perfectly as Randy took Donna into custody, reading her rights as he handcuffed her behind her back. Her chestnut curls had come loose from her updo, sticking out in all directions, her expression dazed. For a moment, I worried I'd hit her too hard, but she was steady on her feet as Randy led her out of the gym.

"Nice work," Finlayson told me. "Where did you learn to punch like that?"

"My father was a cop," I said, rubbing my throat. "He signed me up for self-defense classes at the rec center as soon as I turned twelve."

Stevie and Jolene hurried up to me and threw their arms around me. "Oh, Belinda, that was so scary," said Stevie, squeezing me tightly.

"I thought we agreed after Andy's house that you wouldn't blindly chase after criminals anymore," scolded Jolene, her voice muffled as she hugged me.

"I'm sorry, what was that?" asked Finlayson wryly.

"She's distraught," I said, patting her on the back reassuringly. "Doesn't know what she's saying."

To my amazement, he laughed. "You seem to have that effect on people."

* * *

An hour later, Stevie, Jolene, and I were still at the school. Finlayson insisted that I let the EMTs examine me, but other than a swollen throat and hoarse voice, the paramedic assured me I would be fine. After a brief call to my parents to let them know I was okay (followed by a not-so-brief lecture from my mother about the importance of knowing when to stay in my lane), we sat on the front steps of the school and waited for Trawler to return with his truck. The scene outside the school had calmed considerably, but there were still a few officers milling around, talking into their radios or directing traffic as parents showed up to claim their kids.

Finlayson and Randy stood off to the side, still interviewing witnesses. After a while, they joined us. Finlayson looked more relaxed than I'd ever seen him. "We're just about to head back to the detachment," he said, "but I wanted to let you know that Miss Dickie confessed to everything. She even told us where she hid the shawl and gloves. Officers found them under a loose floorboard in her bedroom."

I turned to Stevie and Jolene. "See? I told you she could never bring herself to get rid of them."

Stevie rolled her eyes. "Yeah, yeah. Rule number four, no gloating when you're right."

Finlayson gave us an odd look, and I remembered he wasn't familiar with our investigation rules. He cleared his throat. "We'll send the items off for testing in the morning," he continued, "to confirm the presence of the victim's DNA. Even without it, we have more than enough to charge her with murder."

Randy reached into his uniform coat pocket. "We also found this." He pulled out a tiny squirrel ornament, complete with walnut body, hazelnut head, tiny black top hat, and fuzzy brown pipe cleaners for a tail.

"Lord Nuttingham!" Jolene grabbed it from him and held it against her chest. "Where did you find him?"

I perked up on the step. "Was it on a secret altar in a hidden room at Donna's house?" I asked eagerly.

Randy stared at me, bewildered. "A secret what? No, it was in her office desk," he said, jerking his thumb toward the building.

"Oh," I said, a little disappointed.

Stevie rolled her eyes at me. "We really need to start monitoring your media consumption."

A familiar black pickup truck drove up to the curb and parked next to a police SUV. Trawler honked the horn twice and beckoned us forward.

Jolene got to her feet with a groan. "Thank goodness. This has been more than enough excitement for one night." She looked at Finlayson. "Unless you need another statement from us."

"Not tonight. Go home and get some rest," he said kindly. He and Randy walked over to the police cruiser. He opened the door, but hesitated, bracing his arm on the hood of the car as he looked back at us. "Thank you, ladies. I appreciate your help with this case."

The three of us shared a surprised glance. "You're welcome," I told him.

He stared at me for a moment, and I thought he was going to say something else. But all he did was give me a curt nod before getting into the vehicle and pulling the car door closed with a snap. Randy gave me a wink and a salute as they pulled away from the curb. Stevie and I watched as the cruiser disappeared down the street.

"You know, Sergeant Finlayson is kind of hot when he's not threatening to arrest us," Stevie said.

Was it just me or was she watching me out of the corner of her eye when she said that? "I guess," I said grudgingly. "If you like the authoritative type."

Jolene turned to us, still cradling Lord Nuttingham against her chest. "I want to say thank you too."

"For what?" I asked. "Almost getting you killed?"

Stevie snorted. "Almost ruining your marriage?"

"No, for standing by me when people thought the worst of me. For helping me to clear my name. For everything." Her eyes filled with tears. "You two are the best friends I've ever had."

Stevie slipped one arm around her shoulders and the other around mine. "I feel the same way."

To my horror, I felt myself choke up. "Me too," I mumbled, looking away.

Stevie gaped at me. "Belinda, are you crying?"

"No," I said, brushing away the sudden tears clinging to my eyelashes. "It's all the dust in the air, and pollen. This is allergies, not genuine emotion."

Jolene threw her arms around me. "You did miss me all these years, didn't you?" she exclaimed.

"Yeah, yeah," I said sheepishly, patting her on the back. "Rule number four, remember."

But when Jolene started to pull away, I squeezed tighter, savoring the newly repaired bond between us. Stevie quickly joined in, encasing us both in a bear hug.

"Okay," I said after a moment, extracting myself from their embrace. "That's enough for one night."

Stevie grinned at Jolene. "Baby steps."

The three of us climbed into Trawler's pickup truck and fastened our seatbelts. A wave of exhaustion hit me out of nowhere, and I let my head drop back against the headrest. "I could sleep for a week."

"I know what you mean," sighed Jolene. "I am so glad Sadie is still with her grandparents. I just want to go home, grab a shower, and go to bed."

"I'll second that," said Trawler, waggling his eyebrows at her.

Stevie groaned, just loudly enough for us to know not to take her seriously. "Please save the married adorableness for when you get home."

While Trawler waited for a signal from the officer directing traffic, I stared out of my window at the school. The flashing lights from the emergency vehicles reminded me of the spinning lights of the disco ball on the night of the reunion. "It's weird," I murmured.

"What's that?" asked Stevie.

"We actually caught a killer," I said. "Three complete amateurs. It almost feels like we had help or something."

"We did have help," said Stevie. "Sergeant Finlayson was with us."

"That's not what I mean." I trailed off, trying to make sense of my thoughts. "Nancy said the high school was the one place where Andy still felt safe. I just think it's odd Donna didn't get caught until she tried to destroy it."

Jolene twisted around to face us. "What are you saying? You think Andy's spirit or whatever had something to do with her arrest?"

"It's not that far-fetched," I insisted.

Stevie closed her eyes and pressed her fingertips to her temples. "Let me get this straight: you don't believe in family curses, but you believe in ghosts?"

"Crime-fighting ghosts," Jolene clarified with a snort.

"Hey," I sulked. "What about the story of Wailing Martha? People believe in her."

The police officer waved us forward and Trawler steered the truck onto the street. As he began to drive in the direction of Topsail Cottages, I figured it was better to be safe than sorry. I rolled down the car window and stuck my head out of it.

"Goodbye, Big Andy!" I called as the school receded from view. "Thanks for the assist!"

Epilogue

On Sunday, almost the entire town attended Big Andy's funeral. The church had to run sound equipment downstairs to the Sunday school classroom to accommodate the overflow.

Stevie, Jolene, and I sat together, hands clasped, while Reverend Kathleen Dexter led the solemn service. After the grave committal, Nancy Perch announced she was hosting a small reception at her home for family members and close friends.

Afterward, Trawler went home to continue packing for his and Jolene's upcoming trip to Niagara Falls, while the three of us walked down to the Right Foot pub.

"Did I tell you that I spoke to Maddie Barclay yesterday?" asked Stevie. "She said Nancy reached out to her about the hockey card. Apparently, she learned how Andy really acquired it and didn't feel right about keeping it."

"I wonder how that happened?" mused Jolene, giving me a very pointed look. "Didn't you have coffee with Nancy recently, Belinda?"

"I might have mentioned it. Not the whole story," I clarified quickly. "Nothing about Kevin's relapse. I just told her the card held a lot of sentimental value to him, and he regretted the deal."

Stevie laughed. "Maddie thought you may have had something to do with it. She couldn't think of anyone else in town who would be so brazen. She wanted me to tell you thank you." She grimaced. "She also said you're still banned from Gull's."

I came to a stop on the sidewalk. "But I helped Kevin get his hockey card back."

"You also took a swing at her with a golf club," she reminded me.

"And accused her of murder," added Jolene.

It was a beautiful day, so we opted to sit on the deck. Jinx was outside distributing iced tea to the members of the Little Blue Harbour bridge club when we arrived.

"Have you guys seen it yet?" he greeted us, his eyes crinkling when he smiled.

"Seen what?" asked Stevie, sitting down at an empty table.

He picked up an abandoned newspaper from a nearby table. "You three made the *Foghorn*," he said, flipping it over to show us the front page.

I snatched the paper out of his hands. "They already ran the story?" I wailed. "But I emailed them about writing it." I'd been confident that despite past rejections, the *Foghorn* would jump at the chance to print an exclusive firsthand account of Donna's crimes.

The headline read, "RCMP Make Arrest in Local Homicide." Below it, there was a picture of Donna being led away in handcuffs, and one of Sergeant Finlayson standing outside the school looking busy and important.

Stevie skimmed the article over my shoulder. "What are you talking about, Jinx? We didn't make the paper. We're not even mentioned."

He pointed to the corner of the second photo. In the background, just visible under Finlayson's elbow, were three unfocused blobs sitting on the front steps of the school. If I hadn't recognized our clothes and Stevie's blue hair, I would have assumed they were prom attendees.

"Not only did I get scooped, but they didn't even bother to give me a proper shout-out for helping to catch the killer." I puffed out my cheeks as I sighed. "I guess it would be considered to be in poor taste to push this, wouldn't it? Andy's killer has been brought to justice. That's all that really matters."

Stevie pulled me to her side bracingly. "You'll find your story, Bel. I know you will."

Jinx took back the paper and tucked it under his arm. "Seriously, though; well done, you three."

"I owe it all to our conversation about magic tricks," I told him.

He cocked his head to the side, looking puzzled. "What do you mean?"

I grinned. "Well, you have to look for what you don't see, right?"

Something shifted in his gaze. "You'd be surprised at what some people can miss."

We locked eyes for a split second, and I realized I'd seen that look from Jinx before. The other night at the pub, just before my sudden brainstorm about the case. He'd been about to say something to me before I rushed off. My heart rate increased, the blood pounding in my temples. *Had Jinx Sutherland been about to ask me out?*

Before I could fully process that possibility, I heard a familiar bark behind me. I spun around in my seat and saw my parents approaching our table, pulled forward by a panting Shelly who looked almost beside herself at the prospect of being around so many tables to beg from. She greeted me with a quick lick on the hand before turning her attention to the bridge club ladies seated next to us, her big brown eyes glued to their deep-fried clams and scallops platter. My father quickly reined her in as my mother gave Stevie and Jolene each a hug.

"I didn't know you two were coming into town today," I said once the hellos were out of the way.

"Would you like me to push two tables together so you can all sit together?" asked Jinx politely.

"No, thank you. We're fine at another table," said my mother, still admiring Stevie's blue hair. "We've got more people joining us soon anyway."

"Randy wanted to take Brady out for a meal before he leaves." My father looked at Jinx. "Is Shelly okay out here on the deck?"

"Not a problem, Ken," Jinx assured him.

We all looked down at the dog, who was once more planted next to the clam platter with zero intentions of going anywhere.

We gave Jinx our drink order and he went back inside, but not before inviting my parents to seat themselves wherever they liked. The five of us chatted while we waited. My mother, much more supportive of our amateur detective shenanigans now that we were the talk of the town, congratulated Jolene on helping to clear her name, while my father told Stevie and me all about his new plans to add a barbeque pit at Topsail Cottages. As we listened, his earlier words jogged something loose in my brain.

"Wait, who is Brady?" I interrupted.

My parents' faces lit up like a Christmas tree. "Brady!" called my father, waving. "Over here."

I glanced toward the entrance to the deck and saw Sergeant Finlayson standing next to Randy in the doorway.

Okay, this is weird, I thought as my parents greeted Finlayson with enthusiasm. *This is like when my mother sold a house to my sixth-grade teacher, Mrs. Vernon, and then the two of them started going to craft sales together.*

Randy, dressed in his usual off-duty attire consisting of jeans and a gray T-shirt with the sleeves cut off, gave us a hearty greeting. Finlayson, once again wearing a suit and tie with his hair neatly combed, looked just as proper as the day I first met him. His usually stern demeanor was more relaxed now.

My parents and Randy chose a table with a better view of the harbor on the other side of the deck, but Finlayson hung back for a moment to speak to us.

"Dad says you're leaving today," I said.

He nodded. "I still have some things to finish up at the detachment beforehand, but I'm driving back to Halifax later this afternoon."

"Can't wait to get out of here, huh?" teased Stevie.

He chuckled. "Yes, I think small towns have proven to be too dangerous for me."

Hannah appeared with our drinks and menus. She smiled at Finlayson as she handed them over. She stepped aside to leave and pointed to him, giving me a thumbs-up. I shooed her away as subtly as possible.

Jolene, ever the good citizen, told Finlayson, "You should come back for a proper visit sometime. Little Blue Harbour has a lot more to offer than just murder, I promise."

He glanced in my direction. "I don't doubt it."

I took a deep gulp of my icy drink to cover the sudden burst of nerves in my stomach. From the corner of my eye, I noticed my parents and Randy watching us with entirely too much interest for my liking.

Finlayson cleared his throat awkwardly. "I should join my table." He extended his hand to me. "It was a pleasure meeting you, Belinda."

"I see we're finally on a first-name basis," I said, taking it. "It certainly took you long enough."

"It's the least I can do for the woman who tackled a criminal into an inflatable mascot for me."

"Speaking of which, the spirit committee is already asking for a replacement balloon. Apparently, Donna's heels ripped one of the seams. Is that something covered by the RCMP? You know, since, technically, I did that on their behalf."

Finlayson leaned forward to whisper in my ear. "I'm letting you slide on the breaking and entering charge, so maybe don't push it."

His warm breath on my neck made my cheeks tingle. "I'll talk to them about setting up a payment plan."

Finlayson said goodbye to Stevie and Jolene, thanked us again for our help, and walked over to my parents' table. As soon as he sat down, Stevie and Jolene rounded on me with expectant smiles.

"What?' I asked when neither of them said anything.

"It would appear as though Jinx might have a little competition," said Stevie.

I rolled my eyes. "There's a long list of things I need in my life right now, and romance is not on it. I've got too many other things I need to sort out first."

"Like what?" asked Jolene.

"Moving out of my parents' house. Getting my writing career back on track. Paying off a group of surprisingly intimidating teenagers."

"Does that mean you plan on sticking around Little Blue Harbour for a while?" Jolene asked hopefully.

"I guess so."

"So, it won't be the last time I have to save your butt after you've jumped headfirst into an embarrassing and potentially dangerous situation?" Stevie asked me teasingly.

I snorted. "Oh, you can count on it."

"If it means we get you here for a little while longer, I'll drink to that," said Jolene, lifting her glass. "Here's to being proven innocent."

"To showing everyone what we're made of," said Stevie, raising her own.

When I left town fourteen years ago, it was because I thought there wasn't anything here for me. But as I sat with my friends, enjoying the sun on my skin, and listening to the sounds of the waves mixing with the conversation and laughter around us, I realized that as far as fresh starts went, Little Blue Harbour seemed like as good a place as any for me to find mine.

I picked up my glass. "To new beginnings."

Acknowledgments

I'm going to fight the urge to hide my true feelings behind a string of jokes and actually be sincere for once.☺

A big thanks goes out to my parents, Evelyn and Brian, for a childhood filled with support and wonder, and for always allowing my imagination to run wild.

My best friend Jill, I'm not exaggerating when I say this book wouldn't exist without you. Thank you for always being there to talk me down when I was ready to throw in the towel, and for putting up with the endless, "Does this joke work??" text messages.

To my husband Ben, thank you for helping me realize where Belinda and company truly belonged, and for always being ready with the perfect nautical pun. A second shout-out to my mother, and to my sister Jillian, for being my favorite—and lol, most brutal—beta readers.

Thank you to all my online writing friends for your support and encouragement while I pushed this manuscript up what was on some days a very steep hill, with a special thanks to Jaimie, Susan, and Christine. I don't know how I lucked out finding such amazing critique partners, but I appreciate you so much!

And finally, thank you to Cindy Birch at Birch Literary Agency and the team at Crooked Lane Books for helping me achieve a thirty-one-year-old dream.